Liliane Thurau
10 Camelot Ln.
East Setauket, NY 11733

THE

BANQUET

BUG

Also by
Geling Yan

•

*The Lost
Daughter of
Happiness*

HYPERION EAST
New York

THE
BANQUET
BUG

Geling Yan

Library of Congress Control Number: 2006926482

ISBN: 1-4013-6665-1

Hyperion books are available for special promotions and
premiums. For details contact Michael Rentas, Assistant
Director, Inventory Operations, Hyperion, 77 West 66th
Street, 12th floor, New York, New York 10023,
or call 212-456-0133.

Design by K.A. Minster

FIRST EDITION

10   9   8   7   6   5   4   3   2   1

To my father, Xiao Ma,
and my mother, Jia Ling

THE
BANQUET
BUG

DAN DONG DOESN'T BELIEVE IN omens. Omens such as an enormous red spider or a double-yolk egg, which the old folks in his home village consider ominous. Otherwise, he would decide against attending the banquet and go with his wife, Little Plum, to get expired canned food that the factory where Dan used to work is giving away. Instead, he just flings his plastic sandal and smashes the spider as it crawls by the makeshift nightstand (improvised from a washboard atop a stack of bricks, all under a crocheted cover), and he pays no attention to the extra egg yolk he eats at breakfast.

So now you know where we are: in Dan Dong's loft room. It used to be an office on top of a cannery in an industrial suburb of Beijing. It's ten o'clock in the morning, and he's taking a shower under a short rubber hose that Little Plum is holding. She stands on a chair, trying to steady the hose. The water comes in spurts and gushes from the rusty pipe that crawls along under the ceiling. That is how they shower, by diverting hot water that is the factory's runoff and merely appears clean. Three years ago, when the factory partially shut down and turned 60 percent of its employees into "reserve workers," collecting only 20 percent of their original wages, Dan came home carrying a soap dish, a comb with missing teeth, and a pair of broken plastic slippers for the public bathhouse, and he told Little Plum that he had cleaned out his locker and would never have to work the night shift again for the rest of his life. He was not worried about getting a job until he found, two months into his reserve worker status, that he and Little Plum only had fifty-five yuan in the bank. Not even enough for the two of them to have a Big Mac dinner at McDonald's.

A couple of days later, Dan saw an employment ad in a newspaper. It said that a five-star hotel needed security guards, and that candidates must be taller than 1.8 meters. As a tall, strong, good-looking man, Dan figured he had a chance. He went to the hotel in his best outfit, a polyester sports jacket atop khaki slacks, with a pair of black leather shoes to match a fake Dunhill bag he borrowed from a neighbor. As he wandered into the lobby, a woman approached him asking if he was here for the meeting. He nodded yes, and she said the meeting had already started. She ran him up the escalator, through an indoor balcony, and out to a ballroom with tables laid for a banquet. A banner hanging over the podium said "Donate Your Wealth, Plant Forests, Fight Desertification, and Take Back Our Green Fields!" The woman asked him to please sit down wherever he could find a seat, then disappeared.

He sat at a table next to the door. The banquet had already begun, and he was starved, so he swept through the dishes in front of him without knowing what they were. A man sitting next to him introduced himself as a reporter from the *Beijing Evening News* and asked which press outlet Dan belonged to. Wishing to be left alone to enjoy the free lunch, Dan answered he was from the *Beijing Morning News*. The guy said he'd never heard of it, and Dan replied that it was newly established. A Web site? Yes, yes, a Web site. After Dan was stuffed and was thinking about slipping out, the reporter asked if Dan would go with him to pick up their fee. What fee? Oh, just the two hundred yuan for their attendance, what they call "money for your troubles": submit your business card and the host will pay you two hundred yuan for the article you might write about the meeting. Dan silently gulped the air: two hundred! That's several times a reserve worker's monthly salary, plus a meal fit for a king. And all it takes is a business card!

Leaving the banquet, Dan went directly to a print shop. He picked out an expensive-looking design and had a bunch of cards made. The card said he was a reporter from some Internet news site. He had made some inquiries at the banquet and found out that many Web-based media outlets were going in and out of business every day.

Up to this morning in early May 2000, when he is taking a shower for the noon banquet that will mark a turning point in his life, Dan has made a nice living eating banquets.

Rubbing himself down with a rough washcloth, Dan asks Little Plum if she believes that he has tasted all the dishes of all of China's cuisines. Yes, she believes he has. He feels a bit unsatisfied. Every time he tries to impress her, she is too easily impressed. If asked whether he qualifies as *the* banquet eating master, she would answer, of course, who else does? She gives him all the wide-eyed admiration he wants, and the lack of challenge bothers him. Looking up, he sees her face red with the effort of lifting the rubber tube. She is twenty-four, small but substantial, with a head of natural curls pulled back into a ponytail, exposing her smooth, still adolescent face.

"But you are wrong this time," he says. "There was one dish I had never set chopsticks on until yesterday."

"What is it?" Little Plum asks.

"I couldn't make out what it was at the first bite. Then I looked at the menu and was shocked." He looks up at his wife through the streams of water. "Can you guess what it was made of?"

She shakes her head, smiling: "Can't guess." Every time she is confronted by a word riddle or a guessing game, she surrenders before tiring her poor little brain.

"The—dish—was—made—of—a—thousand—crab—claw—tips." Dan Dong sounds out every word. "A thousand. Just imagine how they cracked all those claws and shelled them. Imagine: all that meat was once the tiny fingertips of those poor little monsters."

He waits for her to ask how many crabs they had to kill for that many claw tips. But she just quietly absorbs her astonishment.

"When your chopsticks pick the little fingertips, they tremble and jiggle, almost slipping off before your mouth catches them." He lets the water run through his hair, rinsing off the rich shampoo lather. "I hope next time they put the menu on the invitation. If there is ever a crab finger dish again, I will smuggle you in. Trust me, it's worth the risk."

The water pipe begins purring. Then deep burps are heard approaching from inside the pipe, from the depths of an invisible organism, and the water hose twitches. Little Plum immediately reaches up and switches the faucet shut, so the inferno of steam will not boil him. This is the reason she stands on the chair guarding the water.

"It's such weird meat, you know. It's like taking the flavor of a thousand tiny chicken legs and putting it into a single bite. It's so delicious that it's almost unbearable. There's so much flavor it actually makes you a little sick. And nothing is more tender than those fingertips. When you chew on them, it feels like . . ." He tries to describe the texture of the delicate flesh, the subtle contact between the meat and his palate and tongue, the slippery sensation it gives when it passes the entrance of the throat, leaving the oral organs in such wonder. But he has no vocabulary for it. Putting together his education with hers, they can barely write a decent letter to their parents without checking a dictionary.

All of a sudden, the machines downstairs are on. The dark, hairy spiderweb around the overhead lightbulb quivers. The upper story of the building used to have twenty offices, ten on each side of the corridor. Now it houses twenty families of reserve workers. The machines kick into action at random intervals as the factory gets sporadic orders. If the inhabitants of this settlement complain about the noise, the factory manager reasons with them that they should hope it gets noisier, so the rent can drop even lower. The manager also hints that, although their life in a building-top encampment is not ideal, it costs them almost nothing; besides the cheap rent, they can steal electricity to cook with and hot water to wash with and buy meat that has failed inspection. The stolen water even takes care of any urgent need to use the toilet, which is quite an excursion from where they live. One simply squats down over the sewage opening and flushes it out with water afterward. Water is such a nice thing, separating filth from cleanliness in seconds.

A neighbor woman yells outside the plastic curtain, asking what's taking them so long and whether they shower hair by hair. Laughing, Dan Dong yells back that he has twelve toes to scour.

Little Plum helps dry him with a hand towel, her hands gentle and effective. She does everything with such a perfect economy of movement, never an unnecessary footstep or arm stroke. Back in her village, though a little girl, she earned the full wages of a grown man at farm labor. Dan apologizes to the neighbor woman, explaining that he is in a hurry to go to an important meeting. The woman says she will come back to wash her vegetables after he and his wife are done. The neighbors know that Dan has an office job somewhere, but they're not clear what it is. They envy him for wearing a necktie and polished shoes to work.

Before setting out for banquets, Dan always washes and shaves fastidiously. He has two formal shirts, one white and one blue, and he alternates between them. The day after he got his reporter's business cards printed, he borrowed a hundred yuan from neighbors and went to a pawnshop. With five yuan spent on a pair of thick-framed glasses, twenty on a microphone attached to a broken tape recorder, and seventy-five on a cheap camera that he had no intention of loading with film, he set out for the banquets as a new person. He had learned to search for information on conferences by reading newspapers. The first opportunity he found was a grand auction of newly developed technologies. The auction company had invited over a hundred press people and fed them a sixteen-course banquet after the auction. Dan was sitting with a group of "special guests." As more alcohol was consumed and the talk became increasingly indiscreet, he found that the "special guests" were people hired to pose as bidders. They had sat in the auction, raising their signs, bidding against one another just to foment a bidding frenzy.

At the end of the banquet, a huge crystal plate arrived, and Dan learned that the rough-shelled little creatures on it were called "oysters." The waiter told them the oysters had been passengers on an airplane from the seashore barely an hour before. The "special guests" were goofing around, talking about their best performance. It was the auctioning of a weight reduction technology. The initial bid had been fifty thousand yuan. They were bidding like mad and finally got it up to a million. The ultimate buyer was actually the seller himself, who had staged the riot just to get publicity for the product. Now all the media would trumpet how hot the stuff was, selling for twenty times the opening price. Entertained by their stories, Dan tried and failed many times to dislodge the gray, slippery meat dripping with an obscene juice. Finally succeeding, he took a deep breath before putting it into his mouth. He was surprised to discover that the alien-looking, vomitlike substance called "oyster" was actually quite tasty.

The following day, Dan saw the news about the great success of the auction on China Central TV's evening news. It was the lead story in all the major newspapers as well. But in his own memory, Dan only marked it as "the oyster banquet."

With a towel around his waist, Dan rushes into their loft room, leaving Little Plum mopping the floor. When she comes in, he is dressed and posing in front of a little oval-shaped mirror on the windowsill, hunching and squatting, trying to fit his entire face into the small frame. He frowns and fusses over his hair, making some of it stand up.

"Good?" he asks, angling his face in profile.

Little Plum answers yes. She grabs a basket containing dried green peas and starts picking out grains of sand and worm-hollowed pods, resting half her butt on the edge of a desk bearing scrawled red numbers on its legs, inventory numbers of public property belonging to their state-owned factory. When they got married, the factory was changing furniture and sold the broken furniture for next to nothing.

Little Plum picked up a desk with missing legs and another desk with a cracked top. She cannibalized them, transplanting the legs of the one to the other. She also scavenged two wobbly office chairs and made colorful cushions to cover up the ugly red inventory numbers on the seats. There are white crocheted covers everywhere. It is Little Plum's way of unifying and harmonizing all the mismatched furniture. Two glassless hutches stand against the wall, filled with teacups, desk calendars, notebooks, little travel alarm clocks, and other odds and ends. They are souvenir gifts from banquet hosts. Above them, hanging on the wall, is a slab of black marble shaped like a book, with a fine gold logo. The logo is solid, twenty-four-carat gold, according to a famous goldsmith whose signature is carved in the marble. It is their favorite souvenir, from a publisher who donated most of his wealth to save ancient Chinese literary works banned throughout history. Dan always jokes that if they become beggars, they can always sell the gold for food. Across from the hutches sprawls a bed covered with a crocheted bedspread and crowned with a fake-leather upholstered headboard.

Dan keeps staring at the mirror, as if he is about to wrestle with his own reflection.

"Do you wish you had been with me yesterday eating crab claw tips?" Dan asks.

"Uh-huh," she answers indistinctly.

"Such a shame they left the plate unfinished. If only I could eat for you!"

"Eat for me then." She laughs, flipping a green pea at his shoulder. He picks it up from the cement floor and flips it back at her. She arches her back, threatening to charge forward. He surrenders, his hands up and his chin turning to the clock. Time to go to work. Banquet eating is a serious, stressful job, requiring a good work ethic as well as diligence, courage, and so on and so forth.

Watching him take a checkered necktie, the only one he has ever owned, from the clothesline across the vast room, she thinks she has never seen a more handsome man, even including those soap opera stars.

He hurries toward the corner of the room and sinks into one of the swollen, moaning sofas, his knees up to his chin as he tries to tie his shoelaces. The sofas, made of matching fake leather, sit elbow to elbow by the door, like an old, awkward country couple. He has promised Little Plum and himself that he will replace the bed and sofas, their homemade wedding furniture, when he has made enough money eating banquets.

THE BANQUET IS HOSTED by a nonprofit organization that supports young bird-watchers. The hotel lobby is decorated with paintings donated by famous artists. As he walks with the crowds toward the banquet hall, Dan sees the receptionist checking the journalists' ID cards. Her eyes flick between the persons and the pictures as she explains the new policy. Two days ago, a man faked a press pass and got into the Great Hall of the People while the People's Consultative Congress was in session. He was protesting against a provincial Party leader's corruption. From now on, every reporter has to have his ID card as well as his business card in order to attend press conferences and banquets.

Dan walks away from the entrance. The name on his ID doesn't match his business card. He can make the excuse of having left his ID card home, and chances are the girl will let him in. But what if she doesn't? What if her real reason for requesting IDs is to track down people like himself? Maybe others have already noticed some strange journalists who have never published anything but who show up at every conference and eat every banquet?

Staring at an abstract painting in order to avoid eye contact, Dan finds he is one of the few people left in the lobby. Almost all the attendees are already in the banquet hall. It's decision time.

"You like this one, don't you?"

Dan turns toward the accented voice. A fat but well-proportioned man stands behind him. Dan quickly takes in his black shirt and darker black pants, a head of pitch-black hair, and a pair of bloodshot eyes inside multifold lids. He is around sixty, or older, despite his suspiciously dark hair. Dan smiles, realizing the man is referring to the huge painting in front of them. It is a jumble of colors, covering every possible interpretation, from a landscape in a storm to a herd of horses running themselves into a blur.

"What is there not to like?" Dan nods slowly at the painting.

"But *why* do you like it?" The man stares at the painting with Dan.

Dan narrows his eyes, purses his lips, and takes a couple of steps forward, then backward. Is this what people should do when they look at a painting?

"What do you see?" the old man demands.

An enormous chop suey of colors. A melting hot pot of shapes and lines. Or is it simply reality as seen through a starved person's eyes? Dan has not eaten since the double-yolked egg this morning.

"I like you," the man says. "Because you don't say what you see. Rather, you don't say what you *don't* see. What news outlet do you represent?"

Dan offers a card, with both hands, a humble gesture he has learned from his "colleagues."

"Never heard of it. I thought every press outlet had harassed me by now."

"It's a new Web-based media site."

"There are so many of you. Can't keep track of them all. Familiar with my works?"

He says, yes, who isn't, while his mind is distracted by the thought that this man is the creator of this picture. That fat but well-proportioned hand is the very hand that stir-fried this immense dish of dripping ink and spilling colors. Before Dan responds, a group of people swarms over, calling the man "Master Chen" or "Mr. Ocean Chen" and apologizing for not recognizing him quickly enough to save him from waiting. Mr. Ocean Chen turns and calls through the impromptu crowd, "If I'm not mistaken, you are from the Northwest."

Dan says that is correct.

"Ah, that half-barbarous region beyond the Great Wall. That sun-baked string of caravan stops along the Silk Road. Let me guess: Gansu Province?"

Dan nods yes.

The master's hand gives a friendly slap to Dan's shoulder. "Only a landsman of mine would be so tall and strong and straightforward."

When they pass the receptionist, Dan makes as if he is so engrossed in listening to Master Chen that he doesn't see her beckoning to him.

Ocean Chen walks through the smiling crowd, passing by stiff, white-clad waiters and long-haired, dark-clad artists, to a table right below the podium. He motions to a chair for Dan to sit next to him. Fumbling in his pockets, Ocean Chen realizes he has misplaced Dan's business card and asks Dan's name again. Without thinking, Dan tells him his real name. Ocean Chen asks if the given name "Dan" is the Chinese character that means "crimson." Yes, that's right. As in Prince Dan of the Kingdom of Yan during the Warring States Period, around 600 BC? That's right. A nice name. Thanks.

Dan thinks about what he will do. He'll go to a bookstore and check a historical encyclopedia to see who the hell this Prince Dan was, and next time he'll flaunt his knowledge of history like this old fellow.

The appetizers look unfamiliar. Dan picks up his chopsticks, but seeing the old artist elegantly ignoring the dishes, he lays them down again quietly. He has a feeling that he won't have a solid, undisturbed time to appreciate the banquet today. A woman leans toward Mr. Ocean Chen, whispering something to him, her fingers fluttering over the huge crystal plate rotating on the lazy Susan in the middle of the table. Then she repeats it to everyone at the table: the appetizers are made of rare fungi and mushrooms collected during bird-watching trips. To Dan's surprise, they taste meaty and oily.

A girl artist of about sixteen goes up to the podium. The guests listen to her over the sound of hundreds of ivory chopsticks clicking subtly on fine, fragile china, and of lips and teeth moving and grinding over delicate textures. After the girl painter presents her paintings projected on a screen, Dan's initial wave of hunger ebbs. He sits back and begins to recognize faces; faces that appear as frequently as his own, smiling oily smiles at abundant food and at envelopes containing "money for your troubles." The girl painter onstage wears a little red camisole covered by her long, thick black hair. The audience buzzes when she says that she started painting before she learned how to speak. But, she adds, she couldn't speak until age five. Her self-revelation is meant as a punch line, and the crowd laughs on cue.

Dan enjoys the first hot course: minced pigeon breasts with mashed tofu molded into tiny snowballs, sprinkled with tiny tender green scallion flakes. As he puts down his chopsticks to catch his breath, he discovers that the girl painter has become the star of the night. Many guests ask for her autograph. Some want pictures taken with her. As Dan wonders if he should join the majority of the journalists and flash his filmless camera at the girl, Mr. Ocean Chen says that he now likes Dan even more.

"You have a good eye," he says, leaning over to Dan. "And an aesthetic appetite too delicate for this kind of thing." He points his chin toward the girl.

Dan holds his mouth still, thinking the flavor of the snowballs is so delicate that one can only appreciate it fully in its aftermath.

"Look at those horny men, easily seduced by girls like her . . . that's why there are so many of them popping up: girl writers, girl painters . . . This society is sick, devouring her kind with criminal lust . . ."

It is noisy, and Dan has missed half of what Ocean Chen has said. Even if he had listened to him with full attention, he would still have missed something. But he nods anyway, leaning his ear toward the old artist. Occasionally, he expands his nostrils to let burps ease out.

Seeing the receptionist coming toward them with an envelope, Dan pulls out his deaf microphone and mute recorder and places them in front of the artist, hoping she will just leave the fee on the table without interrupting the "interview." But she waits, with an indulgent smile, as the artist's lips foam at the corners from speaking so much.

"What?" Ocean Chen pauses impatiently.

She begs his pardon and presents the envelope to Dan, saying softly, "A little humble money for your troubles."

Dan says nothing but nods his thanks.

"Sorry for interrupting." She does not leave.

"It's okay," Dan says.

"If you don't mind . . ." Ocean Chen's hand makes a brush-off movement toward her.

"Sorry, Mr. Chen. Just one moment, please." She puts her hand on the artist's thick shoulder and turns to Dan. "May I have your ID card? Blame it on the new policy. It just creates more work for us."

Dan says he left it at home. With another apologetic smile at Ocean Chen, the receptionist brushes Dan with a shake of her hair as she turns to leave, saying she will call later to get his ID number over the phone.

She will make a big discovery. She'll find out that the Web-based media site on his business card doesn't exist. They will bring charges against him. What could the charge be? Being a banquet freeloader? All the banquets are sinfully copious, and much of the food would have been leftover and dumped, anyway. What difference would it have made if he had not eaten it? None.

Defending himself, Dan feels a moral strength inflating him, straightening his back. With righteous indignation he surveys the space full of chewing jaws and greasy lips. Do you know what I used to have at mealtimes when I was a little boy? Dark gruel made of tree bark and sorghum. In late autumn after the harvest, we children would dig for days through the harvested yam fields to glean roots with a tiny bit of starch in them. We dug and dug, not using shovels, afraid to cut or chop the roots and waste any little piece. We dug with our fingers, cracking our nails in the half-frozen soil. Dan is looking at the hostess now, trying to engage her attention. The hostess daintily picks up a snowball of pigeon breast with her chopsticks and bites a bit off—a bird's bite. Do you know what we children had for delicacies before the wheat ripened in early summer? We had roasted grasshoppers. And my ma told me to drink water if hunger woke me up in the middle of the night. Dan sees a man sitting across from him turn his head away from the podium to take a drink of beer, and he tries to stare him down. Do you believe that I served in the army for three years because I'd been told that the soldiers would always have pork buns? But it turned out they were cabbage buns seasoned with pork fat. Not heeding Dan at all, the man claps with the rest of the audience at the girl painter's clowning around, throwing his head back to laugh. It makes Dan feel more dignified. Do you know what my neighbors on the building-top slum eat? They eat canned food long past its expiration date. Do you know what their monthly wages are? Less than your daily fee. With the little money they have, they must bargain hard in smelly farmer's markets over a bunch of green onions. They will live their lives without ever knowing such things as snowballs made from pigeon breast. Do all of you think it's fair? Dan challenges the crowd with his silent eloquence, trying to make intimidating eye contact with all the people fussing over the girl painter, who is now making the rounds of the tables, toasting the horny guests with her glass of juice.

Ocean Chen has become sullen. And he thinks Dan's enraged expression shows his alliance and loyalty to him. The artist tells Dan that he is deeply concerned about the moral issues of the art world. The artists prostitute themselves, and the vulgar nouveau riche pay. The media serve as pimps for young female charlatans like this one, who in turn exploit the media. Dan holds the dead microphone, into which the master blows bitter chuckles from time to time.

There are seven hot courses on the table, and all of them are made of animals from remote mountains and forests. According to Dan's experience, there should be one more special dish to wrap up the show.

A group of waiters comes out carrying big, oval-shaped plates.

One male host stands up and announces, "Ladies and gentlemen, the most precious meat of the most beautiful of birds!"

Cheers roll through the banquet hall.

The naked bird is lying on its stomach, its head raised and its beak clasping a bouquet carved out of carrots. There are pieces of daikon radish cut and dyed to resemble feathers. And three real tail feathers with a green and blue sheen stand vertiginously, spiked into its bald, triangular butt, trembling and shivering like undead nerves.

"Is it really peacock?" one of the guests at the table asks softly.

"It had better be. But if they have only one real peacock, they must put it on Master Chen's table," another one says, looking ingratiatingly at the blank-faced artist.

"Those who are not sitting at this table might get chicken instead," an older guest adds. "Ours is surely the real 'Peacock Princess.'"

Dan smells an exquisite aroma from the bird, definitely different from chicken. The waiter holds a bowl of meat juice and raises it theatrically above the bird. He looks around, making sure everyone is with him, then pours the steaming liquid slowly over the bird. Gradually, its beak is drowned, and then the face and closed eyes. Soon the grace and arrogance are gone, along with the mythical aura of the "Peacock Princess." As the waiter's knife lands on the bird, and everyone's chopsticks stand at the ready, the table capsizes. The bird glides across the table and alights on the hostess's lap. The woman screams, jumping to her feet. Her face is flecked with brown dots of gravy, and a star-shaped spatter adorns her white dress front.

"I can't believe this!" Ocean Chen says. He stands upright, one hand clutching the table edge. His face is twisted with anger and physical effort.

Dan realizes it is Ocean Chen who caused the "earthquake."

"You people eat this? The most beautiful bird?" The artist points at the smashed bird. "Are you ashamed? You decadent worms!"

A confused silence echoes around the marble hall. The master flashes angry looks at the hosts and hostesses, at the cadres of various government bureaus, and at the journalists. His eyes glint with tears as he rushes for the door.

The hostess, with the mark of the brown sauce explosion on her dress front, runs and stops in front of Ocean Chen.

"Please, Master Chen! I am sorry . . ."

Ocean Chen turns to face the crowds. "Go on. Eat it. Refine our great Chinese culture with your mouths and stomachs. Thanks to people like you, our glorious ancient Chinese culture has only one part left intact: eating."

"We are truly sorry . . ." A male host catches up with the hostess, trying to block the artist's way.

"*I* am sorry *indeed,*" says the artist.

"Master Chen, it is a misunderstanding."

"What did I misunderstand? Are they peacocks or not?"

"Well . . ."

The hostess and the host stare at each other. They suddenly look ugly in their complete embarrassment and awkwardness.

A man stands up and aims his camera at the artist. All the journalists join in and trigger their cameras. The banquet hall is silent except for the metallic clicks of this impromptu firing squad. On the other side of their lenses, the angry artist stands like a pale martyr amid the lightning of their flashes, lecturing them on how peacocks are hunted and decrease in number every year. "A people that only indulges in oral pleasures is the lowest kind," the artist concludes.

Dan realizes that the energy he saw in Ocean Chen's paintings is hatred. The old artist drives his brush with the power of hatred. Why does he hate so much?

For hours afterward, Dan tries to comprehend the peacock banquet spoiled by the quirky old artist. He goes to a newspaper stall early the next morning and searches the art sections of all the popular newspapers. He sees nothing about the incident. Finally, he finds a minor newspaper that carries a small piece on the fund-raiser for bird-watchers. He buys it and begins to read the article. It contains a line that merely notes Ocean Chen's attendance.

He reads the paper again and again, feeling cheated. The newspaper didn't lie, yet it didn't tell the truth. Before he realizes it, Dan has started scrawling notes and comments in the paper's margins.

During the long winters in Dan's home village, the only recreation the villagers had was listening to folktales. The villagers would raise a few tens of yuan to hire a traveling folktale troupe with two to three performers. The performer young Dan enjoyed most was an old blind man with an expressionless face and raucous voice, who appeared to marvel at the villagers' roaring laughter during his storytelling. Dan remembers how he, as a boy at ten, had followed the old man from village to village, carrying the old man's bedroll and bread sack and keeping the village dogs away from him. Only much later did Dan realize what made this old storyteller so wonderful was his blindness. Because he couldn't see his audience, couldn't take advantage of any rapport with them, he had to rely entirely on his words. When Dan shyly asked the old storyteller if he would take on a ten-year-old boy to be his apprentice, the old man blinked his visionless eyes and sighed.

He said only a blind person would make a good storyteller. Why? Because it is only when one's bodily eyes are blocked that one's mind's eye can open wide, and it makes one see things moving and happening, infinitely vivid and colorful. Then? Then he should write down what is happening before his mind's eye. Then? Then . . . then he becomes a really good storyteller, standing out from those wordy clowns.

Twenty-four years later and here is Dan, squeezing his eyes shut, trying to see a round flowerbed of various mushrooms in a spectrum of creamy white, powder yellow, subtle orange, light and dark browns, all the way to a velvety black. Will he start the article from the appetizer?

"Can't you help me with this damned zipper?" Little Plum asks, face red from trying to fix the zipper on the back of her dress.

Dan pulls the jammed zipper up and turns back to his blank sheet. She watches him curiously. He sits in front of the desk, his eyebrows knitting, one of his long legs folded up with his foot resting on the chair's edge, a posture a peasant takes when smoking a pipe in his home village. He pinches the pencil so hard that Little Plum flinches, anticipating the lead will break at any moment. She sees him write each stroke with the strength of someone carving wood.

"Do you know how to write the character for 'feather'?" He turns to his wife after chewing his pencil butt for a few seconds.

"Feather of what?" she asks.

"There's a special character for a peacock's tail feather, isn't there?" he mutters, hearing Little Plum's plastic slippers flip-flopping down the corridor to a neighbor's at the other end. She comes back again flip-flopping, both hands clasping a heavy dictionary against her chest.

Dan hasn't told his wife about the peacock banquet, about what a disaster it was. He doesn't tell her what he himself has yet to understand. He only understands Ocean Chen as a different man with concerns such as "our glorious Chinese culture" and "a people who only indulge their oral pleasures." He has to grope with Chen's meaning in his own words.

After he finishes writing, he counts the empty spaces where he has skipped the characters he doesn't know how to write. There are more than two hundred of them. He opens the borrowed dictionary and begins to fill in the spaces, one by one. He chuckles to himself, imagining someone reading his unintentional word puzzle. He is not sure what he wants to do with the article; he merely feels compelled to write it because the journalists did not.

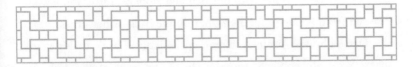

DAN ALWAYS TAKES Little Plum out on his day off. She loves to go sightseeing in vast car lots packed with rows and rows of new or used cars; in immense supermarkets with aisles and aisles of goods; and in multilevel, complex intersections of city streets. She likes the sight of bulldozers lined up, mowing down heaps and piles of garbage. She can also roam the supermarket, admiring stacks of dish detergents, napkins, and bath towels as if they were flower beds or pavilions in a park. The scenes she fancies are expansive, modern, industrially organized, and inhuman.

Standing next to each other by a steel fence overlooking a used-car lot, Dan and Little Plum enjoy the dusty silence. In the distance, banners ruffle in the evening breeze, colorfully advertising big sales. Once in a while, Dan says which car he likes most and which one best suits Little Plum. He comments on the styles and features, haggling with himself over the prices, while the whole time Little Plum merely stands watching with sweet detachment.

"When I have money, I'll buy you that little yellow car."

"Okay."

"You like it?"

"Yes."

She gives him a non-involved smile. The way she smiles makes him think they might as well talk about something as remote as their next incarnation. He gazes at the cars, swearing silently to his wife that he will work harder, eat more banquets, and collect more "money for your troubles." He can't bear to think of her spending her life as their neighbors do, with so many omissions; a life blank as if unlived.

A couple of security guards approach them.

"What are you doing here?" one of them asks.

"Getting some fresh air," Dan answers.

The guards size them up in a way they think will intimidate Dan and Little Plum.

"Go somewhere else to get some fresh air."

"Why?"

"Go away."

Dan turns away from the metal fence to face them. He doesn't want Little Plum's simple enjoyment spoiled.

"There are car thieves. That's why," the guard says.

"Those are petty thieves. I only steal Mercedes-Benzes. The junkers you have here are not worth my trouble," Dan says.

The guards look at each other, then draw their billy clubs from their belts.

"Come with us."

"Why?"

Wasting no words, they wave the clubs lazily. They want Dan to see that the clubs will answer his difficult "whys." They are very young: eighteen or nineteen, fresh out of cornfields or rice paddies.

They take a step forward and Dan takes a step to one side. He grimaces at Little Plum, letting her think he is only kidding them. They raise their clubs and Dan shrugs, surrendering. He tells Little Plum to leave, but she shakes her head and follows them. On the way through the parking lot, he gestures fiercely for her to leave. She sees, and stops. When he turns his back, she follows again.

They pass the cars parked with military precision and reach a row of huts behind the dealership offices. The two guards force Dan into the rear room, rank with the smell of athlete's foot. A small TV sits facing two bunk beds. On the screen one can make out a foggy scene of two characters' fuzzy figures punching each other out with ringing thuds. Obviously, the guards have gotten their education in the way of the warrior from this sort of material.

"You have two choices. You can stay here until we finish investigating you, or you can mop all the car windows," one of them says.

Dan sticks his hand into his pants pocket, wondering whether he should give one of his business cards to them. They probably will let him go if they know he is a "reporter." His fumbling fingers become moist as he thinks of the body search they might give him. If they search him, they will find that his ID card has one name and his business card has another. He would have made a new bunch of cards had he not been distracted by writing the article on Ocean Chen at the peacock banquet.

A car alarm goes off, and one of the guards leaps out of the hut, yelling, "Who's out there?"

The other guard closes the door and latches it from the outside.

Hearing Little Plum's voice, Dan leans on the window and looks out. Under the relentlessly bright lamp, she carries a filthy cat and stands by a car. The cat has set off the alarm.

"Why are you still here?" a guard demands.

"Why not? The land belongs to the nation," she says. She is bitchy and spoiling for a fight.

"You want to go to that room, too?"

"If you invite me."

"Okay, let's go then." They close in on her, one on each side.

She stands hugging the cat, her back leaning toward the car. One guard pushes her, and she jerks away. "Hey, you touched me!" she says shrilly, and the cat shrieks with her, running away as fast as a filthy flash.

"You better watch who you touch, you hoodlums! Trying to feel me up!" she says.

They push her harder.

"You know who this woman is?" she yells, puffing out her chest and slapping it loudly.

They look at each other, then at her.

"Who are you?" one of them asks.

"I'm Dan Dong's wife!"

"Who is Dan Dong?"

"Dan Dong is my husband, moron!"

The other guard grabs her arm and pulls her. Trying to fight him off, she waves her arms wildly, her back arching, pulling backward with all her weight. The zipper on the back of her dress pops open.

"Rape!" she screams. "Somebody, help!"

"Shut up!" the guards say, looking around, glad nobody has heard her.

"Rape! Rape!" she yells louder. "These guys locked up my husband and tried to rape me!"

A few people from the street start to look their way. Fearing that her torn zipper might require some explaining, the guards quickly go to the hut and tell Dan to leave. They stand at the door and watch Dan exit.

"Are you some kind of cadre?" one guard asks.

"No. Just a poor newsman." He hands a card to one of the guards.

He hears a silence behind him as he walks toward Little Plum, one hand at her back to hold the breach of her dress. Dan hears the guards' dialogue.

"What a waste. A newsman marrying a woman like that."

"Did she bite you?"

"No, but she *scratched* me!"

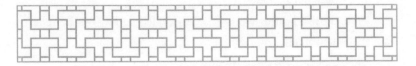

THE REGISTRATION COUNTER sits by the entrance. On both ends are opulent flower arrangements. Real flowers. As Dan bends down to write his much-practiced signature, he sees a business card of exactly the same design as his previous one. It bears the name of the phony Web-based media firm he created and has since abandoned. He retreats from the entrance and tries to make sense of the situation. Apparently another banquet bug has eaten his way into Dan's domain, only he didn't have the dignity to do so independently. He has pirated Dan's intellectual property. Dan sees his hand, shaking with rage, holding a cigarette. In the midst of his rage, somebody must have offered cigarettes all around, and he must have taken one.

A woman waves to him in greeting. He pretends not to see her. There lurks another banquet bug. He has to comprehend the bizarre situation and take stock of it. He has created such a nice job for himself. He has refined and improved it through his observations and diligent learning. He has gotten where he is today through courage and spylike audacity.

Dan asks the girl with dyed yellow hair at the registration counter if she can point out the person who dropped that card. Well, she might recognize him if she sees him. Would she please make an announcement that somebody wants to see him? Sorry, she is too busy. She holds her palm out for his ID. He pulls it out of his pants pocket, a bunch of coins falling on the granite floor, bouncing and rolling as they hit the icy smoothness. He is too distracted to care. The yellow-haired girl throws quick glances between the name on his business card and the one on his ID. He has had some new business cards made, so his name matches that of his ID. Dan doesn't know the risk of it: if someone doubts his identity, he or she can discover the truth about him in minutes. The yellow-haired girl writes down Dan's ID numbers. Involuntarily, he counts. It takes eighteen of them to form his digital existence.

Dan enters the ballroom where the noon banquet is being held. The stage is big enough for a modest-sized orchestra. The hardwood floor can accommodate hundreds of dancers. There are huge posters with the sponsors' names draping from clusters of balloons. A banner hanging over the stage says "Eradicate Illiteracy! Provide Education for Children in Poverty!" Dan has attended fund-raising conferences on this topic many times. They are hosted by super-rich people who have made fortunes overnight, thanks to China's economic reforms. A man in an elegant suit passes Dan, followed by his secretary, bodyguards, admirers, and the smell of an expensive cologne. Dan lurches to get out of their way. He feels insignificant in these supermen's presence. He watches them become richer and more famous through these conferences.

Looking for a place to sit, Dan feels a hand touching his shoulder. He turns around to see a small face under a big baseball cap, framed between two enormous silver earrings.

"I was calling to you all the way from the registration!" She opens her fist and shows him six coins.

Dan looks at her, thinking she must have mistaken him for someone else.

"You're rich, aren't you?" she says. "Six yuan aren't worth your bending down to pick them up, right?"

"Thank you" is all Dan can say.

Dropping the coins into Dan's palm, she dares him with her teasing eyes. "Want to sit by me?" She shrugs her canvas bag up onto her shoulder and whips her chin toward the seats in the front.

Before Dan reacts, the girl pulls his bag, containing the mute recorder and the blind camera, and leads the way through people and chairs. She calls him "Peng," the phony name he invented for himself months ago. As the host announces the start of the press conference, he begins to look for an opportunity to get rid of her.

The doors close. The hosts of such conferences have wised up enough about some veteran journalists who slip out after they register, then slip back in for the banquet and fees. They now guard the doors to prevent anyone's work ethic from slipping. Dan is studying all the exits. Unfortunately, the men's room is inside the ballroom. He sees an exit by the stage that seems unguarded.

He stands up and excuses himself, his long legs squeezing past between knees and chair backs. He knows that some of the guards are watching him. For the first time in his life, he resents his tall stature and large build. Outside the ballroom, a man is smoking.

"Are you leaving?"

Without turning to look, Dan knows the girl is behind him.

"I need to smoke," Dan says, feeling lucky that the smoker has inspired him to lie.

"Do you know what it is about this conference that pisses me off, Peng?" She thumbs toward the ballroom, swaggering toward him. She is about twenty-eight or older, very skinny, no breasts, two big eyes encircled by dark rings, as if she were born with insomnia.

"I don't know." Dan smiles. "Why do you keep calling me Peng?"

Her hands stop short in the middle of gesturing. She is unhappy either with her memory or his attempt to play with it.

"I'm Dan. My family name is Dong," Dan says, dead sincere.

She smiles, saying she has evidence that he is "Peng." Her family name is Gao, with the given name of Happy, bestowed by her parents, who are a pair of somber, pedantic, introverted, bespectacled professors who wanted their daughter to grow with but one aspiration—to be happy. Dan nods and smiles. She goes on telling him she isn't surprised to know he has more names than Peng. Everyone has pen names. Otherwise, who would dare to write polemical, caustic articles? She herself used to use "Deep Gao" as her pen name for articles attacking banquet eating and extravagant gift-giving. She was afraid she wouldn't get invited to banquets if she used her real name. Dan nods more and smiles wider. Could she be the one who used his fake ex-company's card? She says she uses the pen name

"Deep Gao" to mock her parents. That's what they think of them-selves, "Deep Gao"—*"Gao Shen"*—meaning "esoteric."

As she talks, Dan counts the strange words she has used. There were at least three that Dan doesn't know.

She pulls out a business card holder and points a card at him. It is the card he used and abandoned some time ago. It has his abandoned name, Peng, on it. It is the card he saw at the registration, pirated by his secret rival. Do they all conspire to spoil his simple ambition of eating a banquet today?

"You must have gotten me mixed up with someone else," he says.

"Cut it out, will you?"

Happy Gao's (or Deep Gao's) loudness causes the smoker to choke and cough.

"Don't challenge my memory! I never mix up a person I'm fond of with someone else," she says.

Dan stares at her, wondering if her use of the word "fond" is the same as the standard definition in Chinese dictionaries. She is more like a boy than a girl. The dark red lipstick on her colorless face seems out of place.

"I like you because you don't have the phony look the others do." She reaches her hand out and, seeing his eyes blink, wriggles her fin-gers. "Got a cigarette to spare?" He takes the pack out of his pocket and hands it to her. She pulls one out, looks at the label, disgusted, and crumbles it. Dan watches her throw it into a trash can.

"You could use it as mosquito repellent." She thumbs toward the trash can. "Or to smoke fish. Even the cigarettes kids smoke in high schools aren't *that* cheap."

"What press are you from?" he asks, expecting an exchange of business cards.

"I'm freelance," she says, handing him a card.

He nods. What the hell does "freelance" mean? She is telling him about the articles she has written, hoping they'll ring a bell. He nods more, as if reminded. Then she says she wanted to talk to him the other day when he came in with Ocean Chen. They must be close friends, right? She wonders if he can introduce her to the master. Before he denies it, she tells him to stop lying to her; she knows they are good friends from the Northwest accent they share. Don't worry; she won't betray him if he gives her the master's address and telephone number.

"Look, I've got to go." Dan glances at his watch.

"Want to be the first to get the news out?" Happy Gao has produced a sheet of paper from nowhere. "I have prepared it for you. These conferences are all the same. You write one article and you can use it for all of them. Just change some names and a few words." Her eyes are the only innocent part of her cynical face. "You can use this one for your news Web site. I won't accuse you of plagiarism. And you will give me Ocean Chen's telephone number. Deal?"

"Look, I really don't know him."

"Oh yes, you do."

"I don't even understand his paintings . . ."

"Who does?"

"I mean . . ."

"You mean to tell me it's your mission to protect him? I thought you weren't a phony." Her dark red lips bloom into a vicious smile.

Dan hesitates. He can get rid of her, make an excuse and bolt out of here. But he has yet to find the other banquet bug. He must put him under surveillance; destroy the other bug before the bug ruins him.

"Deal or not, Peng?" Happy pushes.

It is unsafe to have someone calling you by the name connected to your previous phantom identity. But it is more dangerous still that someone else has gotten himself hired by a ghost company of your own creation.

"Look, Master Chen is ill. He can't be bothered," Dan says, hoping his lie will bring peace for the time being.

"That I know. The newspapers said he was taken to a hospital two days ago. What I want to know is which hospital he checked in to." So the old artist is ill. Everyone here knew but Dan. "Just give me his phone number at the hospital. I'll give you my article for free."

He shakes his head.

"How about I treat you to a foot massage?" She steps closer, her arms crossed. "I'll get you the best girl in Beijing. She will pamper your feet. Or pamper any part of you. *Any* part you want her to pamper." She proposes it with total straightforwardness, not hinting or suggesting. "For a little extra, you can ask her out. Say, eighty or a hundred yuan. Guaranteed she's clean. And she'll bring her own protection."

Like a trapped animal doing anything just to free itself, Dan scrawls Master Chen's telephone number, an invented one of course, on a slip of paper she has provided. He will deal with the consequences later, he tells himself.

At the banquet he notices, to his relief, that Happy Gao has vanished. Dan doesn't have much appetite until a dish comes into view. In a big oblong plate lie some twenty huge sea snails. A chubby waiter tells them the dish, named "Land within Sea," is designed by a female cook, a winner of the national cooking award. The waiter passes a toy hammer and a metal board to everyone, as he explains how the dish is prepared. You have to take the snail bodies out of the shells, mince them, and mix them with veal and wild mushrooms. Then you season the mixture with secret ingredients, beat it with chopsticks to break the fibers and tenderize it, and stuff it back into the shells. The waiter demonstrates how to hammer the shells open. The guests at the table follow him with intense interest. From the broken shells, the meat comes out in a perfect spiral, exactly the shape of a snail.

Dan sees the yellow-haired registration girl approach. She asks if he has seen the person he was looking for. No, he hasn't. How could that be? She told him that Dan was looking for him. She gave Dan's card to him, telling him what Dan looks like. Is he a middle-aged man? Dan asks. Hard to tell his age. She looks at the faces around the tables. Sorry, she can't find him now. He might have left. Some journalists don't stay for banquets if they have another function to go to. They go to collect one more fee, she says.

A scoundrel. A parasite. A thief who has stolen Dan's business model and intellectual property. Of course he fled when he knew Dan was seeking him out. He fears Dan more than Dan fears him. Analyzing this, Dan relaxes. He finds his eyes lingering on the snail dish. It hurts him to experience such things without Little Plum. Before he leaves the table, which everyone but he has relinquished, he grabs a snail and wraps it up in a napkin.

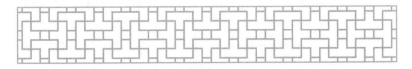

AS SOON AS he steps up the stairs, Little Plum calls out to him. He looks up as she looks downward, her features appearing between the steel handrailings. She says somebody telephoned him. Who? Somebody called the public phone on the second floor, asking for him. Dan realizes that he used that number on his old business card. Little Plum says the phone kept ringing, waking up everyone on the top floor from their long, deep afternoon nap. So she ran downstairs and answered it. It was a woman.

"What did she want?"

"Wanted to know who I am."

"What did you say?"

"I said to her 'Who the hell are *you?*' "

"Well?"

They slammed the phone down on each other.

Happy Gao. Must be that irksome woman. She must have tried to contact Ocean Chen, using the number Dan forged. He hurries down, vaulting the stairs. He reaches the space between the two floors, where a telephone sits on the cement floor, gray with dust. He dials the number Happy Gao gave him and takes a deep breath when it rings. One, two, three . . .

"Hello."

"Sorry, Miss Gao . . ."

"Wait five minutes and call me again," she says, hanging up.

He waits ten, then calls back.

"Another five minutes, okay?" she says. Then he hears a recorded voice from an answering machine. "I can't talk now. I'm in the middle of writing."

He stands embracing the dusty telephone, waiting. He decides to give her fifteen minutes. He looks up and sees Little Plum watching him. He beckons to her. She comes, hopping down the steps. Is she jealous of Happy Gao? Yes, she is. But she shouldn't be. Why? Dan smiles. He wouldn't admit it to her, but he relies on her for everything, including his sleep. There have been nights when Dan would wait for sleep to come, just like waiting for a bus to take him to an important banquet that allows no late arrivals. In sweating anxiety he would listen to Little Plum's breathing, so even and deep, with a soft, regular snore through her nostrils. He doesn't believe anyone could breathe a more relaxed and secure breath. It is the breath of a person completely at peace with the world, who believes she owes nothing to anybody, and no one owes her anything, either. He would follow her rhythm, letting his chest rise and fall coinciding with hers, and his breathing would deepen, and the edges of his anxiety would smooth out. Then he would eventually be rocked to sleep by her breathing lullaby.

After Dan tells about his encounter with Happy Gao, Little Plum gives him two flirtatious punches on the arm. A signal of her reconciliation and relief.

Another five minutes go by and Dan points out Happy Gao's number on her business card, telling Little Plum to ring it. He coaches her to say "Good afternoon. This is such-and-such media group. I'm Mr. Dan Dong's secretary. Is Miss Gao available?" She repeats it again and again, accepting his suggestions and trying to improve. He steps to her side and observes her profile. She pronounces words with child-like sincerity. He pushes her chin back, holds the corners of her mouth narrower, and asks her to try a phrase: "Please hold, Miss Gao; let me get Mr. Dong." He nods at her progress, explaining that this expression will make her voice sound lower, colder, more mature, a totally different voice from her natural voice that said, "Who the hell are *you*?!"

The telephone rings, startling both of them. They spontaneously step back and watch it ring. The ringing is so loud that it troubles the dusty, slumbering atmosphere of the building. He eyes Little Plum to tell her to pick up the receiver, and she smiles, flushing, as if really starting a new job in a big boss's presence. Then she freezes up. He grabs the phone, his palm already clammy.

"Hello . . ."

"Don't tell me you're sorry," Happy Gao says. "I tried that number you gave me a million times. Then I suspected I got one digit wrong or something, so I kept revising, putting the digits in every possible order. I am not going to call you an asshole, even though you are, because I know you tricked me out of protectiveness for the old artist."

Her voice is drowned out by the machines downstairs that have switched on all of a sudden. It is the first order the factory has gotten in a long while. Lately, the dwellers of this building are delighted by this noise, for it reassures them that the factory might pay the back wages it owes its workers and reserve workers. With the noise, they sleep better and eat more.

"What's that noise?" Happy asks.

He cups his mouth and the receiver with his wide palm. He explains that he opened the window to the street. Below his office is a big avenue with busy traffic. He closes his fingers around the receiver tighter. Is that better now?

That's better. She tells him she was impressed by his article. What article? On Ocean Chen's raising hell in the peacock banquet. But how did she get to read it, since it hasn't been published yet? Never mind; she has many secret ways to read unpublished things. Real stuff usually stays unpublished. She laughs, and her dark-lipped laughter beats on his eardrums, hurting a bit. He frowns, moving the receiver away from his ear. The noise of the machines comes between them.

Little Plum stares at him.

Happy tells him it's inspiring to read something so pure, so original, so totally free of brainwashed journalism. And it is honestly objective. It can be refined, and a number of words should be corrected, but the defects are insignificant. What's important is the freshness, which can only happen if one has a fresh, childlike eye. And a nonjudgmental mind.

Little Plum looks at Dan, seeing beads of sweat run down from his temple, sparkling in the sunlight that enters through the broken window glass. She wipes them off with her hand, and he smiles at her. The afternoons are hot in this thin cement structure, and it gets hotter when the factory downstairs is in operation.

"But where did you read it?" Dan asks. A few days ago, he mailed it to some magazines, just for the heck of it.

She evades his question and goes on to say how she enjoyed the way he described the guests, the fashion in which the waiters were dressed and how they served the food, the table setting, the decorations on the back of the chairs, the flower arrangement—and how he touched the flowers and discovered they were not real. And the dishes. The appetizer—the way the mushrooms suggested a peacock's upward-fanning tail feathers. It is visual and full of smells and tastes. All the dishes sound like works of art that the artists themselves would consider sublime and profound. She especially praises the way he pushed the story toward its dramatic climax—he didn't prepare his readers for the crisis, but he didn't do that out of intent; he did it out of innocence. Or out of a higher sophistication.

Dan is surprised that she understands his article much better than he does. She has grasped some meanings that enlighten even him.

"So it is much more striking when the master throws the peacock dish . . ."

"No, he didn't throw the dish; he threw the table."

"Okay. He sent the dish flying at the pretentious hostess . . ."

"No, he didn't. The dish just ends up on her lap without anybody knowing how. And Master Chen—"

"Let me finish," she says. And he lets her.

She goes on praising the parts she is most impressed with. Dan looks at Little Plum, who gazes up at him, sharing everything she can't hear.

"You know what? I have some time tomorrow. I can drop by your office. We can discuss your article further and make it a good profile piece on Ocean Chen. And it will give voice to his concerns about nature, animals, environmental protection, and ecology. I hear he hates banquets and loves simple food. He loathes those who enjoy food too much."

That's a shame, Dan thinks. That's because he can afford to loathe eating.

"It will be a brilliant article with some heavy polishing. We will make it more poignant. Right now it's raw and coarse, let's face it," she says. "I'll come at ten in the morning. Is parking easy around your office?"

He falters. "I'll be downtown tomorrow morning."

"We can meet in your office after you come back from downtown. My schedule is always flexible."

He is cornered. He looks at Little Plum again, as if for help. She looks at him curiously, and his nervousness is somewhat soothed.

"I will meet you in the lobby," he says.

"Good."

He will take her to a coffee shop. He'll make up a story that his office is too busy and noisy. Someone is up there doing plumbing. Or it's in the process of moving elsewhere. How much is a cup of coffee?

What if there isn't a coffee shop nearby? What if she goes there early and finds out there isn't a media company at the address on his business card?

He sleeps lightly that night. In the morning, before he gets dressed for the meeting with Happy Gao, he finds an ugly hole on his pants pocket. A rat came last night. It chewed through the fabric of his pants pocket and the cloth napkin to get at the forgotten sea snail. It also chewed half the shell away, trying to reach the snail's reorganized organs. It must have been a giant rat with huge, sharp teeth that could break such a hard shell. Rats in this building only get to smell noodles and steamed bread; they have never smelled a sophisticated odor like the snail, so pungently delicious. Little Plum has not smelled it either. He watches Little Plum, puffy-eyed and bare-legged, looking for another pair of pants for him. He doesn't have another pair of presentable pants. Little Plum cuts a piece of fabric from inside a pocket and mends the hole. He leaves his shirttail hanging out to cover the patch.

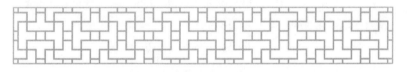

FORTUNATELY HE FINDS a coffee shop just a block away from his supposed office building. Dan checks the prices. It'll cost him twenty yuan for a cup of regular coffee, forty for Happy Gao and himself. He begins rehearsing excuses for not drinking coffee. He is allergic to it. His stomach doesn't take it well. So he'll only have to pay for Happy's cup of coffee. At twelve o'clock, Happy shows up in the lobby.

"No, I never drink coffee," she says to his suggestion. "I indulge in all the vices except coffee drinking." All his scouting and preparation have gone to waste. He offers to take her to a restaurant. Why, is he hungry? She is not. Haven't they been spoiled by all the exquisite banquets yet? How can he propose to eat in a restaurant where the food is common and the hygiene dubious? Besides, she has a function to go to in the afternoon, where she will be fed. She has never bought groceries or spent money in restaurants since she became a freelance journalist.

She talks, leading the way across the street, over a couple of short blocks and through a glass door. It says on an overhead signboard: "Green Grove Club." Happy tells Dan they will enjoy free tea and quiet time here. It turns out she knows the neighborhood of his "office" quite well. The club looks dim and desolate. He wonders if it is going out of business. He hears their footsteps squeaking on the wooden floor of the corridor, on either side of which are small rooms facing one another. The plaques on the doors read "Massage Room." As the passage extends into deeper gloom, the air becomes stale, reeking with the odors of drinking, night meals, and slumbering bodies. An odor of trapped nights.

The massage rooms double as dormitories for the massage girls, Happy tells Dan. A man calls after them.

"Is that Miss Gao?" A man emerges, half-awake, upper body leaning out of a "massage room" at the entrance to the corridor.

"Good evening, Manager Zhu," Happy laughs, turning toward him.

"What time is it?" Manager Zhu asks.

"It's a quarter to one in the afternoon, Beijing time. But does this place run on any normal clock?" Happy says.

"We're on Paris time," says the manager, laughing. He comes out wearing a sports jacket and pajama bottoms.

"Looks like you did good business last night. The girls are exhausted," says Happy.

"We had a tour group from Taiwan."

Manager Zhu knocks on one of the doors and calls a girl's name.

"Another bunch of horny Taiwanese, reclaiming their motherland by fucking her daughters," Happy quips.

Manager Zhu hushes her, smiling. "You're not going to say this in your articles, right?"

"Not until I know it for sure," Happy answers.

"This is . . . ?" The manager looks at Dan, anticipating an introduction.

"This guy is a more formidable reporter than I am," Happy says. "He can destroy your reputation overnight."

Manager Zhu sizes Dan up, reconsidering him. "Let me know if I can be of any help to you," he says, offering his card out of his pajama shirt pocket.

He even carries business cards in his sleep. Dan is amazed.

Manager Zhu continues down the hallway, calling and knocking at each door, but his calls and knocks meet with silence. Manager Zhu turns to Happy. "You go find yourself a nice room, and I'll have tea sent over."

Happy leads Dan down a stairwell to a lower level. The odor becomes thicker and stronger, enriched by some lotions and herbs.

"Does the smell bother you?" Dan asks.

"What smell?"

Dan says nothing, concentrating on overcoming the odor by forcing himself to inhale through his mouth. He has no idea that he is the kind of person more sensitive to smells and flavors than others. Happy pushes a door open to a group of men still asleep on reclining

chairs. The rooms downstairs are the boys' living quarters, Dan figures. The boys are hired to massage women's feet, Happy tells him,
for vitalizing sexual energy.

They finally settle down in a room with two reclining chairs.

"I think you are so sly," Happy says.

"Me?" What is she talking about?

"You wrote about Ocean Chen's egotism with such a poker face,
and with a voice as earnest as a country boy's. But the reader gets a
clear impression of how hurt the old man's ego felt. Oh, boy, is he
hurt! And his libido is still going strong."

What does "ego" mean? What is "libido"? Dan wants to ask but is
afraid to reveal his background as a middle-school dropout. When
the tea and sweets arrive, Happy says she agrees with Dan's article,
that the old artist was actually sore about the girl painter who
snatched all the attention from him. He was outraged not only by the
peacock dish, but by the girl, the audience, and the host as well.

"Still, we can use him to make a great story on the environment.
On how primitively ugly this people is." Happy lights a cigarette and
hands it to Dan. The filter is marked by a dark red ring of her lipstick, which causes a secret shiver in his lower abdomen as his lips
close up on it. "You have to let me see Ocean Chen."

Dan smokes, gazing abstractly into the distance. He gradually
comes to understand what "ego" means. Yet he doesn't like it used in
reference to the old artist. He can't say why.

"This kind of issue is risky, because it will offend both the government and the masses. But if we extrapolate from Ocean Chen's
refusal to eat peacocks, we can make it literary enough to hide what
we are really driving at. If you can introduce me to him, I'll have him
elaborate on the subject. I bet he'll cooperate, just to provoke public

attention. Then I'll make it the lead story in an important newspaper. It's a topic that'll get a journalist noticed internationally."

So she wants attention. Dan scratches the beard on his chin, his fingernails making grassy noises on a week's stubble. He has not shaved since he began to work on the article. She waits. Her waiting is more oppressive than the dense odor.

He says the old artist made him promise not to give out his phone number. Then how about taking her to Chen's place? That is out of the question. Such a shame; it will make him the best freelance journalist. So that's what "freelance" means. A freelancer needs no employer; neither a company nor an office. So he doesn't have to invent them. Deep in his obsession with the word "freelance," Dan watches Happy moving her lips and hands, oblivious of what she has been talking about all this time.

"Once you show me Ocean Chen's door, you can just leave. I will make my own introductions. How does that sound?" Happy goes on persuading, without noticing her words pass right by him.

A freelancer. What a solution! What a relief! He will get rid of that invisible creep who follows him like a shadow, hiding behind the phony identity of Dan's previous phantom company.

He'll be free of all fears and worries. He will get a new set of business cards that say "freelance journalist" before heading off to the next banquet. He'll eat banquets in peace ever after. All he wants is to enjoy the banquets, to make a little money and to save up for a little apartment with a real shower and toilet, and a sofa set that doesn't moan and groan and fight your butt.

"I will polish your article as an exchange of favors. After the publication, you will be famous in the journalistic community . . ."

Then he sees her talk to a girl in a white, loose robe gathered at the waist with a sash. The girl must have come in during his reverie. She carries a red plastic bucket full of hot water in one hand, and a blue plastic basin in the other. She comes toward him, smiling, and he smells her warm body odor preserved and concentrated by a long sleep. It is an aroma directly out of her nightgown and her down comforter. An aroma like sweetened milk. It erases all his thoughts.

"First time here, sir?" the girl asks with a strong South China accent. She is in her late teens or early twenties.

"Yes," he says.

Dan looks at her, then at Happy.

"How do you want it done, sir?"

"Don't be shy," Happy says, a pimplike smile lighting her dark-ringed eyes.

Before he realizes what is going on, the girl sits down on a low stool across from him, one hand hooking a lock of hair behind her ear.

"What are you doing?" he asks.

"Massaging your feet," the girl answers, amused, as if to say she has rarely seen any man so unsophisticated as this Mr. Journalist.

Looking at Happy, he puts his feet back on the stool. Happy winks.

"What would you like, sir?" asks the girl. "Crystal mud or herbs?"

"Mr. Journalist likes crystal mud," Happy answers. "The mud is from Tibet," she tells Dan. "The Tibetans always come up with the most mystical healing materials. It enhances your virility in a flash."

Twisting her cigarette in the ashtray, Happy tosses another meaningful smile at Dan and gets up. Dan comes to understand his situation: he is getting a "massage" that always leads to something else. He has heard some journalists talk about this kind of service. It has a mysterious power of arousal, all starting with an innocent foot massage.

"The crystal mud is a good choice. It is getting to be very popular," the girl tells Dan, bending low to cover the basin with a plastic sheet. To prevent foot disease, she says. Just like a condom, Dan thinks, but for the foot. She pours some hot liquid into the "condomed" basin, churns it with her hand, and adds more. In the hollow of her V-shaped collar, Dan catches a glimpse of her youthful breasts. She sits down on a low stool across from him and begins to untie his shoes and peel off his socks. His feet are naked. How come his feet feel so private? With a shudder he withdraws his feet from her hands, loses his balance, and falls on his back into the reclining chair that suddenly flattens. It turns into a bed for "Full Service." After that, the house presents a big, fat bill, as a journalist once told Dan.

"I like you. You know why?" Happy says, going out the door. "Because nowadays few men would be shy coming here."

"Where are you going?" Dan asks.

"I am going to borrow a tape recorder from a friend. His office is nearby. When I interview Ocean Chen this afternoon, I don't want a single word of his going unrecorded."

He guesses he must have come to terms with her on this "exchange of favors" while he was busy plotting to become a freelancer.

"I haven't much time," he says, raising his wristwatch.

"Two hours?" Happy turns to the girl.

The girl nods.

"But, Happy . . ."

"By the time I get back, you will be so revitalized that you will feel like you got a new flush of youth." She blows a dark red kiss at him from the door, authentically Western. "Don't you worry about the bill; it's on the house."

As soon as Happy's footsteps fade away, he begins to think about escaping from the place and from the girl, whose hands are like seaweed brushing about his feet. Or like the tentacles of an octopus, soft and supple, floating around you until they lock you up inside their intricate, deadly tangles. He feels the strength of these arms grow under the water and as the snare forms. He must escape before his whole body gets tangled up. But he can't move. His feet seem to melt away in her hands. Not only his feet, but his whole being as well. He must leave before Happy comes back, demanding her favor in return.

And yet he is overcome by an indolence he has never experienced. It is brought out by the strange contact between the girl's hands and his feet.

He realizes that it is the girl who has started the conversation. He has gone along with the talk for a while without knowing what they have been talking about. He must have asked where her hometown is and how long ago she left it, because she has begun narrating her life in a village in Sichuan. She left it at age sixteen to join her older sister in Beijing. That means three years ago. Does she miss her parents? Well, she sends money to them every other month.

She pours more of the hot mixture into the basin.

When does she go to bed every night? Depends. Normally she goes to bed at six. Evening? No, morning. She laughs, showing two rows of tiny, uneven teeth. So she only gets five hours' sleep. Sometimes four, but she's used to it. What does she do when she is not asleep? She works. Works for twenty hours straight? Oh, who keeps track?

She kneads his toes gently. Her indulgence makes him hiss secretly.

Does she like her job? She says nothing, but he understands she doesn't. Would she find another job? She is not sure. She doesn't have any other training. So she has had training to do this? Oh yeah, she had to go to school to learn this. Any other schooling? Yes, vocational school, majoring in the travel business. That's a good major, isn't it?

When he feels good, his nostrils puff out subtly, even though he tries to carry on the conversation in a nonchalant manner. Mr. Journalist must have a master's degree from a nice university?

Dan smiles. She admires him as if he were a real master. Her hands go to the center of his foot. Her thumbs reach deeply, touching a sensitive part that he has never discovered until now. He sighs.

Tell her if it hurts, she says. He will. How does it feel now? Fine. Harder? Okay. Too hard? No . . . Oh yes . . .

His limbs feel heavy and his senses swell. He hears her voice coming from afar, telling him to lift his feet; she has to add more hot crystal mud. As if in a dream, he can't respond, even though he is making efforts to do so. Then her hands come, lift his feet, and hug them on her lap while she pours the liquid. His feet feel the softness of her young bosom.

Somewhere down the corridor comes a faint sound of urine hitting the toilet bowl. Then flushing, followed by deep gurgles of the pipe.

When his feet reenter the hot liquid, he hears himself moan. The warmth of the water oozes into his skin and flesh, flowing along with his blood. Each caress of her hands brings more warmth into his body. For a while, Dan forgets they are just male feet and female hands; they have become lives independent of their bodies and souls, playing with each other, innocent of all purposes. He moans louder when she touches the most vulnerable spot, in the hollow of his soles, her fingers going line by line, as if reading a hidden test of his pains and itches, his fatigue and soreness. Never before have his feet been cared for in this way. It is such a strange, unspeakable intimacy which his beloved Little Plum has never shared with him. He feels his arousal.

And he knows the girl knows it. She bows her head, flushing. He must get up and flee.

"Damn, I have a meeting to attend," Dan says, propping up his body on his elbows. The inner force pulling him down is much stronger. "I almost forgot."

"I can finish it faster," the girl says.

"I'm already late!" he says. It is such a job getting up.

"Just five minutes . . . ," she says, slightly pressing his knees.

His feet kick out of the water, almost making the girl fall off her stool.

He is rude. He knows it. But he can't afford to care. As he finds his socks and shoes, he finds the girl in tears.

"I'm sorry," he says. He really is.

The girl just turns her face away.

He watches as she sobs soundlessly.

"Look, I totally forgot about the meeting because you made me feel so good."

He knows his smile is ugly. The girl sniffs hard, her nose all clogged up. He pulls a handkerchief out of his pants pocket and hands it to her.

She bursts out laughing when she sees it is an oily napkin with a big hole in the middle.

Such a child.

"See you again," he says, shuffling to the door.

"Don't see me again," she snaps at his back.

He turns, discovering how pretty she is.

She pouts. "I wouldn't want to see a girl again who bores me to death, telling me about her boring life and giving me poor service," she says.

"You gave me excellent service."

"How could that be?" She looks at him. Her eyelashes are moist with tiny dewdrops. "It's barely started!"

Has it? He looks at the girl and remembers seeing her sweet breasts in glimpses. Three thousand kilometers away from home and here she exhibits her breasts for whoever sits on that damned reclining chair. Her parents receive money from that exhibition, just as his parents receive money from his dangerous career as a banquet bug. The bug could be crushed at any moment, with this shadowy scoundrel lurking around, copying his method of forgery. And then, there is this dark-red-lipped Happy Gao who wants to share his "connections," of which he has none. He just can't be left alone to eat banquets in peace.

"What's your name?" Dan asks.

"Number Ten. Call me Old Ten," she answers.

He nods, feeling a sad smile coming to his eyes. Certainly she wouldn't give her real name to a "journalist."

"Would you do me a favor?" she asks.

He looks at her. He would do anything she asks of him.

"Please tell my boss you are very pleased with my service," she says.

So it is nothing more than this—an endorsement from a VIP customer.

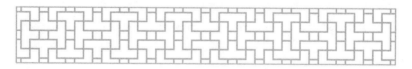

A PERSON CALLED HIM while he was out "interviewing," Little Plum tells Dan as she greets him outside the factory gate. This time it was a man, she tells him, her hands deft with a slim knife, trimming a rubber shoe sole. She makes five cents a pair, cutting off the uneven parts around the edges that the machines have missed. That man is loud, she tells Dan, like a middle school sports teacher. What did he say? Oh, he asked many questions. About what? About Dan's company and work; whether Dan is the boss and Little Plum is his secretary.

Dan stops.

"What did you say to him?"

"I said, 'Are you a policeman or what?' "

"Well?"

"He said, 'I'm a policeman's father.' So I said, 'Then, I'm a policeman's grandma!' "

"You're joking, aren't you?"

"No, I'm not."

He begins walking again. That's it. The investigation on him has started.

"Did you take his telephone number?"

"No."

He goes to their room and sees cases of bottled water piled against the wall. Little Plum sometimes goes with neighbors to busy streets to sell bottled water to drivers stuck in traffic. They also sell maps, cheap sunglasses, sunshades for windshields, and straw mats for car seats. In the summer, they can easily make a few yuan a day. But in the winter, they often carry heavy loads and chant at closed car windows for several cold hours without selling anything. She makes money doing whatever she can.

"He said he'd call you again," Little Plum says. "He asked for our street address and building number . . ."

"Did you tell him?"

"We have no building number. And the street number changed when the highway started construction."

"So you didn't tell him?"

"Of course not."

He hurries to the nearest printing shop and designs his new cards. In an hour they are ready. His real name proudly occupies the center. He is a freelance journalist from now on, and no one can prove he is not. Where have his articles appeared? Oh, a lot of newspapers and magazines. Published under pen names? That's right; who would want to attract the authorities' attention and offend the public?

The following day at eleven a.m., as he hands his new card to the registrar, a middle-aged woman, he has never felt better. He even stays around the registration area and carries on a little chitchat with the woman, talking about a recent soap opera. All his knowledge of soap operas comes from Little Plum, who follows each one of them while he goes to work eating banquets. She was furious when a show she had followed religiously was banned by the government. Rumor has it that the government isn't too fond of stories involving love triangles at the moment, for fear that the stories will lead people to divorce, causing social instability. He and the woman change the subject every other minute, from real estate prices, to how to bribe the police to get a dog's license, to college girls' night jobs as prostitutes. Then they come to discuss the conference's theme. It is to promote the Party's policy of reducing farmers' taxes.

"About time, isn't it?" Dan says. "A peasant farmer is taxed up to fourteen percent of his income. And how much does he make a year? A thousand, if he is lucky. One dish at one of these banquets could cost more than that." Dan lights a cigarette. "Those village Party leaders, they just want to impress their superiors. When you see those beautiful peasant houses along the road, they are just for show. Everything is a mask; it's painted on. Just like what you see on the stage—you can only look at it from the front, and not too closely, but you can't go around and see it from the back. You know what I mean? The houses behind the beautiful masks are mud huts, as shabby as any farmhouse. And where do they get money to do this staging? From the farmers' taxes."

"I thought the Party's Central Committee has sent many inspection teams to check on local authorities and see if they really enforce the tax reduction policy," a young reporter chimes in.

"Once an inspection team comes to a village," Dan says, "the village headman will tell the farmers, hey, each of you has got to come up with money for the comrades' lodging and food. These good comrades don't want to come to your shitty village; they just come because they want to make sure you don't pay too much in taxes." Dan cocks his head and crosses his arms behind his back, mimicking the expression and body language of the cadres in his home village. "And these teams are always made up of officials from the Central Party Committee, from the Provincial Party Committee, plus the Party committees of the district and the county, so they are huge in number. But the comrades don't like simple food, the village headman tells you; they like four-course meals. If they stay for a week, you are going to run out of eggs and chickens; if they stay for a month, you'll go broke."

The journalists coming to register all watch Dan, impressed by his performance.

"You must have gone to the countryside a lot for your research," a young woman says.

Dan smiles. He doesn't need to go anywhere; his family has provided the best research material.

Surrounded by young journalists, Dan spots a hand dropping a card into the tray that the registrar uses to collect cards. The card is modeled on the phony business card Dan stopped using two months ago. He looks up and sees a short man in a pair of khaki pants and a sports jacket. Not only did he pirate Dan's business model, he even pirated his image. Sensing Dan's eyes following him, he looks up and gives Dan a smile of acknowledgment. It looks as if the little man doesn't know it is Dan's intellectual property rights he has violated. Could it be that he saw the design of Dan's old card and copied it purely on the basis of personal preference? The registrar asks the little man to sign for his fee, and he pulls out his fountain pen, a heavy-duty one of the old-fashioned variety, and writes his name. As he heads for the conference room, Dan looks at the signature and is shocked. It is not simply a signature, it is a work of art. He must have had training in calligraphy.

After the conference, Dan follows the little man out of the conference room to the banquet hall. He sees him take a seat at a table close to the rear door. As Dan threads through the crowd and approaches him, the little man stands up and walks out. He is not staying for the banquet. He gets his fee and leaves. Maybe he has another meeting to go to, where another payment of "money for your troubles" is awaiting him. He seems to be more resourceful than Dan in terms of getting information on conferences.

In the lobby of the hotel, a group of enormous foreigners is arriving. Dan has to wait for them to pass. Through the shafts and chasms of the shifting crowd, Dan sees the little man standing in front of the revolving glass door, trying to hail a taxi. A cab drives up and he waves it away, deciding the per-kilometer rate written on the window is too high. He is not rich. Maybe he is also a "reserve worker" and has parents in a poor village waiting for him to send money. He doesn't want to spend too much of his hard-earned money on taxi fares. Dan approves of his prudence.

It is one o'clock in the afternoon, and outside the cool hotel the heat is almost visible. It is so bright that it blurs the outlines of sky-scrapers containing offices, hotels, and apartments. Each time Dan comes downtown and looks around, he finds a new building shooting up overnight. This is a view Little Plum can stare at for hours. But Dan always winces at the sight. It is a concrete forest, a city too sharp and new to be personable.

The little man hails another cab. Again it is too expensive. Two teenage doormen stand stiff, as if frozen by the heat. It is too hot for the little man to go on the street and stop a cab. He hopes to get a taxi that is dropping off hotel guests, but these guests at expensive hotels don't ride cheap taxis.

Dan is inches behind the little man now. He is going to say to him, hello, do you also have another engagement? Dan has learned to use the fashionable word "engagement" for a banquet or function. Dan will then hand him one of his new cards, voluntarily offering to share the copyright of his latest invention. He is sure the little man will understand immediately. He is short and ugly, but he doesn't look stupid. Maybe Dan can let down his guard and openly exchange ideas with him, sharing experiences gained over time through eating banquets fraudulently, so they can improve the quality of their work. And why not? They might become friends or comrades. Dan is preparing the words he will use to initiate this unusual camaraderie.

A heavily equipped photographer comes out the door and slaps the little man on the shoulder.

"I was looking all over for you," the photographer says, very loud. "I wanted to ask you if you liked my photo."

"You mean the one they published in *Beijing Weekly*?"

"Yes."

"Well . . ."

"Your article was ready to go to print when they called me for a photo. It was already nine o'clock at night."

"So I heard."

"It's like they wanted a picture on a fucking whim!"

"Frustrating, isn't it? The way these editors work nowadays. I'm always amazed at their chaotic priorities."

"I give them ten pictures and they choose the least revealing one."

"They can't help that. The Party wouldn't like to see the other nine pictures. The big boys in the Party think those AIDS buggers wouldn't exist if the nosy journalists hadn't gone looking for them."

Dan listens to them, unaware that his mouth has been hanging open the whole time. The little man isn't a phony reporter after all.

The photographer offers the little man a lift. When the photographer brings the car around, the little man beckons to Dan, inviting him to ride with them. He has been aware of Dan's presence. He says they can drive Dan to his apartment. Thanks, but no, just drop him off at any subway station. His mind a blank, Dan gets into the backseat of the car.

As the car tears into the heat, the photographer says, sorry, the air conditioner is out of order. The windows are rolled down and the heat roars in. It's hot, isn't it? the little man remarks. Yes, it is. Dan replies that it feels like an enormous scalding tongue of midsummer licking his face. Good image, the little man praises. Dan watches the little man making confident gestures, raising his voice above the noisy heat, and tries to figure out who he really is behind this short, ugly appearance. At a traffic light, the car stops, and the little man turns toward Dan, a business card in his hand. It is a cream-colored card with dark brown-and-gold print, the design that Dan had used for five or six months. The phantom Internet media firm and its fictional Web-based publication were all his creation. Now it looks as if Dan has not only made up the firm, he has also created this little man, who seems to have gained a life, a real journalist's life, all on his own. Dan wants to scream: "Wait a minute, isn't this company phony?" He feels his tongue drawn back to block the words from emerging.

"I just left my previous company and joined this one," the little man explains without a trace of phoniness.

"Oh." Another phantom company?

He asks some questions about today's conference and Dan answers. Dan participates in their dialogue but immediately forgets what he has just said. He is trying to make sense of the situation. Could it be that it is Dan who imitated the little man, without knowing it, instead of the other way around? Could it be that the little man has taught Dan all along, transmitting ideas to his mind through some mysterious channel?

"How about yourself? What press do you work for?"

Dan hands his new card to him.

"A freelance journalist. That's what I always wanted to be," says the little man. His smile is genuine.

Dan is afraid he is going to ask what Dan has published. He is busy preparing himself: well, he has published a few things under pen names . . .

"Your name looks familiar to me," the little man says.

"Really?" Yeah, right.

"I think I've run across it once or twice."

You lying sack of shit. "You have a good memory."

"That's what we all have to have."

They arrive at a big intersection. Dan asks the photographer to stop the car, and he gets out. As he walks into the shade of tall buildings, he turns to look at the beat-up Volkswagen Santana sedan. Maybe it is time for him to quit the banquet-eating job and find something else to do for a living. He takes off his sports jacket and walks a block with his head bowed. A cool breeze from the subway entrance comes at him and he stops, taking a deep breath. The decision arrives: he will say good-bye to this banquet-eating job after he brings Little Plum to an impressive banquet. He won't let her life pass without knowing what shark fins or sea cucumbers or crab claw tips taste like.

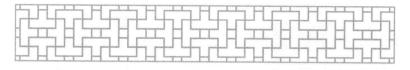

THE FACTORY'S accounting department is jam-packed. Reserve workers are standing in a line that stretches all the way from the fourth floor down to the courtyard below the office building, waiting to cash their salary coupons. The factory has been paying them coupons instead of real money, and they can cash them only when the factory has enough funds. Dan pushes his way up the stairs, through the chatting and laughing crowds. It is the happiest day for them in months. Their sweat has fermented into a sour steam, hanging heavily in the air. Dan bangs into the thick cloud of body odor as he enters the narrow corridor outside the accounting office. He looks for Little Plum, who has been holding a place for him since noon.

He finds her sitting on a stair, leaning against the concrete handrail. She is making a wig, crocheting long black hair onto flesh-colored material shaped like a skull. It is a better-paying job, from a company that produces costumes for movies and soap operas. The wig is close to completion, and it looks as if she is holding a severed scalp. She looks up, sees Dan, and tells him the office will soon open, after the chief accountant comes back from the bank.

People greet Dan as they pass by, slapping his shoulders, arms, back, and butt, quipping that they haven't seen him for ages, that he has turned into such a huge snob, wearing glasses like some big fucking intellectual. They hand him sunflower seeds and cigarettes even cheaper than Dan's favorite brand.

Dan looks at his watch. It is a quarter to five. Most of the people by now are sitting on the floor, some having taken off their shoes and used them as seat cushions. The sour odor gives way to a sort of saltiness, an odor of marinated fish.

The chief accountant doesn't show up. Instead, he makes an announcement over the public address system throughout the factory compound. His negotiations with the bank have failed, so he couldn't get the funds for them to cash their coupons. He hopes this week the factory will pay the interest it owes the bank, and by the weekend the bank will authorize the release of the funds. He apologizes for the disappointment, and he knows it's tough that they have received only coupons for ten months now. The accountant promises that the factory will receive payment from a client, which will soon enable it to pay the interest on the previous bank loan. People stand up, slapping the dust off their butts, and abandon a floor covered with sunflower-seed shells. The chief accountant says everyone will receive half a dozen cans of sardines from the factory as a token of the leaders' love and care for their workers. Stomping down the concrete stairwell, people are talking about the new Lexus the factory manager recently acquired. He has upgraded his car three times in two years. Well, four times, but who's counting? they laugh.

At the exit of the building, two cooks, one male and one female, are distributing sardine cans, naked of labels. The male cook asks Dan if he would please take Maple Hu's share to her, since Dan used to be her late husband's apprentice. Dan says, sure, he'll be glad to. The female cook says, be careful, Maple has just hired another girl, a foxy little thing, pretty as hell. Very classy, too, the male cook adds, and she doesn't look like a whore. People ask him how the hell he knows. Well, once Maple brought her and another girl to the cafeteria, the cook replies. The cute little slut just sat there, not picking up her chopsticks until Maple and the other girl did so.

After Little Plum goes home with their six cans, Dan walks to the factory's residential area behind the two smokestacks. From a distance, one can see the red brick apartment buildings in the turbid afternoon heat. There are ten of them, identically smoke-stained and beat up, appearing tattered with hundreds of faded clothes, ragged diapers, and threadbare sheets fluttering about the balconies.

Maple Hu lives in a one-bedroom apartment on the second floor, inherited from her late husband. The stairway is full of bicycles, jars for pickling vegetables, and murals of children's drawings. Two men wait outside her door, smoking cigarettes. Most of Maple's clients are construction workers from a freeway construction site a couple of miles away. They squat there, studying a spot on the concrete floor, trying to minimize their presence. They are waiting to be "massaged," of course. Dan puts down the wooden box containing half a dozen cans of sardines, knowing the two men are guessing the purpose of his visit. He knocks on the door, newly painted and bearing a simple sign above the door frame that reads: "Maple's Salon."

"The line's back there," one of the men murmurs.

"What?" Dan asks.

"There's a line." The murmur becomes vaguer.

"Can't understand you, buddy," Dan says, smiling, toying with their timidity. "Line for what?"

An old woman comes out the door opposite the salon, holding an infant in her arms.

"Is the brothel closed today?" she asks.

Dan looks at her and sees a faint trace of mirth on her otherwise expressionless face. The two construction workers stare at the same spots on the ground, as if exempted from the question.

"Maple," the old woman yells. "Do you have any cold medicine?"

No answer comes.

"My granddaughter has a little fever!" she continues to yell. "The madam seems awfully busy today."

The two men glance at the door, then at the old woman.

The old woman goes inside her apartment and comes out with a little plastic chair. She drops the chair to the floor and motions the men to take it. As the two men jostle each other for the chair, she brings another one out, still yelling, "Some aspirin will do. Do you have any aspirin, Maple?"

The door opens. Maple steps out wearing a black dress dotted with tiny red roses. She says, sorry, one of her girls went home for her father's operation. They are overbooked today. She is in her early forties, with a cheap nose job and tattooed eyebrows. But she has an extremely kind expression in her eyes.

She asks the two men why they didn't knock and get something to drink. Then she turns to Dan, asking whether his mother's asthma is any better. His mother has a stomach ulcer, but her kind eyes stop him from correcting her. When she looks at you, it makes you think a secret part of her is there for you only; you are special and unique. Residents of this building used to curse her, spitting in her face, and yet no one betrayed her during those anti-vice campaigns.

Two men come out saying good-bye to Maple. The men sitting on the miniature chairs get up and slip inside the door, as Madam Maple continues telling Dan of some folk remedies for asthma that she has collected especially for Dan's mother.

Dan looks at her flabby arms jiggling while she makes gestures.

Then he says something he knows he will regret the very next second. He says she is too old for this. If she wants, he can find jobs for her as a domestic in good households, and the pay will be enough to support her and her boy.

She just looks at him as if he is the one who needs help.

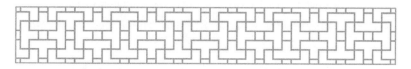

HAPPY SAYS SHE has gotten Dan's article on the peacock banquet accepted by an influential newspaper in Shanghai, after her painstaking polishing. The only thing Dan needs to do is to give the article to Master Chen for his approval. She curses and swears, accusing Dan of being a huge asshole and ungrateful bastard, disappearing on her in the Green Grove Club. But she still forgives him, because he did it out of his loyalty to Ocean Chen.

"It's no secret that he's a horny old fellow and is with a very young woman who might become the fourth Mrs. Chen. So you don't have to guard his privacy," Happy says.

"How do you know he is a horny old fellow?" he asks, realizing he is annoyed.

"Then prove that he isn't a horny old fellow."

He doesn't mind her calling the artist a horny old fellow. And yet he isn't very happy to hear her say it. He doesn't know why.

It has been raining since sunset. The factory is having a power outage. He senses all the neighbors of the top-floor slum pricking up their ears to listen to his telephone conversation with Happy while they are shut out of their soap opera. He grits his teeth and decides he will spend five thousand yuan and buy a cell phone, which for most reporters is still a luxury. He will have to take that sum out of the money he is saving for a little apartment and a sofa set.

"You haven't showed up at any conferences lately. You're afraid to see me, because you feel guilty as hell," Happy says.

"My stomach hurts." He lies without any difficulty of late.

"Too much good food makes one sick," she replies. "Sometimes I can't help but remember Ocean Chen's words. He said it when he left the peacock banquet." She switches on the Northwest accent. " 'Eating is the only legacy we got from our ancient, glorious heritage.' "

"Glorious civilization."

"Huh?"

"He didn't say 'glorious heritage'; he said 'glorious civilization.' "

"You don't have to quote Ocean Chen like he was Chairman Mao."

"But you're the one who is quoting him."

"Good. A good reporter should have an accurate memory and a professional attitude like yours . . ."

"Listen," Dan cuts her off, "I've got to run. Have an engagement tonight." He forgets how many lies he has told within ten minutes.

"Is it the Nudity Banquet?"

What?

"I heard they only invited twenty media guys, and they are all male. The nude beauties are not totally comfortable with women. It is going to be a piece of performance art, with all the seafood laid on stark naked female bodies!" She sounds excited.

"Put food on naked bodies?" Dan exclaims, regretting that he might have shared the information with the neighbors.

"She told you, didn't she?"

"Who?"

"The owner's wife. You don't know? She had a small press conference with selected reporters this afternoon. She did all the talking, babbling about everything from ancient Greek sculpture to African carvings, from Michelangelo to Rodin, spinning a regular philosophy around this porno banquet of hers."

Dan asks Happy how she got the information.

"According to her, nudity is part of this mystical dining experience," she says, not answering his question. She never really answers any question. "Tonight is only a rehearsal. If the girls can corrupt the guys, which means none of them writes totally negative things about it, then the banquet will open to all the media, to spread the philosophy of erotic dining."

A bunch of girls' naked bodies serving as banquet tables? Dan stands in the blackout, taking sips of dark air. One would pick up pieces of dead flesh off live flesh? He hates his vivid, superfluous imagination, but he can't help it.

"When do you think you can deliver the article to the hospital?" Happy asks.

His head still buzzing with the nudity banquet, he asks, "What hospital?"

"Cut the crap, will you?" Happy's words come out of the receiver in spits. "Everyone knows Ocean Chen is at Capital Hospital. And there is only one department for high-ranking Party officials, where they have luxurious private rooms. I'm sure he is in there."

Dan and Happy agree to meet at the Green Grove Club the following morning. While he is waiting, he goes to the clinical part of the club. It is located on the upper floor, right above the lobby. There are six spotless beds in a big, bright solarium that appears unambiguous in its function. It makes you think you have come here only to heal. On the two beds at either end lie two elderly women in translucent paper gowns. The two blind masseurs in dark glasses and blue uniforms look professional. One of the masseurs asks, his face tilting up in the manner of all blind people, whether Dan needs their help. Dan smiles, saying he will in a couple of decades.

He goes downstairs and sits in a little reception area in the lobby. All of a sudden, he notices a shift in his mood. He can't believe it. He actually is longing for the girl called Old Ten. Is she still asleep after a long night's service? What kind of services did she give her customers last night?

He gets up and drifts downstairs, hoping to run into her. It is almost noon, but the place still feels like midnight. Happy is late as usual. She would be late for her own wedding if she ever had one. He feels consumed by this waiting. Because of this hope that Old Ten will show up. If there is one thing he resents, it is this apprehensive hope.

A TV is on somewhere. He follows the sound to a room with its door ajar and sees the two blind masseurs he encountered in the clinic sitting there in front of a thirteen-inch TV, their dark glasses pushed up above their foreheads, watching a United States presidential candidate named Bush. Dan really wishes the aged female clients he saw a moment ago hadn't disrobed, that their shapeless nudity hadn't been watched, even if indifferently, through a layer of thin, dark glass.

Happy arrives at a quarter past twelve. She doesn't even offer an excuse for her tardiness. She says she had to finish an article she was working on, and it's her habit not to leave in the middle of writing. And she never notices the time when she writes.

While tea is served, Happy produces a printed paper, telling Dan it is the galley proof of Dan's article on the peacock banquet.

What does "galley proof" mean? Suppressing his desire to learn, Dan folds the paper, deliberately careless, and slips it into his shirt pocket.

"If you think the word choices I made for you are not quite right, let me know. The editor in chief wasn't sure about some of your word usage, so he changed them. I rewrote some places so your ideas could come through better."

So that's what a galley proof is: approval of others' garbling of your own writing.

"I hope you don't mind my having added my byline to yours, since my contribution is only too obvious," Happy says, giving him a mischievous, sidelong smile.

"Fair enough," Dan says.

So now he has to go to Capital Hospital to see Ocean Chen. He resents this pushy woman who uses a useless person like himself to get what she wants. In the car, Happy says she didn't sleep at all last night because she was reading all about Ocean Chen on the Web. There were more than two thousand dramatic, novel-like pages on him. He was jailed during the Cultural Revolution, you know. That's right, Dan says, feigning a knowing look. The charge was counter-revolutionary remarks, she continues. Yes, he was jailed on that god-damned charge, all right. The old man hasn't learned much, has he? Learned what? He still can't curb his big mouth very well, Happy says, sounding as if she is pitying the old artist, but her face reads differently; it holds an expression of adoration. Dan says, well, he is what he is. But he paid for it, Happy replies; he was in shackles for seven years or longer. My gracious mother, Dan shouts soundlessly, seven years! Hope he still has those window paintings he did in jail, Happy says. What window paintings? Don't you know? The four seasons window paintings. Oh, those—nice, aren't they? Yes, and what a character he is, painting a window with exotic scenery, so he could have a grand view and changes of season in his windowless cell! Sure, he is one of a kind. And what a wonder how his works have evolved since, to such an abstract state. Dan says, well, Mercedes-Benz changes its styles and models every year. That's a dumb analogy, Dan. He says she has to agree that a great artist is a magician, like the Monkey King of the fairy tales, turning into as many forms as he wishes. Happy considers this, smiling. Chen's wife divorced him during that time, right? Right, Dan answers, quietly absorbing the information and storing it away. Then he met his second wife, who had been his worshiper? That's right, he did. But why did she leave him two years into their marriage? She couldn't worship him from up close,

64

that's why. Is that the reason? Oh, who knows? When a woman loves a man, she needs no reason, but if she wants to leave him, she could have a thousand reasons. Happy says she needs no reason when she leaves a man, but Dan's opinion is worth hearing. Not bad, Dan thinks to himself; I'm a quick learner at bullshitting.

As the car leaves the stagnant traffic, turning onto a small street, Happy says they should bring some gifts to the master. She suggests some tonic or famous tea. Dan grunts that he has a bunch of green onions in his canvas backpack.

"A bunch of what?"

"Green onions. Very tasty. My parents got a friend of theirs, a railroad worker, to bring some to me yesterday. I just picked them up at the train station this morning."

Happy has to pull over to laugh. A bunch of green onions! As a gift to the richest and most famous artist in China!

Dan waits for her to stop her asthmatic laughter, to tell her it is a special kind of onion. So special that one won't find it anywhere else.

Before they agree on any gift, they arrive in front of the hospital. From a distance, Happy sees a massive figure walking on the front lawn, shaded by climbing roses. She dashes forward, ignoring a confused Dan.

Only when she and Ocean Chen begin their handshake does Dan realize what she was rushing to. It looks like she is all set, already acquainting herself with the old artist. She no longer needs him. But she needs the article in Dan's pocket that has her name next to his. She turns around, looking for Dan.

"Come over here, Dan."

So he does. The master looks younger in the summer morning. His face looks smoother under a white, boyish baseball cap with a long, protruding beak. Dan wouldn't have recognized him if he had seen him on the street. Ocean Chen steps forward, all smiles, and stretches his arms toward Dan. A handshake becomes a hearty hug, which makes Dan flush.

"How are you, my landsman?" the master asks.

Without knowing how, Dan has taken the green onions out of his backpack and presented them to him.

"From my parents," he mutters, flushing further.

"Our Northwestern green onions?" Ocean Chen asks.

The green onions don't look very fresh. The outer leaves are dry and brittle, the beardlike roots are dirt-caked, and crumbs of soil fall all over the place.

"How did you know I miss these so much? When I was too sick to eat anything, I begged to have onions like this. Oh, this onion, dipped in peppered soybean paste! But they ignored me. They said it didn't have the nutrition I needed." He holds up the onions, and the dirt on their roots smudges his white shirt immediately. "When I called your office two weeks ago, I was going to ask you if you could get me some of these. I even asked for you by the name you told me, not by that silly pen name on your card. By the way, you have a funny secretary, teasing me all the time."

So it was Ocean Chen who called, not an investigator. And the old man took Little Plum's rude manner as teasing.

Ocean Chen invites them to his room on the third floor. A nurse in a white dress and a cute little cap comes to them.

"You missed your medication call, Master," she says, like a child scolding her grandpa. "You look young and handsome today."

"I know," the old artist answers.

"Where did you go?"

"To the public toilets."

Happy laughs loudly.

"You're always joking!" The young nurse pouts.

"No, I'm not. I'm lonely here. At the public toilets, at least you have people to greet you when you do a bowel movement."

"Oh, Master, you shouldn't talk about such things in front of people," the nurse protests.

"Well, these are the things you talk about at the hospital every day, right?"

He laughs, taking a magazine from the newsstand by the nurses' station and throwing it back after one glance, murmuring, "Same old shit."

When the nurse sees the onions he is carrying under his jacket, she frowns.

"You know you shouldn't bring such dirty stuff here."

"Says who?"

"Says the rule."

They stare at each other. They enjoy this kind of fight.

"I pay horrific sums of money to bring in anything I want. Including women."

Happy laughs. The old artist takes off his sunglasses and looks at her, not sure if he likes her laughter.

Master Chen's hospital room is a suite, including a living room, a dining room, and a bedroom. The living room has been turned into an art studio, with walls of new and half-finished paintings. The dining table has been relocated to the living room, facing the sliding glass door to the balcony, through which dusty sunlight comes in. On the tabletop are sheets of paper, jars and tubes of paint, and a vase full of brushes of various sizes. There are dots of color on the light beige carpet and white sofa covers. Inside a longish fish tank on the glass coffee table, a dozen or so tropical fish in flashy neon colors swim around lethargically.

Happy nudges Dan, eyeing a framed photo on top of the TV set. It is of a young woman with a dimpled face—Ocean Chen's new girlfriend, a sweet beauty.

Seeing the artist talking to the nurse, telling her to have the cafeteria make some paper-thin flatbreads and soybean paste for the onions, Happy whispers to Dan, "Don't ask him about her. He wouldn't like it."

It has never occurred to Dan that he should ask the artist anything at all.

Ocean Chen turns back to them, points at the new paintings, and asks them if they like his recent works. Happy says of course she does, they are masterpieces. The old artist looks at her, considering her for a long while. Then he gazes at one of the paintings and says that rooster looks pretty good, doesn't it? Dan is surprised; it could be anything but a rooster. Happy gives the "rooster" a long, grim stare, before she says yes, she loves it, it is such a Picasso-like piece, and it is a flight of imagination. What innovation, using Chinese brush and ink! What a negation of traditional Chinese painting!

The old artist falls onto the sofa with a heavy sigh. Then he starts humming a tune to himself, as if completely forgetting about his guests.

Sensing the artist's mood take a downturn, Happy becomes tense. She is retracing each word she has said, trying to find what she said that upset the artist.

"What about that one? . . . The camel?" With his lazy index finger, Ocean Chen points at a huge painting dominating the wall. "Do you two like it?"

"Um. . . ." Happy considers it, her fist under her chin.

Dan keeps quiet. It seems like an examination for students who have prepared themselves in the wrong direction.

A door opens and a young man appears. He is wearing a white polo shirt with the Ralph Lauren logo on it and a pair of blue jeans. His skin is luxuriously tanned, the skin of an eternal vacationer.

"Hello," he says. His smile is very charming and he knows it.

"How is the golfing?" the old artist asks.

"Okay. I've come to see you before I say hi to Father," he says.

"Honored," Ocean Chen smiles. "How is Father lately?"

Happy gives Dan a pinch on his arm, almost making him cry out. He notices that the young man and Ocean Chen didn't say "my father" or "your father"; they simply referred to the young man's father as "Father." It seems they don't need to specify whose father this is. Is that the way all the Party leaders' children refer to their fathers?

The young man walks around the room in loose strides, looking at the paintings, giving comments once in a while.

"When can I have these?" He points at the "camel" and the "rooster."

"As soon as I can bear to part with them," Ocean Chen says.

As if all of a sudden discovering the two other people in the room, the young man appears a little startled.

"These are reporters," Ocean Chen says, for a moment an old, tired person. "They said the pictures Father calls 'the camel' and 'the rooster' are masterpieces, and very Picasso-like."

The young man bursts out laughing. "Oh God!" he cries out in perfect English. "Father is so funny! Only *he* could make out a rooster and a camel in these pictures!"

"Better than making out nothing," the old artist says.

The young man's cell phone rings. He glances at the number and answers. "No, not next week. Next week I'm going to Australia to golf. The week after is okay." He goes to the bedroom and closes the door behind him. His voice can still be heard: ". . . you promised to sell me five shipments of it. I've already made deals with the Russians. I have to deliver the shipments in ten days! You can't see Father unless you keep your promise . . ." Then the conversation turns into English.

The people in the living room look at one another.

As he walks out of the bedroom, the young man presses the emergency call button. Light, swift footsteps are immediately heard approaching. Before the footsteps reach the door, the young man yells: "No need to come in. There is no one dying in here. Just send us up a pitcher of fruit juice. Freshly squeezed."

The footsteps halt, then turn to leave.

"And a cup of iced coffee. Vietnamese style. Oh, and four pieces of Black Forest cake." He returns to the company, talking to nobody in particular: "I love the Black Forest cake they make here. That's about the only thing they do right."

"Are you . . . ?" Happy stands up, her arm reaching out, a card in her bony hand.

To Dan, Happy has never looked this feminine.

The young man accepts her card and, without looking, slips it into his pants pocket. Before he speaks, his cell phone rings again. He gives the number a quick glance, is reminded of something urgent, and jumps to his feet. He vanishes as abruptly as he emerged. When the food is delivered, Ocean Chen pays.

"I know you want to know who he is." Ocean Chen breaks the long silence. "People would pay two hundred thousand, directly to this young man's account, just to get an appointment to see his father."

Happy and Dan look at him, their mouths stuffed with the chocolate cake.

"There are a lot of prostitutes nowadays," the master says, his head thrown back onto the soft sofa pillow.

Dan and Happy are in a fierce concentration, trying to figure out the relevance of his remarks.

"I am one of them."

Even though he can't see Ocean Chen, Dan perceives a sad, mocking smile on the broad, wrinkled face.

"You see, one doesn't have to sell one's body to be a prostitute. One becomes an even dirtier whore by selling something more precious than one's body. That's what I'm doing. Yes, I do it out of pressure, maybe out of a kind of awe, the awe ordinary people feel toward royalty or nobility. But who made those people nobility? A nobility that takes my paintings to be roosters and camels?" He looks at them without seeing them. He is articulate, but in a scary way. Like a lunatic in a fit of monologue, Dan decides.

Happy pinches Dan's arm again. Dan grimaces. There will be bruises for sure.

"But I let them whore me. Whore my art. My defenseless babies. Let them whore it for free. And it is a prize for me that such-and-such personage has my paintings in his majestic living room. It is publicity for my works. They have the greatest power in this country. I have told others and myself a million times that I never cared about their power. The truth is, I do. So here I am painting more 'roosters' and 'camels' for them."

"You are too hard on yourself. In any case, your art is not for them," Happy says.

"For whom, then?"

"For those who really understand you."

"If an art piece is understood completely, it is not art. Art is something forever between comprehension and incomprehension, and forever beyond complete comprehension. So you think you understand me?"

Happy takes up the challenge and decides to risk it. "Yes, I do. In a way," she answers, "even though I fell into your trap when you told me they were roosters and camels."

Her accusation is playful. Ocean Chen looks at her hard, then surrenders and smiles.

"Then my art isn't the best type."

"Picasso wasn't perfect."

The old artist nods, gazing at her up and down. It is impossible to tell whether he is pleased by her audacity and eloquence.

"What about you, my landsman?" The artist turns to Dan. "Do you understand my work?"

Dan shakes his head, flushing until he feels his ears burning.

"If I let you choose one of my paintings, which one would you choose?"

Dan stares at the pictures, trying to stand still in front of the dizzy colors. He can't feign rapture like Happy did. He only makes sure to face each one of them long enough. It has nothing to do with his liking. His like or dislike doesn't matter; these paintings have been pre-voted, and both his likes and dislikes have been pre-vetoed. It is too far from his life experience, from his Little Plum, who might go through life without even knowing such a tasty thing as Black Forest cake exists. Before he realizes it, he has stood looking at a picture for several minutes.

"You like this one. I can tell," the old artist says. "You can have this one then."

Happy tenses up in anticipation.

"You may pick one, too," Master Chen says to her, making a gesture of invitation.

Overwhelmed, Happy leaps up to hug the old man. Then, biting her dark, red lips, she sweeps the pictures with her eyes and settles on a big piece.

"Now you've got to excuse me. I need some rest," Ocean Chen says in a bored voice, making them think they might have long overstayed their welcome.

Dan stands up and fumbles with his shirt pocket. "I . . . I wrote an article about you."

"Yes, we are close to finishing it." Happy cuts Dan off. "We wonder if we can bring it for your approval when we complete it." Sensing Dan's bafflement, she eyes him and adds, "It will be a sensational piece about you at the peacock banquet."

"You are writing about that?" the artist says, spirited again. "I felt such contempt to see all the reporters keep silent about it. Do you know who the sponsors of that fund-raiser for bird-watchers were? The young man you just met was one of them. He knows what I did at the banquet and pretends he doesn't, still treating me like his closest friend. Either he bribed the media, or the media conspired to protect his image by silencing my voice. I am so glad to see two exceptions from the cowardice of the press."

As soon as they are out of the suite, Dan asks why Happy lied. The article is completed and ready to go—what made her hide it from the old man? She says Dan isn't as smart as he looks. Can't he see what Ocean Chen wants from them? He wants them to write a big profile on his life and career, about his artist's conscience and his eccentricity, not just the peacock banquet. Besides, what they wrote about him at the peacock banquet implied his injured ego, and that might not please him.

"How do you know?"

"Of course I know," Happy says, twirling her car keys on her index finger, a cynical smile blooming under her aviator sunglasses. "Or he wouldn't have given us his paintings. Certainly you know how much you can sell the painting he gave you for. His works are priced at about fifty yuan per square inch."

Dan's hand feels the painting held inside a plastic tube. Its gravity seems to have changed. How many square inches does this one have? Or by Little Plum's reckoning: How many sacks of flour is it equal to? And how many noodles can that make? If Happy looked at Dan now, she could almost see, in his staring eyes, the numbers of his mind's calculator blinking and twinkling like a commodity trading screen. He takes a deep breath. The painting is about twenty by thirty inches, or six hundred square inches. At fifty yuan per square inch, that equals thirty thousand yuan, which equals forty thousand kilos of flour, which in turn yields about eighty thousand kilos of fresh, machine-pressed noodles. Now that's a lot of noodles! The old man is richer than a money press. And that's why Happy picked out such an enormous piece.

"Do you think you can just accept thirty thousand yuan without doing anything to deserve it?" Happy says.

As they drive away, Happy says that in order to write a brilliant profile on Ocean Chen, they will have to do a lot of interviewing. Dan should use the trust the artist gives him, taking advantage of being his landsman. Dan says that to use people's trust is kind of low. She says, with a seductive smile, she is using Dan's trust now—does that make her low? She is certain that Ocean Chen doesn't trust her the way he does Dan, because Dan has the face of a golden retriever.

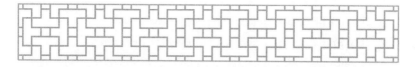

STANDING IN FRONT of her husband, Little Plum turns left and right according to his gestures. She is wearing a white knit top and a knee-length denim skirt, which show her curvy, full figure, yet also give her a college girl's easy, simple charm. The only thing that makes her look sophisticated is her dark red lipstick. He has decided to take her to a shark fin banquet, taking place at noon after a fund-raiser called "Help Those Who Struggle in Poverty."

On the way to the hotel, Dan tells Little Plum not to talk to people. Just answer yes or no. If they bother her too much, she can take out her camera and dash away, as if attracted by the sudden emergence of a photo opportunity. Make sure not to hold the camera upside down. Take the lens cap off before aiming the camera. Close the eye that isn't staring through the viewfinder; it will look funny if you close the wrong eye. Just remember, do anything but talk. Talking will betray her as a banquet bug.

Before they walk up the stairs of the hotel, Little Plum says she has changed her mind.

"Why?"

"I don't like shark fin."

"But you've never had any," Dan says, trying not to raise his voice, and he turns to see whether anyone is in earshot. He doesn't want to be seen talking to her.

"I don't like shark fin," Little Plum says in a low voice, knitting her fingers.

"I am sure you will like it. It costs four hundred in a restaurant for a tiny bowl of it."

"I never bring that much money to a restaurant."

"It will make your skin smooth and white like tofu."

"I don't like tofu," she says, pleading.

He looks at her, taken over by an ineffable tenderness. He thinks about the first time he met her, when he succumbed to that same helpless tenderness.

"Can I go home?" she asks.

"You even bought clothes for this," he says, his face stern now.

She falls silent. It hurts her to think of a hundred yuan spent on an outfit and not making good use of it. That amount could buy five big sacks of flour and feed a big family back in her village for a month. She sighs, summoning her bravery, and faces forward.

"Do you want the shark fin that costs four hundred yuan to go into the waste bucket?" Dan asks.

She exhales heavily.

"It will be easy after this time. Just follow me, but not too closely," he instructs her, walking up the wide, granite stairs. As he reaches the top, he turns and finds Little Plum is only two steps behind him. He gives her a look, warning her to keep her distance.

She doesn't.

He can feel her breath on the back of his neck when he gets to the registration desk.

Having signed his name and given out his card, Dan hisses to her that she will get them both in trouble. She acts as if she doesn't hear. He gives her looks and gestures whenever he can, but she sticks closely to him just the same. Once inside the conference hall, she takes a seat right behind him. His hands turn clammy at hearing a voice ask her if the seat next to her is taken. It is the little man's voice. She says, yes, it is; she's holding the seat for a friend. The little man asks where that friend is. In the latrine, she answers, if he doesn't mind. The little man shoves his way along the aisle in sideways steps and goes to the front row, where nobody wants to sit, since it makes it impossible to stand up and leave the conference in the middle of the session.

Dan changes his tactics and takes the seat to Little Plum's right.

The host introduces the sponsors and announces the start of the conference.

"Take out your notebook," he whispers without moving his lips. "And the pen. Now, look at the guy speaking. Write something down."

"What should I write?"

"Anything."

"But what?" she asks in a whisper, facing the stage, where the president of the fund-raising organization has begun his passionate speech. It is the highest mission for all of us Chinese to support our brothers and sisters who have to stop their children's elementary education because of poverty.

"Write something. Just move your pen."

"The ink isn't flowing."

"Doesn't matter. Keep moving it."

The president has turned livid. It is a disgrace for our nation not to have medical care for poor farmers. It would be an even greater shame to let foreigners, especially Americans, help them before you, their fellow countrymen, lend them a hand.

"Write down what he says," Dan tells Little Plum.

"I don't know how to write most of the words."

"Then write your own name."

She obeys. He glances at her, satisfied. She has completed two rows of her own name, appearing earnest and serious, her lips not closed all the way, her left hand holding the cover of the notebook erect, to block the view of the person sitting to her left. She repeats her name for one page, then switches to drawing circles. When the banquet is served, she tells him not to worry, she can handle the job alone. Before she goes to get her table assignment, Dan tells her there is supposed to be an envelope containing "money for your troubles," about two to three hundred yuan. But don't count the bills right away, it won't look good. She should just show her ID card and sign her name on request.

It is a big banquet, of fifty tables. Some tan-faced farmers' representatives sit close to the stage with the people who made large contributions. There will be a ceremony for the donation of money, medical equipment, medicine, and computers.

Dan is keeping an eye on Little Plum, seated a couple of tables away, when a farmer type in his early thirties approaches him. His name is Steel Bai, a village accountant, introduced to Dan by a middle-aged woman called Jasmine. Jasmine who? She works for the "Committee to Reduce Farmers' Taxes." Dan says, oh, yes, of course he remembers her. He has forgotten to tell Little Plum that shark fin is very slippery; one has to use a spoon as well as chopsticks.

"Comrade Jasmine told me you went to the countryside a lot, to investigate the corruption among village Party leaders . . ."

"I do know peasants very well," Dan says.

"You must come with me."

"Now?"

"Now."

Steel Bai has small but firm eyes framed by premature crow's-feet. This isn't the place for truth, he says. These guys can't represent peasants. They are traitors to peasants. They have embezzled the money donated to the peasants. What's left for the peasants after their theft is less than 10 percent of the funds raised.

"Comrade Reporter, this has been happening in our province, county, district, and village all these years. I will show you the evidence if you will come with me."

Dan stands up hesitantly. He looks at Little Plum, sitting by herself, bored and sleepy. He tells the peasant that he will go with him after he finishes his job here.

"There is no job here for a real journalist," Steel says. He is smart and well spoken for a farmer.

The first dishes are put on the table. All the ingredients are from the ocean, the waiter explains, including the translucent wrappers of those delicate dumplings.

Here one will hear no truth, Steel Bai says. He makes an indication with his chin at the food, saying that's how they spend the donated money. Come on, let's go. This fund-raising organization and those farmers' representatives have conspired to steal poor peasants blind. And the media pretend not to know anything about it.

Dan can't see his way out of this situation. He follows Steel Bai past the tables, catching a glimpse of Little Plum eating the seaweed-wrapped dumplings. He feels happy for her. At least she has made up a bit of what she has missed. He doesn't want the dietary history of her life to begin and end with the same blank slate.

Walking out of the hotel into the noonday sun, Dan senses someone behind them. The little man. He is ten paces from them. Dan suggests to Steel that they take a taxi, but Steel says the place is not very far. After they turn a corner, Dan finds that the little man is still following. Dan leads Steel across the street, using the pretext of buying batteries for his recorder. It is much easier to observe a subject by paralleling him. The little man appears as if deep in thought, stopping to make notes once in a while.

While Dan stops at a stand to buy batteries, the little man also stops, to take a bottle of water out of his bag. Why does this short bastard make it so hard for Dan? He doesn't need to compete with Dan for this banquet bug job, and he doesn't have to impersonate a reporter, since he qualifies as one and even has a photographer to team up with. Dan feels so angry that he imagines himself dashing across the street, grabbing the dwarf by his shirtfront, and punching the living daylights out of him. No, he doesn't want to punch him out, he wants to kill him. Have him wiped out, so that Dan can make a quiet, humble living as a banquet bug.

Steel Bai is telling Dan how these peasants' representatives, a bunch of parasites who call themselves Party cadres, would have a banquet every night with the money donated for repairing flood-damaged roads and rebuilding schools and clinics. Steel says he keeps a secret accounting of the money they embezzle.

"They just eat and eat and eat. Then when an inspection team is sent, they feed them banquets. And the inspection team feeds their superiors with what these representatives tell them."

The little man is at a newsstand now. He flips through a newspaper, asks the salesgirl some questions, then walks on. Dan's anger is seething. His two fists are twitching; they might swing out of control like unleashed Siberian huskies. In the factory Dan's fists were known to unleash themselves on occasion.

"Hello!" Dan yells, taken aback by his own amiable manner.

The little man lifts his head and looks for the origin of the voice. His response is natural and spontaneous. Seeing Dan on the other side of the street, the little man looks delighted. He tries to talk to Dan over a river of traffic, appearing genuinely happy about the unexpected encounter. Either he is an actor of great talent, or he is truly innocent of this spy game.

"Another function to catch?" the little man asks, after the traffic quiets down a bit.

Before Dan answers, Steel Bai says in a soft voice, "Don't tell him anything. It might endanger those you will interview."

"You don't have to tell me," the little man says with a knowing smile. "Want a ride? I've got a second-hand car. Maybe third- or fourth-hand." He points at a red tin box parked by the street. "But I can't afford to park in the hotel's parking lot."

Dan yells, thanks anyway, but they are almost there.

The little man gets into the car, waves at them, and drives away. The game started out with Dan having the upper hand of investigating him, and now it's the other way around. Why does he have to use the phony identity Dan abandoned? Why doesn't he become an honest freelance reporter, which he might actually be? Dan watches the red tin box mingle into the traffic, going under the highway bridge, and imagines himself as a ridiculous character in a dark, mysterious drama directed by this dwarf. He has no way of predicting his lines and actions, much less his fate.

Steel Bai shows Dan the way to a basement dormitory near the train station. He bangs a door open and ushers Dan in. Under an overhead lamp casting morgue-like gray light is a bleak room with six beds, of which only two have bedding. The air smells of dirty laundry and unwashed hair and bodies. Two figures get up from their beds.

"Here is our brave reporter," Steel says to them. Then he introduces the two old men to Dan as Uncle Bai and Uncle Liu.

Dan shifts on his feet, saying he is only a freelance journalist. He notices that the two old men are old enough to be his father's elder brothers.

"Freelance means he doesn't get paid to write what they tell him to write," Steel explains to them.

True, that's what "freelance" is all about. Dan likes Steel's definition of the word.

The two old men look at each other, take a few steps forward, and all of a sudden sink to their knees before Dan.

"Please don't!" Dan panics, trying to pull them up. "Please! I don't know how much I can help you . . ." His pa and ma once did the same when they took his younger brother, dying of a mysterious fever, to the county hospital without bringing money. "Please stand up . . ." Seeing no hope of getting them up, Dan pulls some money out of his pants pocket. If he could, he would have paid a lot more to banish this sight from his memory.

They don't want his money. They will kneel there until Dan promises to write an article for them. Just as his parents knelt there, on a cold, clay floor covered with phlegm stains, until the hospital gave in and took in their dying baby.

"I promise, I promise!" Dan says, pulling up on one old man's resisting arm. He is angry that he was too much of a soft touch, letting this stranger called Steel Bai drag him right into the depths of misery.

You must be careful these days, or you will land in a situation where you collide with misery at every turn. He can't remember how many times he has emptied his wallet and dumped the contents at the miserable creatures with missing arms and legs in subway passages and elevated crosswalks, just to make himself feel a bit better.

"Promise you will publish it in a very big newspaper," Uncle Bai sobs, fighting Dan's hands crutching him by the armpits into a standing position. He says the village heads almost beat his son to death, because he wrote to the county authorities to tell them how much money donated by people all over China the village heads had embezzled. They used the money for banquets and to build new houses for themselves. They built houses with an indoor shithouse where they sit down to shit instead of squatting, and a little bathhouse where they lie down flat to take a bath.

"They had three people beat up, and one of them died on the way to the county hospital," Steel explains. "It happened just before an inspection team arrived in the village. The village heads had arrested a lot of people on false charges of evading taxes, violating the one-child policy, and what have you. Then they bribed the team members with feasts and erotic massages."

"My son . . . ," the old man sobs, "is now paralyzed, and he has two small kids . . ."

"His son would also have died on the way to the county hospital—the nearest one, over a hundred kilometers away—if they had not hijacked a military jeep," Steel says.

Dan's little brother had died on the way back home from the hospital. The doctor had given him some drugs to relieve the symptoms and sent him away. Seeing Uncle Bai blow his nose with his fingers and wipe them on his shoe, Dan's tears well up in his eyes. He hasn't felt this badly since his departure from his home village at eighteen to join the army. They remind him of why he had wanted to run away from home. When he came out with Little Plum this morning, he had expected to have a wonderful time. Now his mood is totally ruined.

While Uncle Bai and Steel Bai are talking to Dan, going into the details of the nightmare, Uncle Liu sets the table—a bare wooden board on an empty bed, covered with newspaper as a tablecloth. He had bought some carry-out dishes from an eatery next door and two bottles of clear sorghum liquor in the subway convenience store. One dish is made of pig's feet and the others of pig entrails and organs. The pig-brain stew wobbles under a layer of red chili gravy. Dan counts the dishes quietly. There are eight of them. As cheap as the dishes are, it is still a banquet. After several loud toasts, all of them become sweaty-faced and thick-tongued. They haven't noticed that their conversations have gone in circles: the villagers went to a lawyer in the city, to file a lawsuit against the village heads. For three months they saw no result until one day each household received a quarterly tax bill with a five-yuan increase. It was to defray the funds the village heads had spent on their defense lawyer. The village heads had been chosen by the People's Government to serve the people, therefore the people had to take care of their legal expenses. Can you believe it? they ask Dan. No, he can't, Dan answers, realizing it's the third time he has said it.

Steel Bai proposes a toast, "To justice!"

With a sharp wheezing sound, they all take a gulp, grimacing as the harsh, 130-proof liquor goes down, burning all the way like a sparkling, hissing fuse. It hurts in an unspeakably soothing way.

"My son told me," Uncle Bai slurs, " 'Justice must be done!' You mustn't let him down!" He turns to Dan.

Dan nods. He feels his pockets for cigarettes, but Uncle Liu has already lit one for him out of a pack. It is an imported brand. They had prepared well for his arrival.

"Write a big article exposing those bastards! Avenge his son!" Uncle Liu says.

"I'll try."

Uncle Bai pokes his finger at Dan. "Don't just try; you *do* it!"

Afraid that Uncle Bai will kneel again, Dan picks up the glass, throws his head back, and drinks the last drops of the liquor. Squeezing his eyes shut and baring his teeth, he swallows the stuff, strong enough to disinfect a wound, and shows the bottom of the drained glass to Uncle Bai as a vow.

Someone knocks on the door loudly. Steel Bai eyes them all not to make a sound.

"Open up!" a woman's raspy voice says, very loud.

They freeze in various postures, their chopsticks poised in midair.

They hear a key enter the keyhole and turn. The door opens, and a middle-aged woman holding a key chain with a hundred keys tied on it stands there.

"Smells good," she says. "I smelled it upstairs."

"This is reporter Dong, very famous," Steel Bai says, referring to Dan.

She is not impressed. She doesn't give a damn that a reporter is gracing her hellish hostel. She doesn't care if you are a fugitive or a whore as long as you pay for your stay. Dan hands his card to her, and she receives it as if doing him a great favor.

The two old men are coughing and chuckling to hide their embarrassment.

"This banquet costs the same as three days' rent. Plus those imported cigarettes," she says, picking up the cigarette pack and examining it. "Twenty yuan a pack."

"No, thirty," Uncle Bai corrects her.

"That's worth another day's rent."

Uncle Liu says they are waiting for the money their relatives sent, which will arrive here any day. They detest people who abuse others' generosity. She's been such a sweetheart to them, and they are pigs if they don't appreciate it. As soon as they receive the money, they will pay the rent they owe her, with interest.

"Now you know the price of being their sweetheart: one month and three days' unpaid rent," she says, looking at Dan.

Dan begins noticing things in the room, registering a crooked washbasin tripod, a rusty clothesline rack, a dusty shadeless lamp, and a picture on the wall. The picture, made up of seashells on dark velvet, looks like a peony bush in its final bloom. One would have to excavate it out of dust to see the shapes and colors of the petals. By the corner bed stands an old, metal-shell thermos bottle, the bottom of which has almost rusted away, giving it a crippled stance. He hears the woman say that one should never deal with peasants. What does any of this have to do with being a peasant? counters Steel Bai, raising his voice. Peasants are stingy, sly, and they all cheat, she yells. Well, no peasant would ever want a woman like her, Steel Bai shoots back, even if she thinks she is better than they are. The rusty thermos bottle poses, one shoulder lower than the other, just like the angry, bitching woman. She shouts that they are shameless, eating a banquet behind closed doors while defrauding her of the rent. Before long, she begins throwing disposable dishes and plates around. Bits and pieces of food fly, a rainstorm of grease and sauce swirls, pelting the floor, walls, and the people. When she is through flinging her tenants'

things, which are very few, she reaches for the thermos bottle. Just as she is about to make a grand explosion, she hesitates, considering the ten yuan it will cost to replace the thermos bottle, and sets it back, not taking her hands off it immediately, as if steadying a lame dance partner after a waltz.

"Here," Dan yells, one hand wiping a streak of grease off his forehead while the other holds out a couple of hundred-yuan bills.

"The rent."

No one takes the bills from him.

"I will write the article for you. I promise."

He throws the bills to the littered floor and strides out the door. Once in the corridor, he breaks into a run. He fears to see their gratitude, which would twist their miserable faces, making them even harder to look at.

DAN HAS NOT gone out for five days, trying to write the article he promised the two old men. His effort results in nothing. It is a week later that he remembers to ask Little Plum how she liked the shark fin banquet. She answers that she enjoyed everything except the fish eyes. There is such thing as sautéed fish eyes? she asks. Yes, they are big and white, full of mucus, like those of folks with eye disease. Little Plum says she went to the bathroom because she felt like puking. She almost left the banquet right there. But she thought of something important, and went back in and found one of the registrars, a girl, very mean, with two pointy tits sticking out under her tight T-shirt. Little Plum asked the girl for her envelope.

"She just stared at me. And I said I know there should be an envelope for me. A big one."

"Usually a big one."

The registrar took an envelope out of a big suitcase next to her feet. She didn't hand it to Little Plum; she just chucked it on the table. Little Plum picked it up and handed it back to her, telling her to do it again. The registrar said, you wanted the envelope and I gave it to you, so what's your problem? Little Plum said, do it again. She told the registrar the difference between handing something properly and just chucking it, and she asked her to do it properly. The registrar gave up and handed the envelope to her, though Little Plum could see that she was calling her "bitch" with her eyes.

"You shouldn't have done that." Dan is all tensed up.

"You told me there is an envelope for everybody."

"Did you leave after you got it?"

No. She opened the envelope and saw only a notebook and a pen inside. She said to the registrar, wait a minute, there is something missing. She stood up and placed her hands on her hips, saying she knew there was supposed to be something else. Something very important.

Dan forgets to breathe.

Little Plum says she wasn't angry or ill-mannered or anything. She wasn't going to make a scene. She just told the pointy-titted, mean-faced registrar: look, I know everyone who shows up here is supposed to get a fee. Then she asked one of the reporters in the crowd who had come over to watch the spectacle whether he had gotten his fee yet. He stepped backward and smiled. So the girl registrar asked Little Plum, who told her there was supposed to be a fee?

Seeing Dan turn pale, she tells him not to worry; she didn't tell the registrar it was Dan who told her about the fee. The registrar went to fetch her boss, and she saw them making faces at Little Plum while coming to her together, asking for her ID card. "Did you give it to them?"

"Why should I?"

Dan sits back in the chair. Good, then, they would not be able to track her down even if they wanted to. He admits to himself that it wasn't such a good idea to take Little Plum to the banquet. She isn't ready. Getting her exposed to nasty, mean people, who are skeptical about everybody and everything, is dangerous. Dan reaches for Little Plum's hand and pulls her close. He puts her on his lap, asking her with his lips in her freshly washed hair, "How did you leave the hotel?"

"They didn't let me leave."

"What?!"

They wouldn't let her go unless she gave them her ID card. And she said she wouldn't let them have it unless they paid her. Dan can't believe what he hears. Dan has seen his wife fight. Most village girls grow up learning how to taunt others, chanting insults with relish and swearing in rhymes if someone tries to bully them or their families.

They let her go after the questioning got them nowhere. Dan runs his fingers pensively through his wife's hair as he thinks the story over. It was such a rotten idea to take her there and leave her alone with the damned staring fish eyes that made her puke, and with those damned bully snobs with staring eyes who always look for innocent country people to harass.

The following afternoon, Dan goes to a conference. There is nothing unusual. Everyone greets him as before. Happy comes to him, asking him to call Ocean Chen, to schedule interviews. She has tried to call Ocean Chen many times, but his fiancée kept telling her the artist was not up to it.

"I want to show you something." Dan pulls her aside and hands her a few pages of writing he has scribbled.

She reads it from beginning to end, then returns to the beginning.

"What is this crap anyway?" she asks, frowning. Happy usually gets angry about lousy, unclear writing.

"It is, well . . ." Dan knows immediately that his writing is bad. "It is written by a peasant."

"No wonder."

Dan searches her face. "Is it that bad?"

She ignores his question, returning the pages to him, and goes back to talking about Ocean Chen's fiancée. The fiancée surely sounds like a bitch, who certainly wouldn't want the old artist to get a phone call from a woman, much less a visit. It is Dan's responsibility to wheedle the master into talking more, so that they can write a world-class profile.

"Don't you think you can help this guy polish it?" Dan persists. "What I like about it is the story. Such a sad story."

"Lousy writing like this will make no one believe the story."

"I believe it. Things like this happen in my parents' village, too."

"See, that's where your limit is. You can't go beyond your peasant narrowness. You are only interested in what concerns your village, your lands, your chickens, hogs, cows, and crops. You can't see what great material lies hidden in Ocean Chen's story. It is material for a reporter who aspires to higher and finer things."

Dan looks at her dark red lips opening and closing, telling him that peasants are the origin of corruption in China. No one can save them from the tragedies told in the article. Because it's no use. There wouldn't be a peasant class if they didn't exploit each other as well. They deserve the bad rulers they have had throughout the dynasties, and they deserve the corrupt leaders they have today, because when they get power themselves, they do exactly the same thing. This country's fundamental trouble is that it was founded by a bunch of successful peasant rebels. Just think about the population: over one billion peasants today. Have their numbers decreased because of corruption? No. Not only have they survived it, they have even thrived on it. Let them kill each other; it's just natural selection and self-adjustment among their own kind. Let them continue surviving and thriving by their—

"Shut the fuck up," Dan says.

And she does. For the first time ever, she smiles a submissive smile at him.

Dan looks at a palm tree in the granite lobby that has a cloth trunk and plastic leaves, green as a post office truck. His mind is full of old, crease-lined faces like Uncle Bai's and Uncle Liu's. Faces with colorless lips and red-lidded eyes. Those faces would crack, smiling so innocently at a newborn calf, or at a field of young wheat that survived an unexpected late snowstorm, or at a chick pecking her way out of an eggshell, or at selling a load of green onions at a good price, making a few more coins than expected. His parents would stand by the government road behind two piles of green onions, baking in the summer sun, looking forward to seeing trucks emerge on the dusty horizon. They really hated to eat the onions they failed to sell; they'd rather have eaten plain cornbread and sorghum gruel and kept carrying the onions, drying up or rotting away, to the roadside every day to try their luck. There are endless lines of onion piles, behind which are old, expectant faces, smiling at a truck rumbling down the gray slope of the road. In his reminiscence, Dan thinks of his parents' guilty eyes accepting their worldly son's scolding for their "foolish, barbarian stinginess," of their shamefaced smiles when promising to eat any unsold leftover onions, which already stung one's eyes with a piercing stench.

"What the fuck do you know about peasants?" he says. His eyes have become moist.

Seeing Dan's Adam's apple bobbing up and down, his eyes red with tears welling up, Happy is scared. His handsome face has never been in such a grimace.

"I would punch you into a pulp if you weren't a woman," he says.

He leaves the conference room, daring not to blink his eyes, lest he touch off the tears. He hates the fact that he knows this woman.

HE GOES TO the basement dormitory again and discovers that the two old men and Steel Bai checked out several days ago. They must have left feeling betrayed. They had come to him as a last resort, and he had failed them. Dan stands leaning against the chipped table that serves as a front desk at the entrance, and he gazes outside. Set off by the dimness of the dormitory, the light outside looks so bright. Dan imagines the two old men going out, all their hopes broken, carrying their nylon market bags, the same type as his parents'. They carry the bags on their shoulders, the same way his parents do when they travel out of the village.

He rewrites the article, imagining the two protagonists as his parents. After he finishes it, he goes to a banquet and shows it to Happy. It is better now, only too sentimental. She asks if he recomposed it for that peasant. He says yes, thanks to her criticism. Can she help get it published? She will try, if he is willing to take out the corny parts. It has to be toned down a lot, and the emotions must be minimized. The more objective it is, the easier it will be for it to pass censorship. It is a very touchy subject, and a newspaper has been shut down temporarily by the government because it published an article on a similar topic. And the newspaper fired the reporter to show its loyalty to the Party.

This noon, the banquet is set for over a hundred media people. The host is a beer company that signed export agreements with some twenty foreign countries. The new logo is going to be designed by a calligrapher, selected from among the best in China, who can sell his calligraphy of a single character for a hundred thousand yuan.

The cold dishes are presented. Each of them is designed as an ancient Chinese character. The most impressive one is a square, red signet character, just like what an emperor would have used on his imperial seal. It is made of raw veal on jellyfish. The intense color of the red meat juxtaposed with the translucence of the jellyfish, set on bone-white, paper-thin china, is so striking that the dish could go directly to an art gallery. Dan regrets that his camera is just a prop; otherwise, he would photograph the dish for Little Plum to share.

"Three chefs spent sixteen hours in a refrigerated room to make these dishes," one of the guests says.

Dan finds it is the little man who is talking. He always seems to know more than the rest of the people and is always showy about it. He is sitting at the next table, his back to Dan.

"I don't think even an emperor would have food like this," a reporter at Dan's table responds to the little man.

"It must cost a month's salary to have it in a restaurant," a woman says. She lifts her chopsticks, looking at her tablemates with a theatrical warning expression, and tears apart the chefs' sixteen hours of work. With a cheer, all the chopsticks begin charging forward. In a few minutes, all that's left on the fine china plate is a few bloody traces of raw meat.

"Haven't seen you for a while," the little man says to Dan, his huge head turning almost one hundred and eighty degrees.

That's right, Dan says; he has been engaged in something else. Does Dan know about the young woman who got caught the other day? What young woman? The little man moves his chair to Dan's table, continuing the story. If she had just eaten quietly, not trying her luck with the fee and souvenirs, she would have gotten away with it. The fee? Yes, she went to one of the registrars, demanding "money for your troubles." Was she bold or what? She sure was, Dan agrees, trying not to avoid the little man's eyes. Her business card says she is a freelance writer. Is that so? Dan can't help an awkward smile. At least that's what it says on her business card. But her camera and notebook, as the girl registrar figured out by looking at them closely, were just props. Really? And also, it seems she filled the pages with her own name. What did they do about her in the end? They had to let her go, but the security guys will do something about it. What are they going to do? To begin with, they can trace down the print shop where she got her cards made. They said they would even find the pawnshop where she bought the junky camera. There are only fifty or so pawnshops in Beijing, and they can just check their recent sales records. The security department might have sent detectives to the shark fin banquet. They are positive that there are more banquet bugs squirming around than just that one young woman. They suspect at least ten or more bugs in each banquet. *Ten or more!*

Dan stares at the chopsticks he is holding. He is furious at these ten bugs, who have been leading a lifestyle that he created.

"I still remember what she looks like," the little man continues. "A cute little thing. With a little chubby face, round eyes and all. The last person in all of Beijing you would take to be a banquet bug. Somehow she caught my attention in the registration area, and I followed her into the conference room. Come to think of it, she was sitting right behind you."

Dan feels a cramp in his stomach. So he *had* been watching them. He had seen Dan move to sit beside Little Plum.

"Why did the security let her go?" Dan asks.

"Instead of arresting her? I don't know. They have their own strategy, I guess."

What is that strategy? To use her as bait? Let her go so she will lead them to a big fish like Dan?

Dan is too distracted to even talk to Happy, who has come to his table to tell him of a publisher she has found for the peasant's article.

Happy acts as if the little man does not exist. She inserts herself between the two men, putting her elbows on the table's edge so her face is level with Dan's.

"He owes me a big favor, the publisher," she says. "So he will publish anything I ask him to. Now you go and tell that peasant to cut out all the corny crap and come back to me with cool, impersonal stuff."

Dan agrees. He tries to make himself louder so the little man, who has turned his head from Dan's table back toward his own, can overhear the conversation. "I'll have the article ready in a couple of days. Three, at most," he says.

"Better be fast. The favor the publisher owes me will expire any moment, depending on the political climate. The climate is mild right now, but it could be wild tomorrow."

Dan thanks her.

"Thanks are cheap," she says.

"I will call Ocean Chen tomorrow." By now, Dan knows better than to expect a free favor from this woman. It is all about exchange of favors.

"You call him *now*." Happy dials the number on her cell phone and hands it to Dan.

Dan can only tell that it is a woman's voice answering on the other end. He gets up and hurries to a window close to his table, his feet snared in the napkin that has fallen from his lap. Following behind him, Happy picks up the napkin and tosses it to a waitress scurrying past with a tray.

She has already hung up, the woman with the sweet-and-sour voice on the other end of the phone line. Dan dials again. No answer this time.

"What a bitch," Happy says. "She believes everyone calling Ocean Chen is asking for a painting for free. She has increased the price of his paintings in the galleries. And they're already overpriced as it is!" She takes out her cigarette case, shakes it, and draws out a cigarette with her dark red lips. She lights up next to the "No Smoking" sign.

"Dan, you have to go there in person," Happy says after a few pensive puffs.

"Now?"

"Why not?"

"I don't think Ocean Chen will like that."

"Why not?"

"His fiancée won't let me see him."

"Don't give me different reasons at the same time."

"If the fiancée doesn't like it, he won't like it."

"I don't understand why Ocean Chen is so pussy-whipped."

You'll become an old maid unless you come to understand it. "Let's not go today . . ."

"We must go. Tell the bitch you are an art collector interested in buying one of Ocean Chen's paintings. I bet she will melt at your feet."

"But that's a lie."

"Everything is a lie. Don't you think Ocean Chen's works are lies? And don't all the critics lie about his works?"

Dan looks at her. He has lost his peace of mind and his joy at eating banquets ever since this woman appeared in his life. She says she will drive him to Capital Hospital and wait outside while he interviews.

Dan meets the fiancée in the reception room downstairs. She questions Dan for twenty minutes, though in a very sweet way, and tells Dan that the master isn't well enough to see anyone today.

"He is sleeping now," she says.

"Let him rest, by all means," Dan says. He sits on the edge of the sofa with all his weight on his legs. If someone pulled the sofa out from under him suddenly, he would most certainly fall forward.

"He needs more sleep," the fiancée says.

"Yes, yes."

"What I do is just guard his sleep. The last two weeks he didn't sleep much, because I went home to Shanghai."

Dan notices that she only refers to the artist as "he." And she has a peculiar way of saying it. Dan can't describe the peculiarity of it, but he believes it is either endearment or awe, just like the way his parents refer to the gods, or Buddha, or Chairman Mao.

She says they can schedule the visit for another time. When? Well, it depends on his health. He is not supposed to get excited, and he can't help getting excited when people are around. He is like a child sometimes.

She is a woman of porcelain beauty, with classic features set off by extremely light skin. Her name is Ruby Li, a common name one would hear a hundred times a day in a schoolyard. Ruby sits cross-legged, one foot dangling, playing with her white, beaded slipper, her toes wiggling subtly inside it. Every time the slipper falls, Dan blinks at the subtle noise. And it has fallen more than twenty times. He can't help watching her stretching her supple leg and poking her toes into the fallen slipper, wiggling back into it bit by bit. Then another round of the game starts all over again. She is too young for the artist. She is younger than the artist's eldest daughter. Dan moves his eyes away, trying not to think about the embraces and kisses between the aged body and the young one.

Dan stands up to bid farewell, asking if Master Chen would like more Northwestern green onions. He can send them through the express delivery service.

"You are the one giving him the onions?" she asks, a real smile breaking out from her measured, photo-like smile.

"Sorry to send such unworthy presents."

"Not at all! He cares for them immensely. Could you send more?"

"No problem."

Dan will buy two cartons of cigarettes for the railroad guy and have him go to his parents to ask them to harvest more onions. Ocean Chen will have the fresh onions in three or four days. He will then do the interview to repay Happy's favor. No, not he—his parents'

onions will repay her favor. As Ruby sees him to the door, her cell phone rings. Dan has never seen a more delicate, jewelry-like cell phone, with a ring tone like a bird chirping. She says, yes, she has thanked the visitor for the onions.

"He promised to bring you more onions next time. He is a very nice man." She gives Dan a sidelong smile, apologizing for talking about him in his presence.

Dan tries not to look at the faint blue veins under the silky skin of her hand. He catches himself wondering about her skin under her white, loose T-shirt. Does it also have delicate veins running underneath? Making her skin faintly blue? What does a hand feel when touching it? Ocean Chen's hand—spotted, coarsened by prison toil, age, and incessant sculpting and painting; is that coarseness going to catch the invisible fibers of this silky skin and damage it? Dan again has to overcome an urge to visualize their entwined bodies. He hates himself for being so obscene-minded, but he can't help it. He really can't. The disparity between the couple's ages and appearance, as well as their life experience, keeps triggering flashes of erotic pictures in his mind.

"Here." She hands the phone to Dan. "He wants to talk to you."

"Hello, my landsman," the old artist says. "You do know the way to my room, don't you?"

Dan mutters some greetings.

"So what kept you from coming here?" the artist shouts.

"I'll come back when you feel better," Dan says.

"Let me talk to Ruby."

Dan hands the phone back to her. She doesn't want him to receive too many visitors, she protests to Ocean Chen. Ruby twists her body, neck, chin, and shoulders, turning in contradictory directions, forming defiant but sweet angles and lines. But, if he insists, she will make an exception, she tells Ocean Chen, passively aggressive, charming to the point that Dan's heart wrenches.

As soon as they step out of the elevator, they hear people talking and laughing. The noise comes from Ocean Chen's room, Dan decides. The door opens not to a resting old artist, but to a party of eight people all holding glasses of wine. Dan recognizes one of the guests as the son of the Party leader. The floor is covered with paintings, and so are the tables. Everyone has to pick his way through in mincing steps. Ocean Chen looks manically happy, calling everyone bastard or son of a bitch. He points to Dan, who is awkwardly looking for a place to accommodate himself, and tells the guests that this dear bastard is his landsman. Then he tells Dan that all the bastards present have big daddies in the Party's Central Committee.

A young woman says Dan looks like someone from the damned press circle. Yeah, she has a good eye. But he is not going to write about their awful misbehavior this evening, the artist promises her. He turns to Dan, saying, this evening never happened, understood? Okay, Dan says, speaking, nodding, and smiling all at once.

Ruby comes to Dan with a glass of wine.

"I'd better get going. I have an engagement tonight," Dan says. He sees no prospect of a serious interview.

"I need your help," Ruby says, placing the glass in Dan's hand anyway. "Would you please go and get some sugar-free cake for him?" She gives him a slip of paper with an address and directions on it. "It's not that far from here. I would have the driver take you there if I didn't have to keep him here for little emergencies that might come up. I'd be grateful if you could help me out. I really don't like him to eat sweets."

Dan says he is glad to run such an easy errand.

"While you are at it, would you go check on his daughter at boarding school? Ask her teacher not to forget she has a piano lesson tonight. Oh, his daughter's name is Snow Dove Chen."

Dan tries to memorize the name. Snow Dove Chen. Wouldn't a dove freeze to death in the snow?

"I'll have you take some fruit to her."

"All right." Snow Dove Chen.

"I really appreciate your help. You can see I can't leave here. These are important guests . . ."

She twists her body again. Her chin, neck, and shoulders remind Dan of a pleasing little girl and a tyrant at the same time.

Dan comes out of the building and sees Happy pacing back and forth on the little lawn. It is getting dark. She lifts her head expectantly as Dan approaches. Has he done the interview? No. Why not? Dan doesn't know if he should say the artist has many important guests or he is not feeling well. And what has Dan done for the last hour-and-a-half? Dan looks at Happy, her sharp features softened by the dusk.

"Ocean Chen isn't feeling well today." Dan chooses to lie for the artist. "I'll come back in a few days."

Happy gives the artist's window on the third floor a sharp look.

"You don't have to lie for him," she says very gently.

Dan feels bad about her. About her waiting for an hour-and-a-half on a mosquito-ridden lawn.

"I promise you, Happy, I'll get the interview done for you in three days."

"Wrong. Not for me. For yourself. For the help you're getting from me."

Happy drives away after she drops Dan in front of the boarding school. The headmaster tells him to leave the peaches with a note saying that the fruit is from Snow Dove Chen's family. The school won't take responsibility if the child gets sick from eating it. On his way to the bakery from the school, he asks the taxi driver to stop and make a U-turn. It has occurred to him that the peaches might not have been washed thoroughly. He takes the fruit back, takes it to a boys' shower room, and washes it in one of the miniature bathtubs, which he has scrubbed repeatedly. Right after he comes out the school gate, he hurries back again. He goes to the boys' shower room and tries to remember which bathtub he used to wash the peaches. If he got peach fuzz all over it, it will give the next boy who bathes in it a terrible itch. He has started to scrub the tub hard when a female teacher of about thirty shows up behind him. He straightens his back, pushing up the two sleeves of his shirt, and smiles. She looks at him, not hiding her suspicion that he might be nuts or a child molester, and asks him in a stern voice what on earth he is doing. He tells her what has happened. She says, incredulously, that she will dump the peaches immediately. He is surprised, asking her why. Why? Can't he see how disgusting it is to wash food in a bathtub? But he had washed the tub many times before cleansing the fruit. It is as clean as a cooking pot. Cleaner than his mother's cooking pot, for that matter. But, she replies, it is still a bathtub, for hundreds of little boys to wash their feet and bottoms and all. Is he out of his mind, using it as a food washing facility? The very idea is mad and makes her ill.

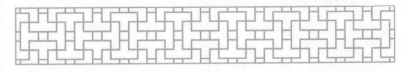

IT IS CLOSE TO eleven o'clock at night by the time that Dan, sugar-free cake in hand, reports back to Ocean Chen's room, which is still boisterous with laughter and jokes. The master, who has obviously had too much to drink, is slurring his regrets about his dog, who died thirty years ago. Ruby makes faces at the guests as she finishes his sentences for him. Please put up with him, Ruby pleads; once he starts his dog story, you know he is drunk. After the guests leave, Ocean Chen goes to the bedroom and stands in front of a closet mirror, glaring at himself. "You whore. No, not a whore—worse: a eunuch! Let them castrate you of your pride and conscience, so you can be a court jester for them. They are a bunch of good-for-nothings, robbing the country and the people blind because they are the spawn of powerful old men. They are the core of evil in this country, and you treat them like nobility . . ." He clutches and tears at his hair, though there is not much of it to clutch. Dan, frightened, runs to hold back his thick arms, while Ruby makes a call to the doctor on night duty. Then she drops the receiver back to the cradle, telling Dan she dare not let anyone hear what the old man is saying. It is enough to get him another seven years in jail. As Dan finally manages to put the old man to bed, swimming wild free-strokes in the white sheet with a red cross printed on it, Ocean Chen sobs, saying, "They are a bunch of ignoramuses who can't tell their asses from their elbows, and still you let them have your paintings! What a bunch of man-eaters, peacock-eaters, shit-eaters . . ."

Ruby turns on the TV and increases the volume, so the nurses won't hear his tirade against the Party leadership. After ten minutes or so, his swimming slows down, his sobbing speech fades, and he drifts into a spasmodic sleep. When Dan goes to leave the master to Ruby, he finds that the old man's fist is clutching the corner of his jacket. He pulls it out gently. In his heart, the master is so much like a child, insecure and clinging. But can he put this in his profile? Of course not. When the elevator arrives, Ruby comes out of the suite, running.

"Please wait," she says.

Dan lets the elevator go.

"Never mind him. That's the way he is, finding things to get angry at, criticizing society or the leaders whenever he gets drunk. So, we agree that you have heard nothing, right?"

Dan nods, and Ruby smiles.

"Tomorrow morning he needs to see an herbal medicine doctor, but I have a meeting with some collectors at nine . . ."

"I will go with Master Chen to the herbal doctor," Dan says.

"You see how much I rely on your help," she says, petting his shoulder subtly.

After a week, even Ocean Chen gets used to asking him for help. Please, Dan, change the water in the fish tank. Dan, go carry this dead plant out and get a new one at the market. Dan, please go settle the checkout bill with the hospital cashier and come back to load the stuff into the car. There will be at least three carloads to move back home from the hospital. Dan, please rip down all the damn curtains in this house and make it as bright as the hospital room. Dan, go tell the cook to turn off that mindless song on his tape player. Less than a week after checking out of the hospital, Ocean Chen feels completely at ease when Dan is sitting in his studio, where he paints, or reads, or talks on the phone, or even quarrels with Ruby. Dan seems to be a content, happy entity, blending into whatever background the artist places him against. It is only when Dan isn't there waiting for chores that Ocean Chen feels the importance of his presence. Sometimes, when Dan returns to him after accomplishing an errand, the old artist is peevish and restless, asking him where the hell he has been. Other times, he stops short in the middle of a brushstroke and stays motionless for a long while, as if trying to retrieve a missing thought. Dan never intrudes on these moments, because somehow he knows they are the most sacred secrets that make Ocean Chen Ocean Chen, and all the other artists the rest of them. Once in a while, the old artist becomes helpless and drops his brush, murmuring that his creativity is completely exhausted, and all that is left of him is a machine that turns perfectly good food into feces. Then all of a sudden he notices Dan, sitting in the far corner of his studio, watching him in a totally nonjudgmental, amiable silence.

"Are you married?" the old artist asks, holding a paintbrush in one hand and pulling at its hairy tip with another.

Dan smiles and says yes. He has told him four times.

"How did you two meet?"

Dan smiles again. He has also told him his love history more than once.

Little Plum and Dan met five years ago in his home village, while he was visiting his parents after completing his apprenticeship at the factory. It was on the fourth day of his stay that he saw a pretty girl in his parents' front yard, sewing something. He had slept in, and his parents had already gone to the fields. She was sitting on a piece of fire log under the rustling shade of an aspen tree. He hollered *"Wei!"*—hello—from inside the window, asking what she was doing. She answered that she had a name, so don't call her *"Wei."* He went out and saw that what she had been sewing was his torn factory uniform.

Dan asked her: How can you sew a strange man's clothes?

She pointed to the old bicycle parked under the eaves of the house. See? Now it's shiny. I cleaned it.

Squatting down across from her, Dan watched her head angle to bite off the thread. The nape of her neck looked so young it was downy. He said: You can't do these things for a man unless you like him.

She looked up and smiled: I like him.

Dan's face was burning. How can you like a man you don't know?

I knew I liked him when he walked past me in the marketplace, on the way to the tavern. I watched him the whole time he drank beer with the village men. He paid for everyone. And he told stories like a folk storyteller.

It doesn't take much for you to like a man. Dan laughed. You know it's dangerous for a girl to say things like that.

Why?

Dan didn't answer. Some mysterious tension made him laugh too much.

A minute passed and he said: You just can't say things like that. He touched her hand, laughing.

Studying his face, she failed to see what was worth his laughter.

He knew he shouldn't be taking advantage of the situation. But he asked nonetheless, would you let him touch you? I mean, you have to prove you like him by letting him touch you.

He *is* touching me, she said, looking at his hand creeping up from her hand to her arm, then to her shoulder. She watched him, strangely detached, as his hand started descending inside her blouse collar, from her shoulder downward.

Just one touch? he asked.

She nodded, letting him open her collar button. Then the button on her chest.

He looked around and made sure they were alone. He pulled her into his arms and touched her adolescent breasts. He found her eyes following wherever his hands went, as fascinated as he was about her body.

106

He forgot all about her until the night he went to the open-air movie theater, and she came, carrying a little stool, and sat quietly beside him. He stole some more touches during the movie, and offered to take her out the next day. They went to a riverbank with a white pebble shore. He laid out some food, including cookies and tangerines he had brought from Beijing. She took a piece of bread from the local bakery and left the rest of the food untouched.

Don't you like them? he asked about the tangerines.

No.

Why?

I've never had them before. I don't know how to eat them.

For a reason Dan couldn't name, he felt terribly guilty about what he had been doing to this girl. She had missed so much in her young life, including the experience of dealing with men, who seldom pass up an easy, sweet thing like her. He had robbed someone who had no clue what robbery meant.

A week passed and Dan was ready for his return trip to Beijing. He went to the marketplace, hoping again to run into the girl called Little Plum. That was the only place he knew he would find her. He looked for her for two days, but she didn't emerge. The night before he left, he went to the tavern and saw her standing at the entrance.

He said he liked her, too. In fact, he liked her so much that he wanted to take her to Beijing someday. She smiled with her usual detachment and said he'd better hurry, because in a few days she would be in Siberia. What would she be doing in Siberia? Her family was marrying her off to a rich Chinese farmer who had established a farm there. He'd hired a herd of Russian field workers and needed a wife to cook for them. Dan couldn't believe it. She said it was her farewell visit to her aunt in Dan's village.

Dan postponed his trip back to Beijing and went to the girl's family, desperately poor, and walked out ten minutes later, beat and disoriented. He had been told that the farmer in Siberia would pay thirty thousand yuan for Little Plum. That night, Little Plum sneaked out and came to Dan's parents' house. He took her to a neighboring county, where they could board the Beijing-bound train.

Dan has never told Ocean Chen the story in its entirety as he does this time. But he isn't sure the old man will remember it.

One day, after a serious quarrel with Ruby, Ocean Chen mumbles how much he misses a love story like Dan's.

"A love story between a village maiden and a cowherd." He smiles a sad smile. "That story died in the city a long time ago."

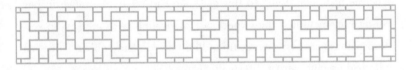

WHEN DAN GETS HOME at night, he sees Little Plum repairing their favorite souvenir, the piece of black marble shaped like a book, edged with gold and with a gold logo. The gold logo has fallen off, and she has been trying to glue it back on. As he helps her, he finds that the logo is too light to be gold. He brings it up to the lamplight and finds it is just a piece of plastic. So the famous goldsmith's signature is also phony. They can't sell it for food after all, as they often joke. With Dan's help, Little Plum finally succeeds in gluing the fake gold back on the black marble. Gold or not, it is nice to look at.

As they hang it back on the wall, Little Plum tells Dan that a man harassed her today. He was in a car stuck in traffic at an intersection where she was selling roasted chestnuts. He asked her if she had been at the shark fin banquet.

"What did he look like?" Dan asks.

All she could see was his head. Kind of a big head, like a dwarf's. Did he wear glasses—dark and thick-framed, out of fashion twenty years ago? All she could make out was his head. It was getting dark and he was a couple of cars away. He yelled over the honks of cars that he was sure she was the girl at the shark fin banquet. She told him to beat it. But he didn't; instead he asked her if she lived nearby. She answered that he should take a good look at himself in the mirror before he asks a woman for her address. And if he's got no mirror, a puddle of his own pee will do. As the traffic started to move, he still tried to say something. She didn't let him. She shrieked at him, beat it! beat it! beat it! And this time he did.

Dan holds her hand, asking if she is all right, but realizing it is he who is disturbed by what she has said. His brain is filled with guesses and debates, shooting in all directions at once. She has been watched. Some creep has been following her. But why didn't he follow her all the way here? He wants to kill himself for taking her to the shark fin banquet without preparing her well. Before they go to bed, he believes he will think of a way out for both of them after he gets a good night's sleep and recovers from the shock.

As the night deepens, Dan is exhausted by the effort of trying to sleep. His feet have turned sickly cold, and his forehead is damp with perspiration. Little Plum has turned her back toward him, curled up with one of her feet touching his leg. The sole of her foot gives off the healthy warmth of a sound sleeper. His arm reaches out and wriggles into the hollow under her neck. There. Now his chest and abdomen and thighs are flush with her back and buttocks and the back of her thighs, curve to curve, fold to fold. In a way he is riding her, riding her sleep. Gradually the waves of her rhythmic breathing pick him up and begin to carry him. He lets her take him, floating, gently dipping and rocking, and he finally matches his breath with hers. The last thought that passes through Dan's mind before he falls asleep is that he will quit the banquet bug job altogether.

ON SUNDAY AFTERNOON Dan takes Little Plum to a construction site. It is also her favorite playground. They climb along the stairwell with no handrails, all the way to the top of the building. Little Plum sits gazing at the unfinished apartment buildings all around, while Dan comments on the architectural design and the quality of the construction. He points his finger, telling Little Plum which unit they will live in a year or so from now, and what kind of interior decoration he would choose for it. If he keeps the banquet bug job a little longer, they might save enough money to purchase a condo. Maybe he can take a chance. It is worth the risk. He looks at Little Plum, simply sitting there, bathing in the early autumn breeze. She has always been strangely content, never wanting anything in particular from him. He is almost shocked to realize how little it takes to make her happy. He pulls her toward him, and she snuggles in his arms.

They sit until their stomachs begin rumbling.

Little Plum cooks homemade noodles for dinner. Since he started eating banquets, Dan hasn't had the food he always enjoyed as a boy. It has been over a year since he tasted Little Plum's hot, soupy noodles. He feels the warmth and softness spread in his stomach, penetrating his flesh and blood, caressing him inwardly. Suddenly he is seized by fear. If he doesn't stop going to banquets, he will lose this loft room with a homemade sofa set and stolen hot showers, and Little Plum, who makes hot, soupy noodles.

Little Plum asks him what the matter is with him, holding his chopsticks in midair like that.

"Don't go on the street to sell things."

"Why not?"

"Because you are being followed."

"I don't care."

"They follow you because they want to get me."

"But why?"

"I'm a banquet bug. They are looking for banquet bugs right now."

Little Plum still doesn't see what is wrong with being a banquet bug. There is so much food! Too much food! It will go to waste if Dan doesn't eat it. And it makes no difference if Dan eats it. It makes no difference whatsoever if a hundred banquet bugs eat it or not. See how much food is left over after everyone is stuffed? Such a waste. If there were no banquet bugs at work, there would be even more food going into waste buckets. And *that* is a *real* crime.

Dan thinks of the apartment they saw hours ago. A small one in a far suburb doesn't cost much. If he keeps going to banquets for another three months, he might be able to make the down payment. After that, he will find a labor job to pay the monthly mortgage. Maybe he can become a taxi driver, as some of the factory's reserve workers have, to meet the expense of owning a condo. And he won't mind having Little Plum's hot, soupy noodles for the rest of his life, from then on.

HAPPY DOESN'T SHOW UP in the underground foot massage parlor. Dan has asked her to come and discuss his revision of the peasant's story. He returned her tape recorder along with the tapes of his interview with Ocean Chen, and she had shrieked with excitement. But she doesn't keep her promise to help him polish the article. So he sits and waits alone in one of the rooms.

A knock comes on the door, followed by a timid voice asking if she can come in. Dan stands up to open the door and there she is, Old Ten. While they exchange greetings, she enters, pushing the door open with her shoulder, her hands full with a bucket of water and a basin.

He has not ordered a massage. Reading his mind, she smiles and tells him not to worry, it is her treat. How has she being doing since the last time he saw her? Oh, just fine. How is her sister?

"Crystal mud or herbs this time?" she asks as she begins to remove his shoes.

He says she must decide for him, since it is her treat. He laughs. She smiles, beginning to knead his calves. He says it is because of her that he has come to like this special "torture." She smiles again. How did people come to know this—that to feel so good, one must hurt a little? He is talking and laughing by himself now. There is a charge in the air between the two of them, and he keeps talking, hoping to release it.

"The crystal mud is a con," Old Ten says. "There's no such thing as crystal mud in Tibet." She strips the socks off his feet, lifts his feet on her lap and tests the temperature of the water.

When the massage begins, he feels the difference this time. She lays his feet farther forward on her lap, and as she bends forward and her arms stretch forth, his toes touch her bosom. In the position she takes, her breasts are relaxed and feel extremely soft.

"You told me last time you wanted to find another job." His toes are in the cleavage of her breasts now. Without warning, a painful thought comes to him. These toes could have been someone else's. Could have been the fungused, callused toes of an old, bald man, flaunting his Rolex watch and his wealth to girls like Old Ten.

"I told you that?" Her hands reach his heels, hurting them in an inexplicably soothing way.

He finds his lips parting.

"So . . . so you say things and you don't remember saying them?"

Her answer is a powerful and deep press into the tendons above his heels. He lets out a soundless cry.

"I don't have a sister anymore."

"You mean you lied to me last time?"

"No, I had a sister then. But I don't anymore."

Dan pulls his upper body up and looks at her. She gazes at his feet.

"She has been killed."

"In an accident?"

"She lent her savings to a man . . ."

Old Ten goes on to explain that it was her entire savings. She lent it to her boyfriend and couldn't get it back. That was all she had saved, working in cities from Guangzhou to Shanghai to Beijing. She had worked for ten years. And her boyfriend took it from her just like that. He wore the most expensive clothes and an expensive jade ring and joined the most expensive clubs, and his wife went to the most expensive salons for her facial treatments every other day, and yet he couldn't pay his debts.

"When did she lend him the money?" Dan asks. The pleasure on his feet that has started radiating throughout his body, reaching the bottom of his abdomen, gradually comes to a halt.

"Six months ago," she says.

It had happened before their first meeting. Why didn't she tell him then? Did she need more intimacy in order to talk about such matters?

"Who killed her? Her boyfriend or the wife?"

She keeps looking at his feet, her hands going up and down; they could be a massage machine.

"Nobody."

"She took her own life?"

"No."

Her numb hands move on his numb feet, up and down, up and down. He doesn't know what else could have happened to her sister. She finally breaks the silence that has lasted for several minutes. Six months ago, her sister tried to poison the boyfriend, but his son ate the poisoned food instead. She was arrested on a murder charge. Last week, she was put to death. She was twenty-nine years old, tall and beautiful. A head of incredible hair that came down to her thighs. She always told Old Ten, her baby sister, that being a masseuse was a path that led to an unknown future. It could be a nice future; you just never know.

"I wanted to tell you the first time you were here," Old Ten says.

But she didn't. She was waiting for him to show up and ask for her the second time. She was sure he would come the following day, asking for more intimate service. Most men would and did.

"I was going to ask for your help. You are a newsman. I heard a lot of unjust cases were overturned because of the stuff you guys wrote. They are afraid of you."

Who is "they"? The government? The lawmakers and law enforcers? All Dan says is "Why the hell didn't you tell me the first time?" As if he were a real journalist, with a formidable pen that could defend the truth. He has never felt the title of "journalist" to be as sacred and as hopelessly beyond his reach. He has never wished to be a journalist as much as he does now.

"What's your sister's name?" As if it mattered.

"Little Plum."

"Little Plum!"

Why is it that he is fated to be involved with poor Little Plums? Why are all the Little Plums in the world pretty and trusting and ignorant of men taking advantage of them? He wants to pray to whatever God there is that no more Little Plums get picked by evil hands.

"I went to visit her before her sentencing," Old Ten says, her hands stopping on his feet.

It was a nice afternoon in early autumn, the kind that makes one hopeful and melancholy at once. Little Plum didn't know she would be executed the next day. She only knew there would be a public trial at which a number of convicts would be judged. She was brought to the visitation room to meet her baby sister, who also had no idea that this would be their last meeting. Little Plum was talkative and giggling a lot, her face wearing subtle makeup. It must have been smuggled into the prison somehow. She asked if her baby sister had contacted the journalist she'd mentioned. And the baby sister had lied that she'd contacted someone else who might help. The baby sister didn't tell Little Plum that she had been rejected by all the people to whom she had appealed. They'd taken whatever she'd offered, pleasure or comfort, and disappeared. The next day Old Ten was giving a private massage in a private room, when the news of her sister's death sentence came on TV. She didn't remember anything that happened after that moment. The moment of seeing Little Plum's gray face pulled out of shape, her hair clutched in two male fists, her breasts misshapen by a crisscross of a rope on her chest. The time from that moment until two days later was a void in Old Ten's memory.

Dan finds his hand on her hair, and her face buried in his lap.

"Cry. Let it out. Don't hold it back," Dan says.

She doesn't cry. It's scary that she doesn't.

A week after the execution, she got to know a person working in that particular court. He told Old Ten everything about Little Plum's execution. They blindfolded her and loaded her on a truck with other convicts. The trucks didn't parade them through the streets as they usually do. They drove directly to a mysterious underground space right beneath the city, several meters deep, lined with a meter of concrete, without a seam for the gunshots to escape, much less the cries and screams.

Much less Little Plum's sobbing plea. Dan's hands run through Old Ten's dyed and permed hair. He can't do anything about it now. He could have done nothing then.

"Please, you must let it go. The tears will help," Dan says, stroking her head.

She holds him tighter.

He scoops her face up and looks at her. She gets up and presses her lips on his. Before he knows it, he feels her young flesh in his arms. She tells him not to worry, they won't be disturbed; she has told the manager she would be giving a long and intimate massage.

She lets him lie down on a bed, converted from the reclining chair. She really means to serve him, using unthinkable parts of her body to contact his, bringing the most shameful pleasures out of him. He has never known his body could contain so much pleasure, each inch of his flesh turning into a private organ of desire.

She is on top of him, her undulating body sleek and moist, answering all his body's inquiries into hers. With such understanding of his most secret needs, she drives him along the path of pleasure, a direction that has never been shown to him until now. The pleasure matures. It spills.

She collapses over him. With a spasm, she bursts into a torrent of tears.

"Cry. Louder. Let them eavesdrop. You'll be on the path toward healing if you let it all out. Let it all out on me," Dan says, taking her inert hand to hit his face and chest. He thrusts his finger between her teeth, wanting them to clamp down in it. He feels hurt; the teeth sinking deep into his fingers, which have also picked sweet plums.

After one hour Old Ten rolls aside, lies on her back, and stares at the ceiling. She sobs once in a while, and when she does, Dan strokes her shoulder.

"I . . . ," she says, and pauses.

"Anything you want me to do for you, just ask," Dan says.

"I wonder if you can write about my sister. It can't bring her back, but her story will bring some justice for her."

Dan has not prepared for this. He becomes sad that she has done all this with him simply as exchange of favors. Just as she has done it with all the other men, from whom she thought she could get help for her sister.

"You should think of yourself. It would have been your sister's last wish in the world that you take good care of yourself," Dan says, throwing his clothes back on.

She tells him the wife bribed someone with a lot of power. They added her sister's name onto the end of the execution list. Her sister had the misfortune to be sentenced during an anti-crime campaign, which is always more of a political gesture than a legal action. It gets people executed in such a hurry that it is impossible to complete the legal procedures. When she speaks, her hair, spilling over her face from the top of her head, is troubled by the words that explode on her lips.

"What's done is done," Dan says. "You've got to face your own life." Or you will be another Little Plum.

"How could you say that?" she says. She has a stronger back-country accent as she gets more excited. "Is there justice anywhere? She was three months' pregnant before her death! And she conceived the baby in prison! Just think who must have done it!"

Dan stares at her. A chill runs down his back.

"They forced her to abort the baby and told her if she ever told anyone about this, she would be sentenced to death."

"How did you know about all this?"

"If you want to know things, you can find ways."

Dan could never have imagined such a thing done by a group of people on whom girls like Old Ten relied for their safety.

"If you help me, I will treat you every day. I like you and trust you. If I ever want to marry someone, I want to marry a guy like you."

"You know . . ."

"I know."

He looks at her.

"That you have a wife."

"Her name is also Little Plum."

She smiles a bittersweet smile.

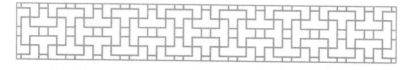

FIVE DAYS IN A ROW, Dan spends the afternoon with Old Ten. He has gotten to know that Little Plum was a top student in middle school, but their parents decided that, as the oldest daughter, she should give up studying to let her brothers continue their schooling. Old Ten's brothers, two and four years her senior, were both admitted to universities, but the family could not afford their tuition. So Little Plum and then Old Ten, the youngest, became their support by working in the city as masseuses.

The afternoon is slow and quiet in the club. All they do is make love and whisper. He discovers that her passion for him isn't pretense, and it increases with each visit he pays her.

Every time Dan leaves, he quietly puts a couple of banknotes into her uniform's pocket. Whether as a tip or a gesture of affection, Dan tries not to define it. They never talk about this money when they meet again. She knows it isn't the fee for her service; it is far less than what he receives from her.

She sometimes asks him in the middle of their lovemaking if he has started writing her sister's story. He lies without wanting to. The further he is into the affair with Old Ten, the less he can muster himself to pick up his pen. He can't even see the relevance of it; it is just a passionate love affair, springing from two equal shares of desire. Dan doesn't want to see it as another exchange of favors; he has seen enough of that, and he is sick and tired of it.

One afternoon, he walks out of Old Ten's room, leaving her in her panties and bra, repairing her makeup, and hears:

"Hey, there you are!"

Dan sees in front of him a crossed-armed, jesting-faced Happy.

"I was looking all over for you. You seem to have vanished altogether from the banquets."

Dan mumbles something, an explanation or a justification of his coming here.

"Don't give me that shit," Happy says. She pushes the door open and sticks her head in. "Hello," she says to Old Ten. "Good morning, beautiful! It's eight o'clock in the morning, Moulin Rouge time."

Dan shoves her aside forcefully.

"Playing savior for these dirty little things?" Happy asks.

"What do you want?"

"Can I want nothing?"

Dan walks ahead of her, leading her away from Old Ten's room.

"Worse than I expected," Happy says, following him to a room that has an "available" sign. "You fell in love with her."

"Shut up."

She goes to a chair, sits down, and slaps the chair next to her. He hesitates, and she slaps harder.

"What is it? Have out with it, or I'll go home," Dan says.

"Your article is going to print tonight," Happy says.

"The peasant's article . . ."

"It is your article now. You shouldn't feel guilty about replacing the peasant's name with your own. Because you completely rewrote the stuff. You are entitled to everything that ensues. Glory or punishment. Criticism or praise. By the way, its title is 'A Normal Day in Bai Village.'"

Dan's mind has gone to Old Ten. Who is she with now? Is she going to massage a man tonight who boasts about his power and wealth? Is she going to part her legs and ride the disgusting man like she did him? But he is as disgusting as all those men, if not more so. Is she going to whisper to them, too? Is she going to press their faces against her bosom as well? Oh, those ugly faces: thick-jawed, swollen-lidded, greasy from overeating and drinking. His own face isn't ugly. Of that much he is sure. At least according to Little Plum, he looks handsome and strong. Little Plum. What a crime he has committed against his beloved Little Plum.

"Don't you like the name?"

He couldn't care less. It is actually Happy's work. She rewrote everything. She made it totally dry and cold, without anger or passion, without a basic moral stance or empathy. How could he write about folks exactly like his parents without empathy and passion?

"It's fine."

"I thought you would like it. It really took some genius to make up that name. I cleared all the kitsch out of the original piece. It now reads like a good, humorous folktale, not omitting any detail, impartial about nobody, giving both the aggrieving and aggrieved equal opportunity to re-perform their roles."

Dan looks at her, lying down with her limbs outstretched like a starfish.

"You'll love the final version of it. It is really humorous. Dry humor, though. A reader with a more sophisticated mind will see those who are harmed in this case would do the same harm to others in other cases, as long as they are limited by their peasant mentality."

Dan is afraid she will lecture him about how peasants are a corruptive force. She can really get on your nerves with that. He has to get going. He lifts his wrist and looks at his watch. Where is he going? She can give him a ride. No, thanks. Rush hour is approaching, and he'd best take the subway. He has stuff to do tonight.

"Hand me that ashtray, will you?" Happy sits up and lights a cigarette. She never cares if you are in a hurry, if you are on your way to your mother's deathbed or if your wife is in labor; she orders you around just the same.

He walks over to the little cabinet below a false window and gets the enamel ashtray for her.

"They caught some banquet bugs," Happy says.

Dan holds the bag he was about to hoist on his shoulder. "What banquet bugs?"

"That's what they call them. Those delinquents coming to enjoy banquets, posing as reporters," Happy says, lying down and slapping the chair next to her. "Come and sit down with me. Have you ever tried drugs?"

Dan sits next to her. So there are other banquet bugs besides himself. What are they going to do with them? Are they going to be loaded onto trucks and driven to an underground execution ground and shot?

"It would be perfect to lie down like this if you'd taken some Ecstasy."

He looks at her, her eyes closed, lips parted.

"I bet you've never tried it," she says. "Such a life, clean as a newborn. If you want to try some, I can arrange it."

"Okay." Would he have been caught as well the day they collared the bugs, if he'd been there eating the banquet?

"You've got to know the right people to get the right stuff. Do you want the mild stuff to start with, or just go for the real thing?"

"Yes." Did they arrest the little man? Or is he a secret agent who has been laying the groundwork for the Anti–Banquet Bug Campaign? . . .

He hears Happy ask him something else, and he answers yes. Then he hears her laugh, her feet drumming on the edge of the reclining chair.

"What?" he turns to ask her.

"I just said, 'Let's strip naked and parade down the street,' and you said 'Yes'!" The laughter almost kills her.

"What did they do about those banquet bugs?" Dan tries to appear indifferent. "Did they jail them?"

"Maybe. Lucky for the bastards that the Anti-Crime Campaign had just concluded. They might get away with just a few years in prison. They are hoodlums and jobless fellows. Some of them are country bumpkins who came as construction workers and stayed on because their bosses owed them back wages."

It depresses Dan to think he is one of them. And Old Ten treats him like an almighty god.

"I was there when it happened. The undercover cops popped up just about everywhere, one or two at each table. Come to think of it, they have been banquet bugs, too. Some faces looked familiar. They must have been hanging around eating banquets for quite some time. The arrest was finished within five minutes. When the banquet continued, everyone had gossip to spice the food," Happy recalls.

What a close call. He could have been in jail by now, eating steamed bread and salted cabbage. He could have been lying on a bare cement floor or torn straw mats, in a room packed like a fishmonger's counter, squeezed between two male bodies reeking of fermented sweat and stale crotch. He could have been black-eyed and swollen-lipped from beatings. He could have disappeared for days before Little Plum was informed. What luck, thanks to his affair with Old Ten.

"After your article comes out, you will be known. It will be the type of article that plays with fire. It either gets you noticed or gets you crushed. Do you really think it is worth the risk?"

Dan doesn't really hear what she has been talking about. He is still imagining his Little Plum, distraught and heartbroken over his arrest, sending hot soupy noodles to the prison and being rejected. And Old Ten would think Dan to be just another one of those men who disappeared into thin air after the flavor of her flesh stopped tasting fresh.

"Have you seen Ocean Chen lately?" Happy asks.

"No."

"Go see him as soon as you can."

"I thought I gave the tapes to you already."

"You've really been fucking your brains out, haven't you? There was a big news story this morning that Ocean Chen's former wife has accused him of evading taxes. Several newspapers made it front-page news. The ex-wife gave interviews to all their reporters," Happy says, flicking cigarette ash everywhere but the ashtray. She is a slob because she thinks being sloppy looks cool. "It will be ugly, I'm telling you. Ocean Chen could go to jail if he is found guilty. He refuses to see the media, even those who are close to him. He will see you, though."

Dan believes the artist will want to see him.

She thinks now is the best time to publish the artist's profile. Only she needs to add this episode. And she will change it to be a more negative piece. Why? Because that's what the readers anticipate right now. Dan has got to do her a favor, she says, and see Ocean Chen again. Try to get as many details as he can, about what he thinks and feels about his ex's betrayal. She bets he is dying to talk to a sympathetic and trustworthy person like Dan. Does Dan think so? Yes, he thinks so. Use his trust. Give him as much sympathy as possible. Ocean Chen desperately wants sympathy from the media, but he has not prepared well enough to win them back after the peacock banquet. That's why he refuses to see them at the moment. She'd bet ten thousand yuan that the artist regrets having offended the media at the peacock banquet.

"You know what? I bet that bitch Ruby has left him by now. Boring, isn't it? All those bitches are so predictable."

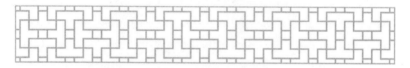

AT THE GATE of Ocean Chen's place, the doorman, who knows Dan well enough to tell him the secret, says the artist has just left for his country house fifty kilometers from the city. Who is taking care of the artist? His driver and cook at the moment. Isn't his fiancée with him? No, she had to go home to attend to her mother's illness. Her mother has taken ill with a heart condition. Is there a bus that runs near the country house? Not that he knows of.

Listless, Dan finds himself again at the Green Grove Club. It is the slow hour. The "blind" therapists are playing Ping-Pong in the reception room, while a bunch of young girls and boys watch a daytime

TV soap opera. Old Ten sits on the floor in front of the TV, painting her toenails. She jumps to her feet on seeing Dan, hopping on one foot toward the door. She doesn't conceal her affection for him in front of the others. She is actually flaunting him to them.

Ten minutes later they are out on the street. She has told the manager she is ill with the flu. Dan should have seen her feign sneezes, she says. He takes her to a subway entrance, and she is shocked that he doesn't drive a car. He has no money for a car. She thought newsmen made good money. Not the ones with old parents in a poor village who depend on the money sent from their son. Well then, she will buy him one if she marries a rich guy. When? Someday. Soon? Hope so. Want a BMW or a Mercedes-Benz? Or a Ferrari? A Benz convertible is rather comfortable, with its top down in the summer and heated seats in the winter, though not as fancy as a Ferrari. She is well informed about cars. Of course, one has to be a fast learner in a city like Beijing, right? Right. She smiles. He smiles with her, wanting to ask if she has ridden in those cars, which always shoot up and down Beijing's streets like noisy streaks, breaking traffic laws and scaring the shit out of hundreds of bicyclists. Has she sat next to a showy guy who has made money fucking people left and right, whose hand lazily goes between the stick shift and her thigh? Come on, her sister's boyfriend liked to change cars often, from fancy to fancier, and she must have been invited to have a ride with them. So will she marry a rich guy like him? No. Why? Because he wasn't really rich; he just pretended to be rich. He looks at her peach-shaped face; a red mole by the left corner of her mouth gives her a seductive look. He suddenly notices her eyebrows. They look different from before. He's heard that some women pluck their natural eyebrows off and replace them with tattooed ones. The tattooed eyebrows all arch at the same angle—the Hollywood angle—and they are supposed to be perfect eyebrows. Dan pictures a nation with a female population of 650 million who have the same perfect eyebrows arching in the same perfect angles. They will end up with too many women and too few eyebrows. She looks older in the outfit she has changed into: a white blazer over a black, lacy blouse, and a tight white skirt. When she walks, her knees don't go all the way straight, and her buttocks drag backward, as if in the process of sitting down. She has not learned to wear high heels properly. Nonetheless she is a very pretty girl who knows how to make the most of her beauty.

It is an early autumn day with a soft breeze and a deep sky. They loiter on the streets for an hour before arriving at Beihai Park. They don't walk hand-in-hand like lovers. The external world seems new to them, as if they have to start all over again to rebuild their intimacy, a different type from what goes on inside the dim massage room. There is eye contact that makes their hearts beat faster. There are moments that his hand or shoulder unexpectedly brushes hers. The fleeting contacts create intense and stealthy pleasures that should belong to more innocent hearts. They shiver at these touches, aching for more.

When they come to the lake at Beihai Park, he asks her if she'd like to ride a sampan. She says, of course she would; she has never ridden in one. They smile at each other: sampan riding is one of the required programs for new lovers in Beijing. At the dock, she sits down and takes off her high heels. He sees two blisters bleeding under her sheer stockings. He puts her feet on his lap, examining the wounds, and scolds her that she should have complained when her feet started to hurt. He tells her to wait and runs to a nearby shop. He comes back with a pack of bandages and some disinfectant cream.

Applying the cream over the wounds, he asks if they still hurt. No, she doesn't feel them too much. She strokes his hair and tells him that an old woman sitting over there on the rock said nice things about him when he went to the shop. What did she say? She said what a lucky girl I am to get a husband like that who really dotes on his wife.

"At least you were my husband in her eyes," she says. "Do you want people to see you as my husband?"

He doesn't dare respond.

"Old women never think you are a good man unless you're a husband."

"Do you call these shoes?" He points at her high heels with lace on the tops. "How can anyone walk in those?"

She says she thought she wouldn't have to walk; she expected to be sitting in his car. She has large and bony feet. He says he dislikes women with small and fleshy feet. Her feet look free and healthy, good for field work. Good for climbing mountains, she says, carrying a heap of firewood on her back, walking up those steep, narrow goat trails. Or a stack of bricks sometimes. She carried bricks up the mountains? Yes, when they were building inns for tourists on the mountaintops. That was a well-paying job that the mountain villagers would kill to get. No wonder she has such strong feet.

He is squatting across from her, kneeling on one knee, her feet on his lap, the same way his feet were positioned when she massaged him.

"Our feet," she says, laughing all of a sudden. "They know each other better than we do."

He is reminded that it is the first time he's seen her laugh openly. God, she is pretty.

The sampans are not allowed to go off into the lake because a windstorm is coming. Disappointed, they go to a restaurant instead.

He holds her as she walks and giggles. She says it would be much easier if he drove a car. Okay, here is a car—he lifts her off the ground and carries her on his back. She struggles to get down and he doesn't let her. They enter a restaurant across from the park, one on the back of the other.

"People are staring at us," she says.

He smiles, letting her down onto a seat with a filthy cover. It's a Sichuan restaurant. A boy carries a teakettle with an enormous spout about a meter-and-a-half long, and shoots hot tea into little cups from impossible angles. There is a split-second pause between the kettle dipping and the tea water spurting out, so one realizes how long the water travels before landing in the cup. Her feet reach out under the table and touch his. He imagines her injured heels under the bandage, the skin scraped off, exposing her moist flesh rich with fine nerves. He has never tried this kind of intimacy. It is a little sultry, definitely adulterous. Her foot goes from his calves to his knees. He swoons.

He lets her do the ordering. She reads the menu and orders shark fin clay pot and spicy scallops. Jokingly she tells the waitress not to cheat them with transparent rice noodles that taste like shark fins. No, they never cheat. Old Ten says she will know if they do, because she knows too well the difference between rice noodles and shark fins. That means she often eats out, Dan thinks. With whom? Someone whose feet and other body parts have been pampered by her? Someone who paid a little extra for additional services?

She goes on ordering. He begins to worry. It has just occurred to him that he only has one hundred yuan in his wallet. He never carries much cash with him. When he has money, he gives it to Little Plum. Little Plum is a good saver. He remembers Little Plum putting a hundred-yuan bill in his wallet before he came out today, along with some smaller bills that he used to pay for the subway tickets and ice cream bars for himself and Old Ten. He could have done without that damned ice cream bar. They cost twenty yuan apiece because they are made in America by some company called Häagen-Dazs. Old Ten certainly knows a lot of foreign things. He should have just let her have an ice cream bar herself and told her he doesn't have a sweet tooth, or he would rather smoke, or given some pretext like that.

He asks the waitress for one more menu, pretending to admire its design. The design is awful. In this restaurant, they are trying too hard to make everything look luxurious. His eyes go straight to the right side of the menu where the prices are marked. He used to make fun of Little Plum reading the right-hand side of the McDonald's menu board hanging over the counter. The shark fin clay pot alone costs seventy yuan. What does a Sichuan cook know about shark fin, anyway? Sichuan is about as far from the ocean as you can get. And if it were real shark fin, it would cost a lot more than seventy. At that price, they would be lucky just to have a shark tail dipped and wiggled in the pot. After the shark fin, there will be only thirty yuan left in his wallet. She tells him a good way to test a Sichuan restaurant is whether they have authentic cold appetizers. So there she is, adding more cold dishes: Sichuan pickled vegetables, spicy beef slices, smoked duck necks, and sesame chicken. She only reads the left side of the menu.

He regrets that he gave all the money earned from eating the last few banquets to Little Plum and let her deposit it. He enjoys watching his wife count money and announce the latest balance of their savings account. Was it five hundred he handed to Little Plum the other night? That would make six hundred with what's left in his wallet. Six hundred! For a meal! It would make his Little Plum's heart ache. He hopes Old Ten will stop ordering. His money doesn't come easily. To lie and fake and be on guard all the time isn't easy. It consumes you. That's why he keeps losing weight even after eating banquets for over a year. Now he hears Old Ten ask the waitress if they have cocktails. A cock's tail? No, she laughs, it is just a name of a drink, a mixture of different liquors and juices. They don't. How about brandies? Maybe; she'll go see.

He hopes the waitress won't come back with a bottle of expensive brandy. Then he will have to lie to Old Ten that he can't drink, because of an important meeting in the afternoon. She is still reading the menu, frowning slightly. She asks him if he likes prawns. No, he doesn't. Good, she doesn't like them either. He feels relieved. How many dishes has she ordered? Six, not including the cold appetizers. There go his earnings from two banquets.

"You're hungry, aren't you?" he says. Is there an ATM somewhere near this restaurant? he wonders.

She looks up at him, smiles, and closes the menu in its silk jacket. He picks up his cup and takes a sip of tea. The scalding temperature makes him shudder. She's started talking about her sister again. He takes her hand and caresses it. He thought today would be a tiny vacation from talking about her sister. He squeezes her hand tightly when he sees her tears threatening to spill out. They spill out anyway, dropping on the glass plating that covers the tabletop: one, two . . . three, four.

The waitress comes back to tell them they have brandy. To Dan's astonishment, he is glad they do. He'll find an ATM machine and he will have enough money to pay for the meal and brandy. If Old Ten is happy and doesn't keep talking about her sister, he doesn't mind spending money. He'd give anything to make her forget about the article she has asked him to write. It gives a strange flavor to their relationship.

"What brandy is it?" she asks the waitress.

"It's just brandy."

"I know. But there are many different kinds of brandy at different prices. Which kind do you have?"

"We sell it by the glass."

She gives Dan a frustrated smile. "What kind of brandy do you like?" she asks him.

"Any kind," he answers.

Dan doesn't know any kind of brandy. Old Ten orders, and the waitress brings two glasses of brandy. Old Ten is sophisticated in drinking. She must have gone out drinking a lot. Or did she learn that from Hollywood movies? From Hollywood movies, he wills. She has a sexy way of holding the glass, her hand lazy, almost inert, letting the stem of the glass dangle between her middle and ring fingers. Their glasses, with gold rims and some gold patterns around the bottoms, look turbid. Apparently they washed them in the same greasy water that they had used to wash a few dozen oily dishes. No, she didn't learn drinking from Hollywood movies. Watching Hollywood movies would be too high taste for the guys seeking her services, Dan deduces. Those fat-ass wealthy guys have taken her out and given her an education in cocktails and brandies. What would they do after they had drunk their fill? Dan is tipsy after the first glass, but Old Ten is fine, poised and cool. He watches her dainty fingers holding the foggy glass, trying to figure out how she has developed these habits. She has developed them where his eyes cannot penetrate, in the course of shady relationships like the one between them now. Every day the trains enter Beijing loaded with country girls, and the pretty ones like Old Ten form a city underneath the real city, establishing a life that is in secret symmetry to the actual life. A life that is invisible to wives, to children, to people who make humble salaries and go to work on bicycles. Dan would have been among those people, and would never have gotten to know this kind of life that includes a beautiful girl called Old Ten and his ardent desire for her, if he had not impersonated a journalist. He could have owned her, at least for a while, if he had been a powerful journalist with fame and money. He looks at her, realizing he has been feeling jealous of his impersonated self.

"Hey," Old Ten says to the waitress, "this brandy is fake."

"No, it is not!" the waitress protests.

"Have you tried it?"

The waitress shakes her head. It looks as if she couldn't tell the difference even if she tried it.

"Shall we have Chinese clear sorghum liquor instead?" Old Ten turns to Dan.

Dan nods, smiling. It will add another fifty yuan or more to the bill. Is she going to stop there? Or will he have a lot of explanation to make to Little Plum? It is very unusual for him to spend that much money by himself. And Little Plum has an acute intuition for lies. Old Ten is satisfied with a Sichuan liquor priced at eighty a bottle. And off she goes again, talking about her mother pressing her for news of her sister; the mother is the only one in the family who has been kept in the dark about Little Plum's execution. She can't tell her anything until Dan raises his voice for justice. She holds his hand under the table. He has the feeling of being crushed by the pressure from her eyes. Even if he had been a real journalist rather than a banquet bug with basic folk storytelling skills, he still wouldn't want to write her sister's story. How could he write it when he is physically exploiting Old Ten, just like other men? How can he cry out for justice while taking the bribe of her flesh? He can't write it unless they can change everything and start their relationship over afresh and anew.

The brandy is genuine imitation. His head and stomach are throbbing. He gets up and stomps across the floor, heading for the door.

"Where are you going?"

"To the toilet."

"The restaurant has one."

"I'd rather use the one in the park."

"Why?"

"It smells better."

He blows a kiss to her, stepping over the threshold. He knows his behavior is exaggerated, but he can't help it.

He finds a cash machine in the park. He tries to insert his card, but it keeps spitting it out. He asks a cleaning lady if there is another machine close by. No, the park isn't a good place for cash machines. Not safe. He walks in the opposite direction and sees neither banks nor cash machines.

The wind is picking up speed. An old man, about a hundred years old with a mummified face, wobbles across the street, pushing his cart full of puffy cotton candy. A torn, dirty plastic sheet comes flying, lands on one of the candy balls and sticks to it, batting and rattling. The old man tries to tear it off his candy, but gets tripped by a concrete lump on the ground. The cart capsizes. The old man disappears under the colorful, puffy balls of cotton candy. Dan runs toward him but stops short. The old man begins wailing, trying to rip fallen leaves, popsicle wrappers, and cigarette butts off his cotton candy puffs. God, it looks miserable. Dan goes over, pulling his sole hundred-yuan banknote out of his pants pocket. If it takes this much to shut him up, so be it. He thrusts it into his ancient, gnarled hand and turns to run away.

Near the lobby of an office building, he finds a bank with ATMs outside. He runs across the street toward it and sees metal stanchions and velvet cords fencing off the area near the revolving door. Without thinking, he swings his leg over the velvet rope. As he makes his way to the ATM, a voice shouts: "Where do you think you are going?"

He stops and turns. A lean man in an ill-fitting uniform stands outside the rope holding a metal lunchbox in one hand and chopsticks in the other. He pokes his chopsticks downward. Dan sees behind him a string of footprints on a wet concrete surface. The lean man tells him to take a look at what he has done. Dan says he already has. Too late; one should always look before stepping into a roped-off place. That's right, Dan agrees, one always should. His legs are stiffening from standing in his own footprints. It took five workers doing backbreaking work to finish this damned job right before the windstorm, and it took him ten seconds to destroy it. Six. What? It took him six seconds to ruin it—the twelve footprints are evidence of that. So he thinks six seconds means a lower fine than ten seconds? The lean man is incredulous and enraged. No, no, no, Dan corrects him, it only means he'd realized his mistake much quicker. No use arguing over six versus ten seconds, because he is going to pay for the damage either way. How much? That's not up to him; the building manager will decide the price.

Dan stands trapped in his own footprints, feeling the alcohol now working its full effect. The sun is hot, and the driving wind grows stronger and drier by the second. The cement will soon dry with him rooted there. He says to the lean man that he needs to get some cash so he can pay for the damage. The lean man says he will definitely not let him ruin the rest of the pavement. What does he want him to do? Simple: just surrender his money to the building manager. He will if he allows him to go to the cash machine. Then the price will double because he'll have left another twelve footprints.

The lean man grunts something into his walkie-talkie, making descriptive gestures to his unseen interlocutor. People swarm over, their pants and skirts beating the wind that has begun turning into a storm, and ask one another what has happened.

What must Old Ten think of him by now? Is she thinking he's run away from paying the bill? All of a sudden, he breaks out in a sweat at the thought. He takes a step toward the rope, and the lean man calls out: "Don't move!"

He stops, his arms drawing circles in the wind for balance.

"You want to pay more, don't you?" the lean man says.

"No," he answers.

People laugh.

Maybe Old Ten is looking at her little watch and finds he has been gone for half an hour. She is shaking her little head and her adorable cheeks are going up to form a sneer. Such a man, scared off by a restaurant check. She will ask for the check and peel a few bills off a wad of money earned by massaging feet and God knows what. Another proof of the futility of her efforts to get any help from men.

Two more uniformed men come out from the revolving door. They make a detour around the rope and join the lean man.

"Here. This is my card. I'm a journalist," Dan gives his card, his last hope, to one of the men.

The lean man stands motionless before taking the card from him. He moves his lips to read Dan's card, then passes it to his colleagues.

"How do we know it is real?" the lean man asks.

"You want my ID, too?" Dan offers.

The lean man says yes and Dan hands his ID card to him.

"Can we keep them?" the lean man asks.

"Why?"

"Just to make sure we can get hold of you when the manager decides how much the fine is."

Any hesitation will cause suspicion. So Dan tells them to go ahead, keep whatever they need. He chuckles, smelling the brandy on his breath. Just produce a receipt for what they took from him. One of them gets out a receipt book.

"That's how you extort from people, isn't it? Putting up no warning sign. Letting them fall into your trap. Then making them pay the fine. Nice little sideline business, huh?" Dan makes intimidating eye contact with one of the three, then moves on to the next one after staring down the first one. "Taking my ID may have consequences." The alcohol helps a great deal with his performance.

The three of them exchange some words in a whisper.

"Okay, you may come out now. Just be careful not to make any more footprints," one of them says, lifting the rope.

The lean man keeps staring at the title on Dan's card: "freelance journalist."

Dan doesn't move.

"I won't move a muscle until I have my ID card back."

They have another quick exchange before they say yes. He retraces his steps one by one toward the rope. He has to walk pigeon-toed so his feet can fit into the footprints facing the opposite direction. It is ugly and awkward to take reverse steps that force him to point his big toes toward each other. Up to this moment, he has never realized that he doesn't walk straight at all; he walks with his big toes pointed far apart and his heels almost rubbing together. So he has a Chaplinesque gait. Like a fat duck. It depresses him to know he has a ducklike manner of walking. He walks back to the restaurant trying to make straight steps.

To his delight, Old Ten is still there, talking to the owner of the restaurant, a forty-something ex-farmer in a black suit, in Sichuan dialect. Dan sits down. How is he going to tell her that he couldn't get money and that, even though he ran through the windstorm looking for a cash machine, he gave his sole hundred-yuan bill to an old cotton candy peddler to shut up his wailing? He takes a noisy sip of the brandy left in his glass, and the noise surprises him. The owner turns to look at him, smiling, and leaves.

"Excellent!" Dan yells to his back.

The owner whirls around and looks at him.

"The dishes are as good as those at the National Banquet," Dan says.

"You were invited to the National Banquet on National Day?" the owner asks.

Dan sees Old Ten's eyes glint at him.

"We poor newsmen have to work while others eat."

"So, Mister is a journalist?"

"By training," Old Ten adds.

Dan hands one of his cards to him. He always carries an excessive number of business cards. Sometimes they are more useful than cash.

"What an honor!" The owner reads the card and extends his hand to him.

Dan says the restaurant needs publicity. It really does. Nowadays publicity is everything. Absolutely right, the owner agrees; they have never reached out to the media. Remember the old saying? Dan asks. It goes something like "People will eventually smell good wine brewed in the depths of the deepest alley." That's an old Sichuan saying, Old Ten reminds them, very proudly. Is it? Dan retorts. Want to bet? Only Sichuan has ancient breweries and narrow, deep alleys, she replies. Anyway, Dan continues, it is an old saying. Too old to be a virtue, though. Too old to retain its moral value. Mr. Journalist is absolutely right, the owner says, one should believe in the media. Wouldn't it be a blessing to have Mr. Journalist write something about the food here?

Next thing Dan knows, he is tasting hundred-year-old Sichuan liquor. The owner has opened the bottle in his honor. The meal is on the house. The owner asks Dan to please write down what he has just said about the dishes and publish it in a newspaper. Certainly; the dishes deserve much more praise than what he has just given. Mr. Journalist has an open invitation to dine here as long as the owners live.

Dan swaggers out of the restaurant, Old Ten's hand in his left hand and a hundred-year-old liquor in his right. The manager sees them off in the diminishing windstorm. Dan spots a rip on the elbow of the owner's black suit. They get into a cab, and the owner bows to the taxi's closed door, his wrinkled, shabby tie hanging out, dangling in the sandy air. His life hinges on Dan's promise to write about his restaurant and the dishes, which are crude and trite compared to those of the banquets Dan is accustomed to eating. Dan closes his eyes. The owner's eyes sparkle with hope, and his bowing figure in the torn suit and wrinkled tie make Dan nauseated.

Why does one look so miserable when he is desperately hopeful?

And people are always desperate with all sorts of hope once you tell them you are a journalist. There are a lot of jobs Dan doesn't mind doing. He can see himself as a taxi driver, a food peddler, a street sweeper, or a gangster. But now he knows that he *does* mind having to be someone's hope. The hope of a restaurant owner. The hope of this young, beautiful foot massager, snuggling by him, massaging his limp arm and fingers with her lips, asking if he will please write about her sister soon. He tells himself to stop going to see Old Ten. She has turned him from a real person into her desperate hope.

"You know what? I can't write for shit," he says proudly.

Even in darkness, he can see how big her staring eyes are from the shock. She lets go of his hand. He turns his whole face toward her, a gleeful smile pulling up the corners of his mouth and leaving his white, square teeth glistening. Alcohol is a good thing; it makes him honest, and brave enough to face the consequences of his honesty.

"I never went to university. I was a middle-school dropout. And I wasn't a good soldier when I joined the army."

She keeps staring at him, scared.

"I can dog-ear a dictionary before I finish a piece of writing. Because I have too many words to check. And because I lick my finger when I turn the pages, and I lick it too wet." He is glad to see her in such disillusionment.

She giggles all of a sudden. "You are funny when you are drunk," she says.

"I am not drunk."

"Yeah. All the drunks say they're not drunk. And all the lunatics say they are not crazy." She comes leaning tight against him. Even with the layers of their clothing in between, his body misses none of the shapes and curves of her figure.

He wakes up next morning beside Little Plum, terribly depressed, thinking about how he will survive his longing for Old Ten, since he has decided not to visit her anymore.

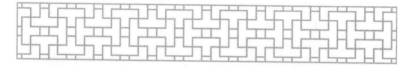

HAPPY IS WAITING for him. She is in a public park surrounded by a mass of residential buildings. From a distance, he can see her pacing back and forth, talking on her cell phone, making polemical gestures. As he advances further, he sees the bead-fringed sleeves of her blouse whipping forcefully. She tells the person on the other end to hold on and switches to call-waiting. Can he (or she) make a decision in twenty minutes? Publish it as is, without any cuts or changes. That version is the least offensive to the government, and there is no point in publishing it at all if it is toned down further. Take it or leave it, just give her an answer in twenty minutes. She makes a subtle gesture to tell Dan not to interrupt her. She switches back to the first caller and finds he has hung up. She curses through her clenched teeth that the president of the newspaper has just graduated from an eight-month training program at the Communist Party Academy of the Central Committee. He happened to see Dan's article as it was going to press. He stopped it and wanted some parts cut.

"So I contacted another newspaper."

She dials the number and waits. Someone answers. She says she might have the author consider rewording some of the sentences, but the real names of locations and people involved in the event have to stay in. Without warning, she hands the cell phone to Dan.

"Tell him it is reportage after all, not fiction," she says under her breath.

Dan has no idea what "reportage" means. He notes the term and parrots Happy with perfect precision.

"Are you Dan Dong?"

"That's me."

"I'm Editor Wang."

"Honored to talk to you, Editor Wang. How are you?" Dan says. He feels that Happy is giving him a look.

"I enjoyed your writing very much."

"Nice of you to say that . . ."

"But Dan, it's really unfortunate that our president doesn't like some parts of your article."

"Well . . ." Dan looks at Happy, who glares at him.

"If you are going to stand by what you have written, I understand. We'll look forward to your future writings. It won't be the end of our relationship; it will be just the beginning . . ."

His voice is drowned out suddenly by Happy shouting into the phone: "Don't try to make him compromise. He is a man of no compromise."

The editor disregards Happy and goes on talking to Dan.

"We regret that it won't work out this time. We would love to see more of your brilliant pieces in the near future. Good-bye."

"Good-bye. Many thanks . . . ," he says.

The editor has already hung up.

"All set?" Happy takes her cell phone back.

Dan looks at her. "He said he regretted it didn't work out this time."

"What?" Happy shrieks. "He's not going to let your stuff go to print tonight?"

"I guess not," Dan says.

"And you said thanks to him? You *thanked* him for canceling the publication of your article?" She turns to walk away from him, goes a few steps, then turns and walks back, suddenly remembering she parked her car there. "How could you let him get rid of you so easily? How could you waste all the time and energy and breath I spent talking him into publishing it? Once he has promised, hold onto his promise with your lousy, rotten teeth and crumbing, filthy fingernails. Don't let go. Don't *ever* let go."

"I can't force him."

"You're hopeless. To be a journalist, you have to be brave, thick-skinned, cold-blooded, tenacious, and intimidating." Happy has started dialing the phone before she has finished her lecture.

She stares at Dan without seeing him, puffing her lips and tapping her fingers on her car. She is extremely impatient with anyone who makes her wait. She hangs up, thinks for a few seconds, then dials another number. "Come on, come *on,* you fuckhead, your twenty minutes are up. Pick up the phone!" She gives up and dials another number. "Editor Wang is an asshole, but at least he confronted us like a man," she says while dialing. "And this one told me he would make a decision in twenty minutes, and now he is sitting there, listening to the phone ringing, and trembling." She continues talking as she puts the cell phone to her ear and listens. "Chickenshit . . . Oh, hello! This is Happy!"

When she finally hangs up, Dan has come to understand that Happy has made enough intimidating calls to land a magazine that is interested in the article. But it is too late for the next issue, which goes to print two days from now. The space for this type of reportage has been filled.

Having hung up, Happy calls again. "It's Happy. Ask me if I've had dinner. No, I haven't, because I am fed up with chickenshit. Did you submit an article to *China Farmers' Monthly*? Good. I figured you were the contributor. Well, only ten of you guys write for their lousy pay. Do me a favor, will you? . . . Pull your article out. Tell them you have significant changes to make. I'll get your book published. How does that sound? I have stuff that *must* be published now. It can't wait, and yours can. Deal?"

She takes a deep breath, hanging up the phone. Now Dan understands what the word "tenacious" means. Rolling down her fringed sleeves, which had been rolled up above her shoulders during her conversations, she smiles at Dan.

"Do you want to learn how to drive?" she asks, throwing the keys to Dan. "I can teach you." She looks at Dan, completely resuming her femininity. "Now? Now. Tomorrow I may be a bitch again, too busy to do sweet things like giving one of my potential boyfriends driving lessons."

Seeing his eyes dart away, she laughs.

Before Dan gets into the car, he asks why the article can't wait. Because the political climate is going to change soon. How does she know? The president of the newspaper told her. So she knows the president personally? No, she doesn't, but his response to Dan's article is indicative of the Party's new policy. The president of the newspaper had recently attended the Party Academy, the cerebral organ of the Party, so he must have felt the political shift in the air. The Party thinks the media have had too much freedom lately. It wants to restrain some big mouths among the journalists, who are getting on their nerves by nosing into the corruption of Party cadres, including the cadres in rural places like Bai Village.

"If the article doesn't get published this month, it will never get published," Happy says.

She puts her hand on Dan's and moves it to the emergency brake. The car lurches back slightly.

"Ever drive a car?"

"I used to drive a tractor back home."

She laughs, her hand squeezing his hand a couple of times. Hers is a skinny hand. As she leans closer, he smells some strange odor. An odor of smoked duck or pork. She has smoked the whole evening while talking to people on the phone to get the article published. Dan feels a tenderness toward her. She seems embarrassed at being good or nice, but Dan suspects that she has more goodness in her than she cares to show.

"Okay, start the tractor now. Just drive fast, honk loud, curse whoever is in your way," Happy says. "Go. Good. Change the gear. Hey, not bad. Faster. See, I'm not even putting on my seat belt. If we crash, I die with you. What are you afraid of? Faster. Honk. More." She rolls down the window. "Folks, look at this perfect picture of communism: a tractor driver with his girl."

Happy doesn't look bad when she stops trying so hard to look cool. He remembers liking her when she appeared vulnerable on the lawn below Ocean Chen's hospital room.

"Hey, you can do it. The two of us would make a perfect team. You interview, I write. You drive the tractor, I make intimidating phone calls. You can really get people to trust you with your golden retriever face. And I benefit from their trust in you."

A car rushes from the intersection, where it should have stopped and waited.

"You idiot!" Happy yells, pressing her hand on Dan's knee to help his foot hit the brake. Her metal-framed sunglasses, pushed over the crown of her head, fall after scratching Dan's cheek.

Dan's hand goes up in a reflex to protect his eyes, and the car twirls to the sidewalk and jerks to a stop with one front wheel over the curb. The supple branch of a tree sticks into the window, and Happy leans over Dan's shoulder, letting out sobs of laughter.

"Your driver's license, please," a voice says.

A policeman stands straddling his motorcycle, totally faceless thanks to his helmet pulled extremely low.

"Officer, you should go after that jerk. He almost got us killed."

"I was following you and saw you do a dragon dance with your car," the policeman says. "Your license, please."

Dan doesn't know what to say or to do, while Happy whispers: "Stop flashing that moronic smile at him." She opens the door, twists her body out of the car, and takes a few sexy steps toward the police officer.

"We weren't drinking, Officer."

"Did I say you were drinking?"

"We are just too tired. It has been a long day."

"License."

"It's not easy to be a journalist nowadays, you know."

The policeman bends over to Dan, ignoring the sexiness of Happy, who poses like a standing snake.

"Do you want to give me your license, or do you want to pay a visit to our station?" he asks. The lower half of his face surfaces out of the shadow of his helmet. It is a very young face.

"He forgot his license. Here is mine." Happy hands her license to him, her fingers making contact with his hand.

The young policeman feels the bills between her hand and his. He winces a little, and an expression of swallowing a fly appears at the corners of his mouth.

"We are very sorry," Happy says, and theatrically bows her head.

"Be careful. Don't let me catch you again," the young policeman says. He turns his self-loathing into hatred for the people who made him loathe himself.

"Thank you, Officer."

Without turning his face to them, his hand gives them an impatient wave.

"How much did you give him?" Dan asks. He has switched to the passenger's seat.

"All I had. About five hundred, I think," she says. She inserts a CD into the car stereo and her body moves with the music. "Boy, were you scared!"

"No, I wasn't . . ."

"Yes, you were. Whoever puts on that smile is scared. The way a sheep smiles at a knife slashing down at it. Have you seen those sheep smile in slaughterhouses? My great-granduncle was a butcher. I was scared, too. I have things I didn't want the policeman to see. The things that really are going to get me in trouble."

He wants to ask what these things are. But he says nothing. He doesn't know how to deal with Happy's smoky body odor. Old Ten has a unique body odor as well. It is like sweetened milk, just beginning to turn sour. The smell alone can drive him crazy. He wonders why Little Plum doesn't smell like the first time they met. She smelled like wild grass and flowers mixed with home-brewed wine.

You could get drunk on that smell. But the smell has become fainter and fainter, fainter than a memory.

"For example, I have diplomas from two universities. Neither of them is real, of course. And five kinds of business cards," she says. She pulls out the CD and puts in a new one. She changes music a lot. "By the way, do you need a diploma? It's a handy thing to have. Especially when you want a job from someone who knows nothing about talent and ability but only cares about a stupid diploma. I have a friend who makes them. He makes identification cards, too. If you get that little foot massager pregnant and want to get an abortion, he will even make you a marriage certificate."

"Really?"

"Sounds like you *are* going to get that girl pregnant."

Dan doesn't respond right away, considering whether or not she deserves the truth. He decides she does.

"She has asked me to write a story about her sister who was executed last month," Dan says.

"That will be a novel. Like Thomas Hardy's *Tess of the D'Urbervilles* . . ."

Dan doesn't know what she is talking about. Part of the reason that Dan is unable to like Happy is because he has to listen to her and pretend to understand the things she says about which he has no clue. He suspects that she loves to say things people don't understand. She probably enjoys saying things that she herself doesn't really understand.

"Let me know if you need a marriage certificate for the abortion. My friend can give you a discount," she says, slapping his thigh.

Dan jerks his leg away.

"Don't be shy. Nowadays who wants to sleep with his wife? No one except handicapped people and penniless losers."

Dan sees a subway station entrance and asks Happy to stop.

"That hotel," she says, pointing her finger, "is called Five Continents. It has a very nice bar. You know what? You will find the most beautiful whores there. They say they are college students," Happy says. "Has your cell phone ever received text messages from them? They'll tell you they are good at all kinds of conversation, and they are nice traveling companions when you are away from your wife in the U.S., or Canada, or Hong Kong, or wherever."

She drives past another subway entrance. When she wants to do you a favor, you don't have much choice but to be grateful. She is so pleased with her own ability to arrange things for you, to make the best choice for you. If she drives him all the way home, he will go to a new apartment compound near the factory and pretend he lives there. He will tell her he's sorry; it's getting late. Otherwise he would invite her up for a cup of tea.

Following his directions, Happy drives on the wide avenue crossing the fourth ring road. Beyond the fourth ring road is considered Beijing's suburbs. The traffic is thinner, and the vehicles clinking-clanking along are mainly trucks and minivans that are not allowed to enter the city. Caked with mud, they all have angry horns, eye-blinding headlights, and oily exhaust. Occasionally, vegetable fields and orchards that have not been overtaken by the city's expansion swallow the deep night.

The car comes to a sudden stop.

"Sorry, Dan, I can't drive you home," Happy says. Seeing Dan at a loss, she adds: "I have something to take care of." She reaches into the backseat, grabs Dan's bag and jacket, and puts them on his lap.

Dan looks around, trying to see if there is a taxicab in sight.

There is none. The subway has split from this avenue and will join it only at the end.

"I said I wanted to take the subway," he says. He hates her for making him pay the taxi fare.

"Close the door carefully," she says. "I'll call you. Don't forget to interview Ocean Chen tomorrow."

DAN'S CELL PHONE RINGS. He squints at the clock on the makeshift nightstand. Five o'clock in the morning. Little Plum tosses and covers her head with the quilt. It is still dark, and he doesn't recognize the caller ID.

"Hello?" he says.

"Dan!" an unfamiliar voice says. "It's Ruby."

Who the hell is Ruby? "Oh, hi."

"Did I wake you up? Or haven't you gone to bed yet? I know journalists write during the nights. He always stays up late painting, too."

Dan is wide awake now. Of course, Ruby. He gropes around on the nightstand while Ruby is talking about her mother's illness.

"You don't need your glasses," Little Plum says, giggling.

He realizes he is groping for his glasses. They are just a mask. But Ruby's voice makes him spontaneously want to put on his costume. Anyone who only knows his false identity makes him want to put on the costume.

"Do you think you can stay with him for a couple of weeks? I can't leave my mother right now," Ruby says.

Dan can see her making a beautiful twist with her body again. He says yes, he will try to stay as long as Master Chen needs him to.

"I don't trust anybody else. The first time I saw you, I knew I could trust you if something horrible happens to him."

Dan is so flattered that he feels the blood rushing to his face. She trusts him, with the heart under her white silky skin with faint blue veins showing through it. She is telling Dan to make sure the driver and cook don't steal his paintings. She trusts neither of them. But she trusts Dan. The word "trust" coming out of her pink-lipped mouth, making subtle vibrations go through her perfect teeth, becomes something else. If she doesn't give him her love, he can make do with her trust. Dan can't help getting erotic or romantic about Ruby, a woman of a class he is so unfamiliar with. She goes on. The driver and the cook will steal if you don't watch them closely. And he is absentminded all the time. If anyone visits him, don't let him hand out paintings as if they were candies.

Little Plum sits up and looks at him.

When he hangs up, she asks nothing. She knows her husband has become more and more important. Throwing on clothes, Dan sees her worshipful smile and pinches her nose. They soon topple each other in a tickling wrestle, choking with laughter. He can be silly with no one but Little Plum. With Old Ten he is a journalist and a savior, a man who can right wrongs and call down justice. He can't be silly with her. Happy treats him as a colleague, even though not at her level. There are moments when he longs to be free from all these roles he plays, to be silly and goof off.

After breakfast he calls Ocean Chen's cell phone, and no one answers it. On the fifth attempt, the driver answers, saying Master Chen is asleep after a night's work. The master is still painting? He paints fourteen hours every day, only getting two hours' sleep. He talks to no one and walks mile after mile through the fields. So he is doing okay? He is, much better than when Miss Ruby is here.

The driver thanks Dan for offering his help, but he doesn't think the artist needs company. He is very much in the mood for painting. Every time he is in a difficult situation, he takes refuge in his painting. The driver thanks Dan again and again, rejecting Dan's offer to visit the artist. Dan says he is available anytime; please give him a call when Master Chen needs either him or his onions. Or both.

At noon Happy calls.

"Are you with him now?"

"Who?"

"Ocean Chen, of course!" she sounds accusatory.

". . . Yeah." Don't sound like you are my boss.

"Can you excuse yourself and find a little privacy to talk?"

"Umm . . ." There you go, bossing me around again.

He doesn't want to talk to her at this moment. She will intrude on the last corner of his life he shares with Little Plum.

"Go outside and tell the old man you can't hear well in the room."

"I . . . I can't."

"Okay, I understand. Just listen, don't respond, and make sure your face stays blank."

Dan makes a faint "Umm."

"Rumor has it that the investigation is not going in Ocean Chen's favor. Some galleries that did false bookkeeping in order to share profits with him got found out by the tax authorities. What is probably going to happen is they'll hold a public hearing."

"When?"

"Don't utter a sound. Is he looking at you? No? Good. What is he doing?" she asks, forgetting that she had just told him to make no response whatsoever.

"Not much . . ." He gives Little Plum a pinch on her butt as his thanks for the tea she has put in front of him. He smiles as she gives him a false dirty look. "He paints and paints, that's all."

"Don't speak," she says.

"I'm outside now."

"Good. What does his country house look like?"

"Nice. Big . . . Many weeping willows. A pond. Ducks and all." Dan's dream house is like this. "And a lot of water lilies," he adds. Then it occurs to him that water lilies are out of season. "All withered. Turned brown."

"What turned brown?"

"Water lilies."

"Look, you've got to make him tell you why he divorced his first three wives. It is useful material for my writing. It will project his personality. Maybe it will explain why his last ex-wife hates his guts. Given that all his women are greedy, including the pretty young thing he has now, it might help him if you allude to the greediness of his women, so people will know the tax stuff is simply a personal vendetta. I heard that following the Anti-Crime Campaign there's going to be an Anti–Tax Evasion Campaign. Tell the old man to stay calm and tough it out. If he survives the campaign, he can play tax tricks as long as he lives. Just tell him there's no right or wrong in China; it all depends on who you know. Will you tell him that?"

Dan says he will. He sees Little Plum stand on tiptoe trying to reach a large paper bag hanging on a nail above the window. He rushes over and takes it down for her.

"He might want to spend money on bribes. Buy cheap cars and motorcycles and give them away as gifts," Happy says. Dan answers with umms and hmms, watching Little Plum taking five completed wigs out of the paper bag. He remembers her telling him the glue used on the wigs smells sweet, so the rats might like to chew on it. No wonder she hung them so high up there. "Those low people don't know the value of his paintings. Don't let them profane art by being given his works. And make damn sure he doesn't bribe anyone with cash. That will make him liable."

Dan says, okay, he'll make damn sure. Now she is running Ocean Chen's life as well.

"Now go inside and try to get the secret of secrets out of the old man."

Dan hears a dial tone in the cell and realizes that Happy has hung up. What Happy has asked him to do feels terribly dirty. Secret of secrets? Does he have to sell *that* in order to make a living? Do they *all* sell that to make a living? Come to think of it, that's what journalists do. They expose the unexposed, using every means, base or noble. They can make someone infamous overnight. It is a nasty job. At least it has a lot of nasty aspects.

Dan shuts off the cell phone. Today is the day he has planned to take Little Plum to see a new apartment compound, farther out in the suburbs than their factory. When they arrive, there are at least ten salespeople in the sales office. They all approach Dan and Little Plum. One of the salesgirls invites them to see scale models in a little sandbox, telling them that they are very lucky, because the prices have just been lowered. Her name is Miss Wang, she tells them. With a telescoping collapsible pointer, she points at the models, showing where there will be a wooded park in one year, and where there will be a little lake in two years. So they are selling something that's not there yet, just like most of these new living compounds, Dan thinks, but he can't bring himself to say it to the girl, who is as serious as a new actress with her painstakingly re-hearsed lines.

"It is only one thousand and nine hundred yuan per square me-ter," the girl says.

That's the only attraction. Dan enjoys window-shopping for con-dos. When he walks on the street and receives hard-sell fliers for sub-urban apartments, just like this one, he takes them home and studies them. If it is not too far out of the way, sometimes he goes in for a lit-tle window-shopping. And Little Plum always enjoys the enormous construction site anyway. They follow Miss Wang to the "elevator," a bare platform with no protection around the edges, and stand beside a pile of tools. Miss Wang hands them two construction helmets, apologizing that the real elevator is not yet in operation, so they have to share this one with the tools.

Once inside a "condo," a space walled in by cement blocks, Miss Wang becomes more animated. She points at a hole in the floor and tells them it is the Jacuzzi in the bathroom of the master bedroom suite, and a concave area is a walk-in closet. Floors are made of hard-wood, and the kitchen is covered with Italian ceramic tiles.

"I'll be glad to answer any questions you have," she says, a smile of anticipation on her face.

Dan looks at Little Plum, who is in her happy, content detach-ment as usual.

"Where she is looking," Miss Wang says, motioning toward Lit-tle Plum, "is a tennis court. Beyond that is an indoor golf range. Come this way, please."

She walks with great care so as not to stick her pointy high heels into the gaps between the cement slabs on the floor.

"Here, right below your window, is a creek flowing down from the fountain at the main gate. It will go around every building and return to the fountain purified. On the banks of the creek are roses and lilies. Up north is a supermarket with local produce, which is much cheaper and fresher than that of the city."

They follow her to each side of the apartment and see with their mind's eye what the compound provides.

"I know there is a chicken farm to the north. The air pollution here is heavy, right?" Dan asks her, not realizing he is in "journalist" mode.

"That's the reason why our prices are unbeatable. But we are going to do something about it. We will get them to move. We are negotiating with them now. If we succeed, we will buy the farm and tear it down and put up more apartments. Then the price of your condo will double."

"What if the negotiation fails?" Dan asks.

"The government will work on pollution before the 2008 Olympics. I assure you, the pollution problem is the first priority on the government's agenda. By then the chicken farm will be all gone. The smell will improve considerably."

She points near and far, her hand also much rehearsed. She is like an instructor of Marxism, teaching beautiful ideas of communism, helping you see things far beyond the way they appear now, so you can enjoy them in advance while they are still beautiful ideas. She doesn't seem equivocal about any question Dan asks, and she promises him cable TV with foreign movies and a community hospital that will be operational within five years. Dan thinks she believes the words she articulates, but not necessarily that she knows what she is talking about.

"Okay, I like it," Dan says. The only thing he likes about it is the price.

Miss Wang is delighted, telling them to follow her back to the office, where they can get materials on bank loans and the government's mortgage regulations.

As they ride in the open lift descending from the top of the building, squeezed in between loads of disposable lunch boxes and empty buckets, Dan looks at Little Plum. She gazes dreamily, smiling to herself, at the galaxy of lights, switched on suddenly for the construction workers on the night shift. She will be the only one who won't protest if the promises remain unmet. She never wants to know what is missing from her life, whether shark fins, sea snails, crab claws, or cable TV with foreign movies. Or a basic human living space with running water and a flush toilet. She doesn't know that while her husband has been missing from her for two weeks, at least part of him has been elsewhere with another woman. Dan extends his arm and pulls her gently to him, building a guardrail for her on this wall-less, acrobatic elevator.

When they get back to the sales office, a group of people are standing in front of the door, chanting a rhyming protest slogan. It is a group of buyers demonstrating against the developer of the compound. The rhyme says the developer has cheated them; they have no legal long-term lease on the land they acquired from the chicken farm, and the chicken farm is suing them. If the farm wins the lawsuit, the down payments on their condos will go down the drain.

Miss Wang forces her way through the crowd, motioning Dan and Little Plum to follow.

"Don't listen to them," she says. "They raise hell so they can force the price down further."

The demonstrators tug at Dan and Little Plum, blocking their entry.

They are telling Dan that the owner of the compound is a swindler. He only had a one-page agreement with the previous head of the farm, who recently died of a heart attack.

"And his successor doesn't honor the deal. He said his predecessor took a bribe and made a personal deal with this developer."

"They said they would buy out the chicken farm. But the truth is that the farm is expanding and has imported new equipment."

"Even if the chicken farm's new head takes a bribe, and the long-term lease eventually gets settled, there will always be millions of chickens running around, stinking up every cubic meter of air. Just imagine!"

"Once they've got your down payment, they'll never refund it to you, even though they promise they will."

"Don't be another sucker!"

"Don't let them take you in!"

Miss Wang tries to pull Dan free but fails.

"We will call the police," she threatens.

"Go ahead. Call the newsmen, too, while you're at it," someone shouts.

Dan pulls Little Plum through the crowd into the office. All the other salespeople have gone for the day. They sit down by the sand-box diorama, continuing to study the beautiful ideas materialized into the miniature models.

"Please have some tea," Miss Wang says, placing two paper cups of tea on the edge of the sandbox. "I know it's messy. But the government policies are messy. Never a clear law on land leases, and ninety percent of all suburban housing developments have problems like ours."

Dan keeps looking at the models.

"I can give you two percent more," she says.

"Of what?" Dan asks, frowning, his eyes narrowing behind his thick-framed glasses. He doesn't know that in Miss Wang's eyes he looks rather intimidating.

"Discount."

"When do you think we can move in?"

"Anytime. As long as you can do your own interior."

"I thought the price includes the interior."

"It does, if you wait until next summer."

Moving her deft finger on a calculator, she tells them it will be a honey-sweet deal for them with just a few tens of thousands down.

"And your monthly payment is only one thousand three hundred," she says. "If you have a good job, the banks will have a catfight over you. What do you do?" She looks back and forth between Dan and Little Plum.

A brick breaks through the window glass and lands in the middle of the floor. The girl pulls the sandbox into a corner. Out in the dimming daylight, the chanting grows louder.

"Don't worry. They will leave in ten minutes," the girl says. "That's the time they get hungry. Sometimes they come back for another round if the soap opera isn't good. What is your job? Do you teach college?"

"I have no regular job."

"You don't?" she says, staring at him. "Do you think you can go to a friend who has a company or something? Any company, no matter how small. You go ask him to prove that you are working for him, and your monthly salary is, say, five thousand a month. Then I will take care of the rest."

"Just a piece of paper?"

"With his company's stamp. Do you have a friend like that?"

Dan thinks of the person who makes all kinds of documents and certificates. He will give Happy a call, asking her for an introduction.

"Yes. I can have that ready in two days," Dan says.

Before they leave, there are five bricks on the floor. The chanting is over, as the salesgirl predicted. Dan places one of his business cards on the table and gulps down the remaining tea.

"Oh, you are a freelance journalist!" the sales girl cheers. "You write for newspapers and magazines?"

Dan nods. Little Plum looks at him, full of pride.

"I know a person who is a freelance journalist, too! He is rich. He gets paid by all kinds of people who ask him to write. People even give him airline tickets and hotel rooms to stay in. His family name is Deng. Do you know each other?"

She is the kind of girl who thinks people with the same job are all classmates or office mates. Dan smiles and says he might have met him on one or two occasions. He notices that he lies just about every other sentence.

"In that case, you don't really need anybody to prove your salary. I'll take care of the bank loan."

She asks for his identification card, runs to the other end of the office, and makes a couple of photocopies of it. She goes back to her own desk, finds a form, and tells Dan to drop it by tomorrow after filling it out. She promises that she will hand over the keys to his apartment in a month.

"I thought it takes two weeks," Dan says.

"Two weeks means you have to give the bank guy some gifts—say, a TV set or a gold jewelry set, including a necklace with a heart-shaped pendant and a pair of earrings. I don't think it's worth it."

Dan doesn't think so either.

On the way home, Dan thinks he might sell Ocean Chen's painting for the down payment. After they get home, Dan's cell phone rings. It is Miss Wang. She says her boss wants to invite Dan to a casual lunch tomorrow. Dan accepts the invitation and tells her to thank the boss. She says they will meet in the restaurant's reception room.

Dan arrives twenty minutes early. It is a nice day, fresh and clear, with a high sky and perfect temperature. Beijing only produces three or four days like this in a year. The restaurant turns out to be anything but a place for a casual lunch. There are two rows of young girls in eighteenth-century European attire standing in symmetry on either side of the door, their deep purple silk skirts ballooning up and their long trains mopping the dusty floor. And they wear red-and-gold sashes diagonally across their bodies. The gold inscriptions on their sashes say "Coming here is like coming home." In broad daylight they look completely out of place. Nowadays one sees these girls everywhere, whichever way he turns, in expensive hotels and restaurants and department stores. They stand by gates, by counters, by elevators and escalators, outside and inside the restrooms, behind the dining seats and in front of the corridors, dressed like characters from a certain stage drama, embarrassed and stiff, shifty-eyed if caught spying on you, with a fierce curiosity that only belongs to someone fresh off the train from a far-off place. Dan often finds himself annoyed by these girls, who make him feel not so much attended as watched. They should be responsible for Dan's frustration that he can hardly find any privacy; privacy to take a break from faking someone he is not, to pull himself together for more faking or make a quick repair on his camera that has stopped flashing. Or just to be blank for a while. Being blank discharges the intensity built up doing his banquet bug job. It is hard to find a quiet spot to turn oneself totally blank when you know there are girls somewhere watching you. And there they are, on the top step, watching him creep up the stairs. Dan feels as if he is falling into a web woven by the rays from their eyes. He smiles, asking the two homely girls (in fact, they are all hard to look at) standing nearest the entrance whether they are sisters. They first turn to look at each other and then both turn to face Dan, outraged and in shock. Neither of them believes she bears any resemblance to the other, whom she considers ugly. Dan changes his course and walks back down the steps. Are these girls supposed to stimulate one's appetite? Or are they meant as a symbol of class or a gesture of hospitality? No one knows and no one questions. Maybe it is just to create jobs for superfluous female labor swarming into the city from the countryside. He would certainly object if he had come here on his own to enjoy good dishes and these girls in their elaborate costumes and hairdos were part of his expenses.

He takes a stroll around the little side garden outside the reception room. He looks into the elegant reception room through the picture window and sees a youngish man on a very angular, impeccable white sofa, picking his nose. He sits cross-legged, a newspaper on his lap. Dan figures that either picking his nose helps him concentrate on his reading, or else reading makes him more focused on picking his nose.

At the agreed time, Dan gets into the restaurant and gives his name. He is ushered inside and is introduced to eight people around the dining table. He discovers that the nose picker is the president of the real estate development company.

"This is President Wu," Miss Wang says. "This is Reporter Dong."

President Wu stretches out his hand (Dan knows where it has been) and pulls Dan to the chair next to him after a long handshake. Dan sees a big jade ring on the middle finger of his left hand.

"I love to sell houses to people like you. I hate to let low-class people move into my compound," the president remarks, laughing.

All the others present laugh with him out of loyalty. Dan laughs, too. He notices he can now laugh for no good reason. The jade on the president's ring is as green as a drop of spinach juice.

"Did you tell Mr. Dong he has neighbors like soap opera stars and pop singers?" He turns to Miss Wang and then turns back to Dan before she has time to reply. "Some days ago, a soap opera star came to me, asking to buy one of the condos. I ignored him. He wasn't even polite to me. And he has started an affair with an actress. I don't like my clients to sleep around on my compound."

Dan says Mr. President is a man of high morality. He actually is thinking about what Old Ten told him: her sister's boyfriend had a precious jade ring. Is that man also a real estate developer?

"Here is what I want you to do: I want you to write an article about how you love my compound. You wanted to live in it as soon as you first set eyes on it. Tell people why you have chosen our compound over all others. Make it a big piece and get it into a big newspaper."

He looks Dan in the eye, not letting a flash of his thought escape. If you know what it feels like being fixed in the crosshairs of a rifle, you know the feeling. Dan will do anything to escape the rifle scope of this man's eyes.

"Yes, I think the price is very . . . ," Dan says.

"I care about high-class people's opinions. Those who come to throw bricks are hoodlums," President Wu says. He is the kind of

163

man who cuts people off a lot, speaking but not communicating, following only his own train of thought. "Miss Wang told me you can't wait to move in, can't wait for the interior to be finished. Write about that. Make people believe *you* instead of those rioters."

Dan nods, thinking that Old Ten's sister was a top student. She let a hand with a jade ring like the president's pick her like a juicy little fruit.

". . . How does that sound to you?"

Dan realizes the president has been asking him questions and he has missed all of them. All the guests around the table look thrilled. The president must have proposed something exciting.

"But if you don't keep your promise, I'll take my condo back," President Wu says.

So that is what has been going on. The president will let him live in one of the condos under the condition that he writes a big article about his compound and publishes it. Dan's immediate reaction is that it will save him from all the dangerous adventures at the banquets. He will let Little Plum have the one thing that has been missing from her life, a real residence that has a kitchen, a bathroom, and a closet. She will never again need to stand on a stool and hold a tube for him to shower. Nor will she have to squat over the sewage opening to pee. This president is a very generous man after all.

"You are too generous, Mr. President," Dan says. "When do you think is a good time for an interview?" He doesn't want to appear desperate. He takes out his little notebook and pretends to check his schedule. "I have some time the day after tomorrow . . ."

"I have a few compounds in the city. They are all billion-yuan investments. Sometimes my wife nags at me, saying I am living with my compounds instead of her," he says, disregarding Dan's questions.

After the remnants of the appetizers are withdrawn, the president calls the waitress to change the predesigned menu. Some dishes are too mediocre, some are too rich. Does the restaurant have something that's rare but not filling? Something that keeps one's mouth busy, taste buds excited, but doesn't stuff the stomach quickly?

The waitress giggles and says she will have the chef work on that.

"Just shock me. I can no longer find a single restaurant in China that will surprise me with dishes I haven't tasted. No imagination," the president says.

It is a banquet of sixteen courses. The president spends more time talking on his cell phone than eating. When he recognizes a certain person's caller ID, he rushes to one side and faces away, cupping his mouth with his hand, a flirtatious smile all over his back.

Then comes the last dish. People guess at it while the waitress smiles mysteriously. With his back to the table, the president is still talking away. The guests wait for him to finish talking and try the dish. In the silent curiosity, the president's whisper can be heard.

"Be my little one and wait for me, hmm? . . ." he says. His hand cups the phone and his mouth, and the jade ring catches the sunlight streaming in from the window. It is a vulgar hand, the hand of a butcher or a pimp.

When he comes back to the table, he stares at the new dish.

"What is this?"

"Something to shock you," the waitress says. She knows that on most occasions, she can get away with her cute smile. Especially with a man like President Wu.

"Just tell me."

"Pigeon tongues."

"Are they rare?" His face darkens. "They are not rare at all. But they cost like hell! What is this place? A clip joint? A place for suckers who are worried their money will grow musty if they don't spend it quickly enough?"

The waitress spontaneously takes a few steps toward the door. Looking at the guests, she tries to find eyewitnesses. Dan looks away.

"But, sir, you didn't want me to tell you beforehand . . . ," the little waitress says, her eyes an intense plea.

"I don't like a waitress who talks back," the president says.

"Sorry, sir . . ."

"That's a better attitude."

"Thank you, sir."

"You've got to learn how to talk and how not to talk."

"Thank you for teaching me, sir."

It could have been Old Ten, standing by the door, body cringing, eyes brimming with tears, yet still attempting a trembling smile. Dan withdraws his eyes and stares at the hundreds of tongues, stir fried or sautéed, with bright red pepper shreds and white wild chrysanthemum petals sprinkled all over the tiny organs. All the little triangles of meat form a huge chrysanthemum on a crystal plate. What a work.

"I have never tried pigeon tongues," Dan says. He feels the little waitress's tearful eyes turn to him.

"Yes, they are rare to Mr. Journalist," someone among the guests says.

"Pigeon tongues! I will boast to my wife that I've had pigeon tongues today, thanks to our president!"

The waitress knows she is rescued. She gives Dan a long, piteous look of gratitude and bows out quietly.

Dan finds that the president eats as many pigeon tongues as everyone else, even though he still remains sullen.

After the meal, the president's mood recovers. He says he is going to read Dan's article in a week, and Dan is going to have the keys to the apartment soon afterward.

IT LOOKS MORE LIKE a ruin than one of President Wu's newly built compounds. Dan holds Little Plum's hand and walks among scattered cinder blocks, torn cement bags, and dried lumps of plaster. The buildings are barely completed, yet some walls have already cracked. There are Styrofoam lunch boxes everywhere. On the first floor, some rooms have smoke-blackened walls and clotheslines. They have served as shelters for homeless people or construction workers.

President Wu has three building phases under construction in the suburbs, and this is one of them. What impresses Dan is the enormity of his plans. This compound, like the other two, has ten high-rises, each of which has twenty-eight floors.

Dan doesn't understand why the president leaves them all uncompleted. There is a sales office in a makeshift house, its door locked and windows shuttered. Dan forces the door open and steps in. The sandbox diorama has collapsed, and the miniature buildings litter the floor along with bricks. The water cooler has a few drops of turbid water left, and a number of paper cups are marked with brown rings of dried tea. There are two old computer monitors. Dan and Little Plum walk from one end of the room to the other, each of their steps causing a tiny dust storm. In the pale ray of morning light coming in from the jagged window, the dust particles fly like mad. The place looks haunted. As soon as they step out, Little Plum cries out.

"Dan, look!" she says, her finger pointing upward.

Dan sees several dozen heads in construction helmets, popping up from windows on the top floor. Soon, helmeted heads emerge from the windows of other buildings.

"Please wait!" a man shouts.

He comes running toward Dan from one of the building entrances. Behind him runs a gang of helmeted men.

"Please, tell us the truth: When are you going to pay us?"

"Pay what?" Dan asks, wondering how Little Plum and he have already landed inside a perfect siege of helmets.

"You promised last week. You said you would pay us Monday. But today is Friday. We don't want to be trouble for you. But our wives and kids are waiting for us to send money home."

At a loss, Dan looks at the faces under the helmets. Their faces look identical, with the same lack of expression. Their deeply suntanned skin sets them apart from ordinary Chinese. They look like South Pacific aboriginals. They are city drifters. Leaving their women and children behind, they have drifted into the city from villages, to find jobs that the city men don't care to do.

"I am not with the development company. I am here to shop for a condo."

"Please. We have waited for a year. You guys said last August you would pay us before the Autumn Moon Festival. Now you owe us two years' pay. We've slept on a bare cement floor and eaten thin rice gruel for so many months, just waiting for you to pay."

"Really, I don't know what you are talking about," Dan says.

"We saw you touch the computer in the office," another man says. "The boss sent you here to see if we had left."

"Look, I have nothing to do with your boss."

"You all say the same thing!"

His arm round Little Plum's shoulder, Dan tries to charge through the crowd but ends up in the center of a tighter siege.

"We heard the big boss is a very rich man. He has enough money to build two Tiananmens and three White Houses. How come he just keeps not paying us? We are so cheap; it probably costs him nothing to get us paid!"

"Did the big boss promise last August that he would pay you?" Dan asks.

"Every week he has promised to pay."

"And he's never paid?"

"No."

"How do you guys live then?"

"You *see* how we live. We don't need much food when we're not working, anyway."

Dan sees a young boy leaning on a crutch. An old man wears a coat made out of a cement bag. On closer scrutiny, they don't look alike at all.

"What if the big boss never pays you?" Dan says.

The crowd explodes.

"Did he say that?"

"He told you that?"

"That's what we fear he might do to us!"

"We'd beg him for mercy! We have hungry children at home!"

"My mother is having surgery!"

"My wife is expecting a baby!"

Dan's jacket is pulled and tugged. Little Plum peels off the fingers grasping onto Dan's tie. One of his only two ties.

"Listen! Please listen to me!" Dan screams. Sweat has broken out on his back. He tells them to be patient and logical. Their boss wants the buildings completed, doesn't he? He will pay in order to complete them.

"No, the boss can hire new workers," a man says. He seems to be the leader of the construction crew.

"Some bosses in Beijing have done that!" the boy with the crutch says.

"They kept promising and kept delaying payment," the leader says.

He tells Dan that many bosses are cheats. In the end, the workers go home when they can't wait any longer. They use up the last penny they have, or they get sick or something. Then these bosses recruit new workers. They do the same thing all over again to the new workers.

Dan says he will see to it that these heartless schemes get exposed. He wants to get rid of the workers immediately. Or he will have to shut his eyes and plug up his ears. He is scared to be amid so many helpless beings. He hates being a container into which these miserable guys spit and vomit their bitterness and sadness. Why the hell should he want to know that so-and-so's mother is waiting desperately for money to have her belly cut open? Hasn't he seen enough of country wives, huge with pregnancy, tending fields because their husbands have drifted elsewhere to work, promising to send money home? He was having a perfect day when he came out here with Little Plum, and now he is upset.

"Look at that building," Little Plum says, very loudly. "It isn't straight; it leans to the west." She is louder, flexing her palm, putting it vertically in front of her nose ridge and moving it slowly from her face toward the building.

Everyone turns to look.

"It looks all right to me," the old worker in the cement-bag coat says.

"If you keep looking at it for ten minutes, you will find it tips this way," she says, her hand in front of her nose ridge inclining a little. "That's what I do. I always keep looking at these new, tall buildings for a while, and I find none of them is straight."

She tells Dan on the way home from the construction workers' siege, which they finally succeeded in tearing open, that she finds that not a single building is absolutely straight. Nor is there an absolutely straight nose ridge. She was studying the faces of the besieging workers and found that all their nose ridges were crooked. She says she has been doing this since she was a child. She has never seen a person with a hundred-percent straight nose ridge. Just as you can never find a tree, a wall, a table leg, or a telephone pole that is a hundred percent straight.

"What about *my* nose?" Dan asks, teasing her.

"Of course it's not straight. You don't walk straight, either. Everybody walks leaning to the left or the right."

There is something to that, something deeper than what she says, but Dan can't figure out what it is.

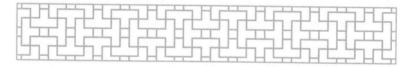

ONE EVENING a week later, Dan has the article on the housing development ready. He asks Happy to meet him in a little public park near the Asian Games Village. Happy comes in a thin down coat, under which he spots the uneven train of her lacy nightgown. She sleeps and works in complete disregard of society's norms. Dan paces back and forth behind the park bench she sits on, watching Happy read under the indifferent white light of a street lamp. A cheap stereo is playing a love song by Deng Lijun—also known as Teresa Teng—a

Taiwanese singer popular in the late seventies, and the choked, amorous expressions thunder through the whole park. Through the bushes and tree branches, Dan can see some shadows waltzing in pairs. The dancers were young in the seventies, and they become young again each night when they come to dance to the love songs. They hold each other's thick shoulders and waists, gazing at their partners' dreamy eyes under balding foreheads and thinning, permed hair. They turn and swirl through the night air that they stir up with their high heels and freshly polished shoes. Dan is moved. When the music stops, they remain in each other's arms, instantly sad about growing old. He turns back to Happy.

She frowns, either at the love song or at the article she is reading.

When Dan was writing the article, he had to squeeze his eyes shut and try to see the fountains and creeks, the lake and the putting green, and the rolling slopes dotted with little flowers and mushrooms to be gathered up by elfin youths in white and sweet maidens in red. He had gone to the big department stores and subway entrances where people hand out real estate flyers that read like fairy tales. He ended up taking these writings apart, reassembling the sentences and paragraphs, stringing them together with some of the words from Miss Wang's presentation and changing it from third person to first person. He was pleased with his editing job.

"What is this shit anyway?" Happy throws it away like a dirty tissue. "Pop lyrics or some shit like that?" She thumbs toward the dancers.

One of the pages flutters over the ground and Dan hops behind it, his tall body bending low.

"Will you polish it for me?" Dan asks, picking it up.

"It is too polished already. It is polished with cream and syrup.

Good thing I didn't have dinner, or I would throw up," she says. She is in a mean spirit.

"What do you mean by 'too polished'?"

"How much did you get paid to write this?" she demands.

"Well, I can split it with you."

"Better be a million."

Dan thinks about it. He can't publish it without Happy's help.

"How about one tenth of a million?" he asks.

"You mean a hundred thousand?" she says. "That's too little."

"It is half of what I will get."

Happy looks at him, smiling queerly.

"So they'll let you live in one of their condos, right?" She leans back on the bench. "They have too many condos on their hands. It costs them nothing to let you have one."

"How do you know?"

"They won't allow you to sell it, though," she says.

"But it's a gift . . ."

"The hell it is."

Dan stares at her.

"So you want to share your 'gift' with me?" She looks at him, smiling widely. "You know, it is such a great sacrifice of decency and grace to polish your lie."

"We can rent the place out and share the rent," Dan says. He knows he looks desperate.

"You will never outsmart those people, my boy." She pats his shoulder lovingly.

"Are you in or are you out?" Dan says.

Happy fumbles in her purse for cigarettes but withdraws her hand immediately.

"So many things have happened during the last week. I quit smoking, fell in and out of love," she says, standing up from the bench, stretching her arms.

"Well, if you do it, do it with simplicity," she finally says. "You used to have it. It touched me when I first read your piece on the peacock banquet. Use the dictionary and get those words right, for heaven's sake. There are about a hundred wrong words in this piece of crap. This is my help to you. You will repay me with the private details you get from talking to Ocean Chen. How many days did you stay with Ocean Chen in his country house?"

"I was there for five days. It is a beautiful place, very quiet." He would have gone there if the master's driver had not talked him out of it. "But Master Chen didn't talk to me once. He was painting like a madman." His lies go more fluently than the truth nowadays, and he doesn't feel his face changing colors as it used to.

"Go there again. Stay for another five days and see if he talks. Talk to his cook and driver. Tip them each time they feed you information."

She walks toward the park's entrance, sticking her hand into her purse and pulling it out again without a cigarette pack. She keeps forgetting she has quit smoking.

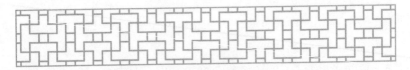

DAN GOES TO President Wu's office with the article. The secretary tells him the president is at his own hotel, which isn't far from here. Dan sits down on the broad leather sofa and reads the article for the last time. The secretary asks if he is going to wait here for the president. Yes, he is. But the president is not coming to the office to-day. He isn't? No, he has some people over at the hotel for a business meeting.

The hotel is small. It has a pair of golden lions at the entrance and plastic flower arrangements all over in the little reception area. The smell of it reminds Dan of the basement hostel where the peas-ants from Bai Village stayed, except it is belied by the pungent, phony fragrance of air freshener. There is a statue of Kuan Yin inside the cashier counter, and another of Jesus standing in symmetry next to it. On the wall are some dusty photos. Framed with golden metal, some parts faded, the photos feature President Wu standing beside the vice mayor of Beijing in one of his compounds, under a sign that reads "Provide Affordable Housing for Those Most in Need." There are also a few photos of him with some sports stars and soap opera stars, posing in front of a red ribbon.

A girl in a uniform leads Dan up the stairs, along which are little niches in the wall with nude goddesses of the West and East posing in them. As they reach the third floor, Dan sees a sign that reads "Presi-dential Suites."

From the end of the corridor comes the rattling sound of mah-jongg tiles. Dan remarks to the girl that President Wu has an unusual mah-jongg schedule; while others like to play in the evening, he plays in the morning. No, he only starts playing at midnight, she replies. He has been playing since last night? No, he started playing the night before.

The door is ajar, and Dan can smell alcohol and greasy food. There is no sound other than the slick bone tiles clicking against one another and rattling. He can hear the quiet tension inside. The girl tells him to go in but not utter a sound until the game is over. The president hates anyone intruding in the middle of his game. When he plays, he doesn't eat, talk, or rest, and he only drinks water and liquor.

A woman in thick makeup receives Dan in the doorway of the suite. Can she help him with anything? she whispers. He has an appointment with President Wu. She hesitates for a second, then tells Dan to wait for the president to finish this round. She is about forty and wears tight stretch pants that show her underwear cutting across the cheeks of her full buttocks, giving her four butt cheeks instead of two.

Beyond the doorway is a big living room furnished with gold-framed velvet sofas. There is a square table covered with a velvet tablecloth fringed with golden tassels. There are two snoring shapes lying on two sofas under blankets. A girl stretches out on her stomach in front of a huge TV, watching a mute soap opera. Dan sees President Wu pick up the tiles with his left hand while flinging matchsticks with his right hand. He props a matchstick between his middle finger and thumb, and he pushes the matchstick with his index finger, making it taut, letting the two ends drill into the thick flesh of his fingers. It's as though he is trying to see how much pressure it can withstand, or how much torture he can endure. Then, as the stick is about to break, his middle finger gives it a flick and shoots it across the floor. There are times he breaks the matchsticks and makes himself shudder a little. Dan secretly wishes he would stop short of breaking the sticks.

The game is over, and President Wu stands up and goes to the bathroom. When he comes out, his hands still zipping up his fly, President Wu asks the woman, now picking up matchsticks fallen all over the floor, whether he is wanted. Dan stands up from the chair he has been directed to sit on, and smiles. President Wu stares at Dan, his eyes bloodshot, lips cracked, and beard overgrown.

He isn't just pretending; he has truly forgotten who Dan is. Dan reintroduces himself, somewhat awkwardly, and redelivers his business card. Wu raises his eyebrows and stretches out his hand.

President Wu says this isn't a very good time to go over the article. He suggests that Dan leave it with him, and he will read it as soon as he has time. Dan reminds him that it is he who wanted it done in a week, but Dan knows his company certainly has much more important things to take care of than this article. When does Mr. President think would be a good time for him to come again to discuss this article? Anytime after today.

President Wu tells the woman with the four-cheeked butt to show Dan out, as he returns to the mah-jongg table without saying good-bye.

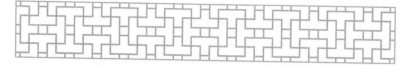

DAN HAS HEARD nothing from President Wu for a week. He goes to the hotel in a suit and tie, hoping he can find the president there playing mah-jongg. No, the president has not shown up here for several days, a different girl at the reception tells him. He leaves the hotel for the Green Grove Club, but it is Old Ten's day off. Does anyone know where she went? he asks a girl called Old One. No, Old Ten has many secrets, Old One tells him.

On his way home, Dan sees posters and banners lining the street for about a kilometer. A drug company is holding a press conference at the Hotel Five Continents, promoting a new medicine against a deadly flu. It is a new-age drug, made of pure natural ingredients and a special kind of water.

Within a few minutes, Dan finds himself inside the Five Continents' banquet hall. He looks around, smiling at the familiar and not-so-familiar faces. There doesn't seem to be any sign of vigilance. It looks as if the Anti–Banquet Bug Campaign is over. Nor does he sense any tension among the crowd. In suits and ties, the doctors from famous hospitals roam among easy-mannered journalists. As Dan is looking for a place to sit, a man with purple pimples on his forehead comes to him. He stands close to Dan, clearing his throat several times. He is warming up for a talk. Casually, Dan turns for the exit. He doesn't want to run the risk of encountering an investigator on the banquet bug case.

"Hello," the man with purple pimples calls to him.

Dan keeps walking toward the lobby.

"Why are you leaving so early?"

Dan still pretends not to hear him.

"Does it mean you don't like our product? Or you don't have faith in it?" he asks, only two steps behind Dan.

"Sorry," Dan says. "I didn't realize you were talking to me."

"I know we could have chosen a better hotel. The banquet hall looks cheap, doesn't it?" he asks. He presents his business card, which says he is the director of the drug company's PR department. "I'm Director Yang. Which hospital are you from?"

"Why?" It has to do with the suit and tie that he has put on for the meeting with President Wu.

"Why?" He laughs. "Because at this event you are either with the press or you are a medical professional. And I can tell a reporter even without his equipment."

Director Yang is a charming fellow, in spite of his pimpled forehead. He convinces Dan that today's banquet is unique in many respects: every dish is a remedy for one ailment or another.

Dan follows him back to the banquet hall and sees that the guests have started on the appetizers.

"This gelatin is made of bull penises and seahorses, seasoned with several kinds of herbs. It enhances virility."

Dan picks up the jiggling substance with his chopsticks and takes a bite. The texture is very delicate and the flavor is sharp with herbs.

"Good?"

Dan nods. It is good. Manager Yang tells him that it takes seventy hours to make it. Dan chews slowly and studies its texture with his tongue. He discovers a hundred secret flavors hidden within the initial one, and none of them is ordinary. Such a complex of tastes.

"Here, try this," Director Yang says.

It is a soup with tender yellow, half-transparent flowers floating on top.

"They are frog uteruses. A female aphrodisiac. You would have a great time if your woman were here with you," he says, winking.

Dan becomes sweaty eating the hot, sticky substance. A little bit oily, it evades the tongue, and his teeth work on it. It is subtle and delightful. Does the human uterus taste like this? Dan feels a churn in his stomach.

"Medicinal cuisine doesn't have to taste awful, does it? Even though it's medicine, it doesn't have to be *like* medicine in the conventional sense."

Dan nods and smiles, so that he doesn't need to stop eating to participate in the conversation. He has really missed good banquet food. Absent from the banquets, he often thought of food like this. It drives him crazy to imagine how much exquisite food he could have enjoyed that ended up as leftovers in the garbage pails. The Anti–Banquet Bug

179

Campaign has ended with the sixteen bugs' arrest, and peace seems to have been restored.

". . . You want to think about it?" Director Yang asks.

Dan has not really paid attention to what the director was whispering to him. He nods slowly, pensively, disguising his rapture in eating. Why do people have to hide behind such a beautiful feast to conduct business? They negotiate and argue, collude or betray, over tables on which delicious dishes are laid—dishes that could have taken days of creativity and craftsmanship to make. Dan hears Director Yang say something like "fair share." He swallows the food and wipes his lips with the napkin. Here goes another deal, all in the name of appreciating the art of fine food.

"You don't have to prescribe it. You just recommend it to your patients. Make strong recommendations, that's all. Then you tell them where to buy it. Here." He lays his card on the table. "Here is our Web site. They can order the drug online. We make overnight deliveries."

Dan has missed the major part of his proposal.

"I know you can't really prescribe it, because once any medicine made of natural ingredients has chemicals added to it, it has to get the approval of the Ministry of Health. I only expect you to recommend it. Strongly and authoritatively recommend it. And if you don't agree to the number of shares I just proposed, let me know. We will work things out."

It suddenly occurs to Dan what Director Yang has been proposing. And now the president of the drug company is at the podium, giving a speech to thank the doctors and the media for their support.

"The media is our great friend. With your help, with your articles in every major newspaper, the drug is going to work wonders for the masses," the president says.

Dan asks Director Yang if the media know that the supposedly herbal medicine is actually mixed with chemicals. The man with the pimply forehead smiles and leans closer to Dan.

"Do you think today's media cares? Not even the media in Western countries care. In America, they let swindlers sell anything they want on TV, as long as they pay for the time. The only thing they tell you is that *you* are responsible for what you buy. Look, these banquet eaters here are just cogs and gearwheels in a propaganda machine. They say anything you want them to say, as long as you feed them a feast and stuff their pockets with 'money for your troubles.' "

Dan feigns a look of surprise.

Does he think 20 percent is fair? Dan realizes that he must have agreed to the percentage as he concentrated on eating. He looks at the director as he explains the deal, his pimpled forehead radiating nervous energy. Once a patient of Dan's orders the drug from the company's Web site, the 20 percent goes to Dan's account automatically. They will open an account for him—secretly, of course—once the terms are agreed on. How does the company know that so-and-so is such-and-such doctor's patient? That's easy. The company gives each doctor a "doctor's code." The patient puts his doctor's code number on his order, and each order gives the doctor a credit.

"If your patient's condition improves after taking the drug, we will get the press to publish the story as a letter to the editor."

So that's how it's done. Dan sees that kind of letter from patients every day in various newspapers and is amazed at how well they write and how effectively they dramatize their experiences.

Dan looks at the revolving lazy Susan on the table and watches as the last soup is delivered to each guest. No one has room for the soup except Dan. People have already started on their dental hygiene.

Blocking their mouths with the backs of their hands, they use tooth-picks to dislodge the remains of the feast, sucking the cool, clear air through the spaces between their teeth, and heaving satisfied sighs.

Some people begin leaving. Dan sees the little man stand up from a table by the exit. As always, the little man has secured his escape route before taking his seat.

"Hello," Dan says.

"Oh hi," he answers, waving his short, thick fingers. "Haven't seen you for a while. How have you been?"

"Out of town." So you are not among those sixteen crushed banquet bugs. "I was interviewing some peasants in the countryside," Dan says, offering the information.

"I was out of town, too," the little man says. "To investigate a very interesting scandal. You'd be surprised how smart people are."

"Is that right?" I wonder if you still hand out cards from the phony company I created.

"Are you leaving?" he asks.

"Yes," Dan says.

They walk out of the banquet hall, toward the rear door.

"There is a company that makes delicious soy sauce. Their products are even exported to over twenty countries abroad. Do you know what their products are made of?"

Dan looks at him. He seals his lips and prolongs the suspense. Dan sees, all of a sudden, that his eyeglasses, just like his own, have no optical correction. They are cosmetic as well.

"Their products are fake. They make soy sauce out of human hair. Animal hair can also be their raw material, but it is inferior. They figured out that hair contains similar chemicals to soybeans in terms of flavor. After fermentation and extraction, the flavor is even

182

more intense. They defend themselves by saying that human hair is organic; it comes from the human body and returns to the human body, so it is not harmful to human health."

"Is that right?" Dan asks.

"I told them, whether or not it is harmful to human health remains unknown. They said in a country with one point three billion people, there is always a latent food crisis. Finding new food sources should be encouraged. And I said they should tell people the truth about the 'soy sauce' being made of human hair, then let consumers make their own choices."

He takes another pause. Dan hates it when this man talks like a cheap folk storyteller of his childhood, holding this damned suspense, making children follow him from village to village.

"The soy sauce company is facing a big fine and bankruptcy. They owned up in court that they collected human hair from hair salons, barbershops, traveling barbers, and hospitals. It's creepy, isn't it? Flavoring your noodles with the dark juice of hair from surgical wards. You can't look into anything too deeply nowadays, can you? Everything could be false, could turn out to be something else."

"Are you going to write about this?" Dan asks.

"It has gotten enough exposure," the little man says. "What I am interested in is not how they fooled people for so many years . . ."

A hand taps Dan's shoulder. It is Director Yang. He pulls Dan aside and produces a brown paper bag with something bulging inside.

"So, we made a deal, didn't we?" he says.

"Sure." What is it? A wad of crispy, new bills? How much is it?

"Some humble gifts." He presses the brown paper bag into Dan's hand, and a sheet of paper with lines, which are filled with signatures. "Do me a favor. Sign the receipt. Your name here, your hospital here."

After Dan signs his name, legible only to himself, and scrawls the name of a hospital, Director Yang asks, "Did I give you my card?"

"Yes, I think so," Dan says, his fingers weighing the contents of the bag. One thousand? Two thousand?

"Here is another one." He inserts a card between Dan's thumb and the brown paper bag, "just in case you've lost the one I gave you a moment ago."

"Thank you," Dan says, thinking he will throw the card into the trash can behind him.

"Don't throw my card into a trash can, okay?" the Director says with a mocking smile.

"Why would I do that?" Dan says, smiling.

He laughs, and leaves.

"One of the fake medicine makers?" the little man asks when Dan comes back. "They really squandered so much money on this banquet."

When they are outside, the little man says that what interests him is the soy sauce company's knowledge of the raw materials. How on earth did it occur to them that hair had similar proteins and chemical components to soybeans? It is no less genius than Einstein's Theory of Relativity.

Dan nods in agreement. From the weight, the bills feel more like three thousand. Enough for the sofa set Little Plum and he wanted to buy at a shopping club. He will take her there tonight. He will borrow a pickup truck to haul it back, and have the neighbors help them get the furniture upstairs.

"It is such a great discovery that human hair tastes good," the little man says. "That is what really fascinates me."

"Yes, it's fascinating." They will get rid of those homemade sofas that always poke and punch your butt in the wrong places.

"You want a ride?" the little man says.

"Thank you, but I'd rather walk." He wants to go to the men's room and lock himself inside a stall to count the bills.

"I can drop you off at a subway station on the way to my next engagement."

Another engagement. Which means one more banquet and an extra fee of two hundred yuan. Again Dan declines his offer with thanks.

Dan soon finds himself following the little man's car in a taxicab. He isn't clear why he has started this car chase. Either he wants to share the little man's resources and sneak into the next function for the fee, or he just wants to reverse his passive role in this unintended pas-de-deux. At a traffic light, the little man hops out of his car, rushes to the front, and lifts up the hood. As the light changes, the cars he has blocked clump together, honking in a choir. His car has stalled out. He hurries back inside the car and emerges with a magazine, which he rolls up to form a funnel. Dan throws ten yuan to the driver and gets out of the taxi after they have passed the little man by a hundred meters. The little man is at the front of the car again, pouring some oil through the improvised funnel into the crankcase. The traffic splits and pushes past. A driver hollers at him: "Hey buddy, I've seen better junk melted down in a steel mill!"

Amid the ruthless current of traffic, the little man standing by his dead car looks like a hapless character in a comedy. Dan is now in a small eatery, sitting by a window over a chilled beer he has just ordered. He watches the little man run into and out of the car, trying different tools on different parts, wiping sweat off his forehead with the sleeve of his sports jacket. When Dan finishes his beer, a tow truck comes. Watching his car being pulled forward, the little man runs after it for some distance, as if seeing a loved one off to the surgical ward for a critical operation.

After half an hour, Dan climbs up a subway staircase with the little man some twenty paces ahead of him. Outside is a touristy area where foreigners as well as locals shop for fake antiques. Dan follows as the little man threads his way through the street, packed with people like movie crowds, and arrives at an ancient-looking structure. It is a fancy restroom made to look like a pavilion. Between the signs for ladies and gentlemen is a guy sitting behind a desk, guarding the door and selling toilet paper. Dan goes into a shop and walks upstairs, where two chairs and a table are set by the window for customers to sit back and examine the merchandise. Dan sees the little man talking to the restroom attendant, and from his excited expressions, Dan figures he is telling him about his broken-down car. Pretending to appreciate some "Tang Dynasty" pottery statues the owner has shown him, Dan examines the merchandise piece by piece by the light from outside. He sees the attendant and the little man switching places, as one stands up and the other sits down. The attendant's indolent pose reminds Dan of someone he knows. It is the photographer he met with the little man a couple of months ago. Dan watches them over the pottery he holds in his hand and sees the little man count money in a small box: the revenue from sales of toilet paper. Then the photographer disappears into the restroom and reemerges wearing the vest with numerous pockets, shouldering his bag of photo equipment. Dan realizes these journalistic partners are also teammates in the public toilet business.

Two foreigners come with a hundred-yuan bill, and the little man shows them the cash box, gesturing that there isn't enough change to break the bill. The photographer fumbles inside his camera bag and digs out some change. After the foreigners leave, a Chinese couple shows up in a hurry but immediately balks at the fee and the price of the toilet paper. They turn to leave, making outraged comments.

It doesn't make sense. Why do they have to sell toilet paper and guard a restroom, fancy though it is, when they make a respectable living as journalists? The only answer is that they are imposters, just like Dan. And they must be as poor as Dan, if not poorer.

"Is there anything else that interests you?" The shop owner becomes impatient with him.

Dan feigns an admiring gaze at a pottery horse.

"That is a real Tang dynasty piece," the owner says.

Like hell it is. "No wonder it caught my eyes just now."

"About eight hundred years old."

Yeah right. Perhaps you buried it yesterday, and excavated it this morning. "Yes, I know."

"I can give you a very good price."

"Let's hear it."

"Fifty percent off the original price."

"Well, I'll have to think about it. You know, I was taken in the other day." Dan motions to the restroom across the street. "That short guy sold me a phony piece just like this one. As the Chinese saying goes, short guys are short because they have too many twists."

"You must be mistaken," the owner says, looking out the window. "I've known him for years. He has never sold antiques. He used to have a stall here, where he did calligraphy. But he gave it up because he couldn't afford the fee for his stall. There is too much competition: if you fired a gun randomly on this street, you'd probably kill a person trained in brush-and-ink painting or calligraphy. It is the most cultured street in Beijing, where cultured people aren't worth much. So after the restroom was built, he became an attendant."

Dan sees the little man talking to a group of Chinese tourists, who are infuriated by the price and have started bargaining. Dan leaves the shop and immerses himself in the crowd.

Dan has to admit these two are better banquet bugs than he is. They know the advantage of organizing themselves, so one can cover for the other, just as the other day the photographer-impersonator covered the little man when they sensed Dan was stalking them. It explains the frequent encounters between Dan and the little man, in which the little man has made friendly overtures toward Dan. It was their way of paying professional courtesy to him. They've admired Dan's work so much that they copied Dan's card and his self-image, and they wanted to thank him for that. Or they wanted his advice or to give him advice. There is always room for improvement. Or perhaps they wanted to recruit him as another teammate. Maybe their team is much larger than just the two of them, and that was how they survived the campaign against the banquet bugs. Those who didn't make it through the campaign were individual bugs. But what if they wanted to take Dan somewhere to bump him off? Having pirated everything from Dan, maybe they were ready to kidnap him and take him to some suburban building site—one of President Wu's will do—and rub him out. After all, nobody needs competition for any job opportunity in the city of Beijing. Fortunately, Dan has never let them drive him far.

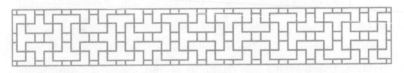

DAN SQUATS DOWN, pretending to retie his shoes. He sees the feet in white sneakers behind him faltering. He whispers to Little Plum to go ahead, he will catch up with her. They came to this outdoor market to buy a coffee table for their new sofas and found they had been followed. In a men's undergarment section, Dan dashes behind a curtain used as a fitting room. He looks out through a rip in the fabric and sees the guy crane his neck and look back and forth. He doesn't look like an undercover policeman in the conventional sense. He is heavy and slow, and his orange windbreaker looks like a borrowed costume. He has this sloppy way of walking, slouching along, scraping the ground with his fake Nikes. Dan sees Little Plum stop to talk to a furniture peddler, checking the goods with her hands while haggling over the prices. She shakes her head and turns to leave. The guy follows her. Does it have to do with the campaign against banquet bugs? Isn't it already over, with sixteen bugs crushed? Then why is this creep lurking around here?

When Dan comes out of the fitting room, both Little Plum and the creep are lost in the crowd. Dan moves toward the exit of the marketplace.

There they are. By the exit, the guy has stopped Little Plum. He is asking her something, and she shakes her head, forcing her way past him. The creep quickens his step and is now walking shoulder-to-shoulder with Little Plum. He can be graceful and swift; his sluggishness is just a disguise. He bothers her again with some questions, and she takes a small detour to avoid him. Dan sees her give an anxious glance toward the market with hundreds of heads bobbing up and down behind her. There is no sign of Dan, so she is relieved and goes along the food stalls lining the walls near the market. The guy makes another attempt to question her, and she walks in a semicircle around him to show people she is trying to get away from this man who is harassing her.

When they reach the bakery opposite the food stalls, Little Plum becomes furious. She calls out to the people on the street, telling them that this hoodlum has been chasing after her for an hour. Dan knows she can be bitchy if she chooses. He stands about fifty meters away and watches them. Little Plum makes gestures that the man has touched her arm and shoulder. She is raising hell. A circle of an audience has quickly formed around the bakery's glass door. Dan's view is blocked.

As he breaks through the thick wall of onlookers, he sees Little Plum in the guy's custody and ready to leave. The man holds out a police badge and tells the crowd to part. The crowd reluctantly clears a narrow path, then follows them with increasing enthusiasm. The whole scene rolls forward like a roving theater.

Dan is so panic-stricken that his mind freezes. He follows the crowd mechanically, trying to peep past the heads and shoulders to watch Little Plum. What is this plainclothes policeman going to do with her? Is he going to take her to a detention room? Are they going to send her to jail, mixing her with thieves and killers? What are they going to charge her with? For showing up at the shark fin banquet and eating a free meal? Is she going to be smart enough to say that she was supposed to attend another banquet, a wedding feast, but was confused and ended up eating at the wrong one? What's the big deal about it? People sometimes do go to the wrong banquet, since there are so many of them. They must have been following her ever since the shark fin banquet. But why didn't they come for her during the campaign, when they caught the sixteen banquet bugs?

"I am not afraid to go with you," Little Plum says loudly. She doesn't seem to know how serious this is. She still behaves like a village girl, having a row with someone just to kill boredom. The girls and young men back in her village enjoyed this game and called it "word battle." "But you'll have to drive me home in one of your big Benzes."

"Sure. A big Mercedes-Benz," the man says, giving the crowd a grimacing smile, meaning they should pay her no heed because, unlike her, they are sane.

"That's right," Little Plum says.

"How about a Rolls-Royce?" a man in the crowd asks, making a clownish expression at the audience.

"No, anything cheaper than a Benz won't do," Little Plum says.

The crowd roars with laughter.

"Rolls-Royce is much more expensive, dummy!" another man yells.

"And your boss will write me a letter, saying how sorry he is to have wronged me," Little Plum says.

"Okay," the undercover policeman responds.

"What if his boss is illiterate?" a woman asks.

People laugh again. It is the kind of situation in which people become easily amused and find inspiration for laughter at every turn.

Are they going to torture her? Is she sensible enough to own up to everything they want from her and spare herself from beatings and God-knows-what else? Dan regrets that he has dragged her into this. She used to have such a simple and clean life. And she was so happy. Her life lacks nothing as long as she doesn't know how many experiences a life *can* contain.

"Hey, if your boss doesn't write me a letter, he must treat me to a nice restaurant. He will give me a shock-soothing banquet. Even bandits give that kind of banquet if they have wronged someone," Little Plum says.

"No such thing in Beijing," someone says.

Dan elbows his way forward, trying to stop the undercover policeman before they reach a car hidden behind a half-collapsed makeshift shop. With its windshield glistening in the shade, the car looks sinister.

"Hey, where have you been?" Dan asks, leaping forward, grabbing Little Plum's shoulder. "I was looking all over for you!"

Little Plum looks at him as if he is just one of the audience.

"Watch your hand!" she says. He reads her eyes. They say: "What the hell did you show up here for?"

"Let's go home." Dan pulls her gently toward him.

"Who are you?" she says. What she really says is: "Don't you see I've been playing decoy to cover for you, and I've been doing a great job of it? And now you've ruined my efforts." She isn't a naughty word battler anymore. She is a little mother tiger, protecting her cubs regardless of her own unpredictable situation.

"C'mon." Dan doesn't let go of her. He wants her to read him, too: "I won't let you go with him."

The undercover policeman stands between them, his face, expressionless now, turning left and right, the way one watches a Ping-Pong tournament.

"Are you a relative of hers?" the police spy asks.

"I am her husband," Dan says.

"She doesn't think so," the police spy says.

"That's because she's angry with me. We had a fight at home."

People quiet down, their riveted faces also turning left and right like Ping-Pong fans.

"Did you have a fight?" he asks Little Plum.

"None of your business," Little Plum says.

The undercover policeman thinks the situation over.

"What's her name?" he asks Dan.

"Little Plum Chen."

The police spy looks at Little Plum. "Well, she had a different name ten minutes ago."

"I can have as many names as I please," she says. "And I only fool fools!"

People laugh, and the comedy resumes. Every day these people look for somebody to make fun of, and if they can't find an object, they make do with dirty jokes about the Party leaders or the police.

"Any identification you have with you?" the undercover policeman asks. He gives the people a dark look, trying to dispel their comical mood.

Dan pulls out his card, and the police spy snatches it from him.

"A freelance journalist?"

"That's right."

He stares at the card.

"A freelance journalist," he repeats.

"It means I am . . ."

"I know what it means," he snaps. "Would you mind coming with me? Both of you?"

"What did we do?" Dan protests.

"You know very well what you did," the police spy says. One hasn't experienced genuine intimidation until he has seen this police spy's face.

"It's not against the law for a couple to fight, is it?" Dan says.

The undercover policeman smiles—he is doing them a great favor not unmasking them in public.

"You can't just round up somebody from the street for no reason," Dan says, his face turning to the crowd.

"The reason is what we are going to find out," the police spy says.

"They don't like comrade journalists!" someone in the crowd says. "That's the reason."

"Who said that?" the police spy roars. "Show your face!"

The crowd winces a little.

As Dan and Little Plum sit in the back of the police car on the way to the police station, Dan's cell phone rings. It is Ocean Chen, yelling and panting, saying that something terrible has happened in his house. Before Dan has time to say anything, the undercover policeman says he is not allowed to answer the phone. Dan repeats it to the artist.

"Who is that?" Ocean Chen asks. "Give the phone to him."

"Ocean Chen wants to talk to you," Dan says, handing the cell phone to the undercover policeman in the driver's seat.

"Hang up."

He is loud enough for the other end to hear.

"Who is that?" the old artist yells.

"A police officer," Dan says.

The police spy snatches the phone away from Dan.

"You can't talk to him!" barks the policeman at Ocean Chen.

"How dare you be so rude! Do you know who I——" the old artist says. Dan can hear his shriek.

The police spy turns the cell phone off and slips it into his pocket.

"Don't be a fool. Once you are in this car, consider yourself halfway inside *there,*" he says. "There" is a code word for jail, like "gone" for death, "convenience" for excreting.

When he talks, Little Plum peeps at the undercover policeman's face in the rearview mirror. Whenever Dan shows up from backstage, taking over the lead role, she steps aside, resuming her usual detachment, watching things develop. She looks at Dan, full of admiration, as he puffs dry, defiant chuckles through his nostrils. Dan sighs and chuckles, to show the police spy how he marvels at the absurdity of the whole thing.

The district police station is inside the Second Ring Road. Even with the siren on, it takes them an hour to cut through the mad traffic. On the way to the interrogation room, Dan asks if Mr. Policeman can make a call for him to Ocean Chen, the artist. No, definitely not. The artist is old and ill and all by himself at the moment; he might have called from the emergency room. Please? No, he will not let him call, and he will not make the call for him. Please? No. Is it so hard to understand a police officer's "NO"?

A uniformed officer walks hurriedly past them, reading a document.

"Hey, do you know of an Ocean Chen, by any chance?" the undercover policeman asks.

The uniformed officer looks up.

"Oh, Officer Lu." The uniformed officer greets the plainclothes officer.

"He is a painter," the plainclothes officer says, turning to Dan, "isn't he?"

"He is," Dan answers. "Also makes sculptures."

"You're not talking about *Master* Chen, are you?" the uniformed officer asks.

"That's him," Dan says. He is excited, his eyes darting between the two officers. He loathes himself for being so pathetically hopeful. But he can't help it. "He calls me his landsman!"

The undercover policeman, whom they now know as Officer Lu, glances at Dan, meaning for him to calm down. What's the big deal? It's just some guy who makes useless things like art.

After escorting Dan into one room at the middle of a corridor and Little Plum into another at the end of the corridor, Officer Lu orders the doors locked. He doesn't say whether he will make a phone call to Ocean Chen or not, but Dan figures he will, if only to satisfy his curiosity.

The daylight fades away and footsteps are heard running down the stairs, along with jokes and laughter. The police officers are getting off work. It has been at least three hours that Dan and Little Plum have been locked up here. Several times, Dan walks to the door with a strong desire to plead: Please check and see if my wife wants to use the bathroom or if she is thirsty.

Once in a while there are footsteps passing in the corridor. They tap along the granite floor, echoing hauntingly as if in a movie. Dan holds his breath and listens until the echo dies gradually. A flash of fear runs across him: he has already learned to distinguish footsteps. This is how it must feel to be an inmate, to learn footsteps, nasty ones or friendly ones, coming with an order to pluck someone out for interrogation or for a secret transfer. Or to an underground execution site. Footsteps approaching with food or water, with insults or comfort, with letters from wives or parents. He is scared by his instantly acquired knowledge of the footsteps—he can already tell if they concern him or not. At a quarter past ten at night, he hears footsteps again. They climb the stairs with a steady, stately rhythm. They advance with sensational echoes, ringing through the hollow building as in a dream. Dan knows these black-leathered, rubber-soled footsteps of an officer's boots are coming with a decision for him and Little Plum.

The door opens. Officer Lu, in full uniform, comes in with two pages of paper.

"Did you call Ocean Chen?" Dan asks.

"What?" Officer Lu seems not to remember why he has been gone so long.

"You called Ocean Chen, didn't you?" Dan asks.

"Oh that. No."

"You didn't call?"

"Sign here and we can all go home." Officer Lu puts the paper on the table.

Hiding his surprise, Dan goes to the desk lazily and picks up the pen. He sweeps the simple form in a quick glance. It is a form for personal property, saying that you have checked every item that was taken from you and they have all been returned to you. Dan signs his name.

He feels strangely depressed at seeing Little Plum, her head bowed and her shoulders droopy, as if all her energy burned out during those silent hours, walk toward him along the long, sterilized corridor. The light is so white it is slightly purple. Little Plum smiles at him, and her smile, her face and skin are bleached by the light. Her life doesn't have to contain an experience like this.

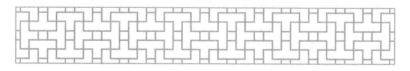

OCEAN CHEN TELLS DAN that he doesn't trust his secretary anymore. He wants Dan to go over to his country house to supervise the outbound shipment of some of his new works. He wants them shipped to a cottage that was his friend's love nest before the friend emigrated. Ocean Chen has found that his wastebaskets have been scavenged and some crumpled paper with his casual sketches stolen. So he wants Dan to do him a favor by helping him ship the new paintings.

They will ship them at midnight. This has to take place secretly. Dan will watch over all the garbage cans and wastebaskets and ferret out the scavengers hidden among the workers.

Ocean Chen greets him by the road leading to his country villa. He is wearing a red baseball cap and a white smock smeared here and there with watercolors and colored ink. He has been waiting for Dan ever since he sent his car to pick Dan up. He laughs, slapping Dan's back and shoulder with his color-stained hands. His happiness is so contagious that Dan feels his own worries subsiding as he strolls beside him toward the house.

"Sorry that police officer was rude to you yesterday," Dan says.

"What police officer?"

"The one you talked to yesterday."

"I did?" he asks.

"He yelled and hung up on you," Dan says.

"Did I yell back at him?" The master is incredulous.

The artist has no recollection of the brief phone conversation in the police car. He had been too wrapped up in his own misgivings to register Officer Lu's insulting behavior toward him. This is why he usually appears forgiving and big-hearted.

"Master Chen, did you receive a call from a district police station last night?" Dan asks.

"No," he answers.

"Are you sure?"

He stares at Dan as they walk along the road, and his eyes gradually intensify. He becomes frightened.

"What did they want from me? The police?"

"So you did get a call last night."

"Did they want to interrogate me over the phone?"

"Did they?" Dan asks. He wants to rule out all possibilities and find the real reason that he and Little Plum were released. If the police called the artist, that would explain everything.

"Just go ahead and try!" he yells, poking his finger at the autumn afternoon. "How dare you!"

Dan looks at him.

"What the hell do you want from me? You miserable cops in synthetic uniforms? My lawyer won't let you overstep your authority."

Dan realizes the master has been obsessed with his own matters. He figures that Officer Lu didn't call last night. But where did he go while leaving them in the interrogation rooms for hours? Dan is distraught because he can't see where he stands in this invisible wrestling match with the police.

"What's the matter?" The artist is irked by the silence.

"Nothing."

"Tell me."

"Oh, it was just my wife, who got into a fight with an undercover police officer. That's all," Dan says, preparing for the master's further inquiry. "My wife sometimes . . ."

"I wonder why it is," the master says, cutting him off. "They all seem nice and honest when they first come. Then the thefts and betrayals begin right under your nose." The old man has gone back to his own thoughts. He wasn't really listening when Dan answered his question. He is the kind of artist who stops listening as soon as he finds out that the matter doesn't concern him. The old man stops short in the middle of the roughly paved road, disrupting his own remarks with a song. An old love song from his student days. Then he cuts off his singing with a speech that seems connected with the previous one.

"Can't work without women. Just can't. They are an inspiration when they are fresh. Then they all become the same type. Don't know why they are so original and different in the beginning, then end up being all the same. Oh God, they are such bores in the end! I can deal with anything but boring creatures."

Dan now sees the reason that Mrs. Chen Number Three hated him so much that she betrayed him.

"Yes, Ruby was my muse in the beginning."

Dan feels goose bumps popping up on his forearms, spreading over his shoulders and the nape of his neck, moving down his back and ending around his butt. Although the words "inspiration" and "muse" are no longer strange vocabulary to him, they have an odd effect on him; they actually embarrass him. Why can't these artistic guys face the naked needs of men? Why do they fool themselves with words like "inspiration"?

Once Dan is seated in a rustic chair in the enormous living room, Master Chen presents him with a box of sweets, an exotic dessert from the Middle East sent by a collector in Paris. Before Dan has had time to try them, Ocean Chen comes back from the kitchen with a plate of venison jerky. It is gift from one of his students. Then he gets a bunch of paintings from behind a big cabinet and lays them out on the floor one by one. He hushes Dan while tiptoeing over to close the door.

"Come here! Take a look at my latest works. See if you can find anything new." As Dan calculates the time he needs to stand before each painting, and prepares himself for deep speechlessness, the Master says: "Aren't they tasty? Made of Middle-Eastern honey and dates. I saved them from myself just for you!" he says, tugging at Dan's arm that holds a piece of the flaky dessert.

"Why don't you try the venison jerky? It's heavenly!" he says.

With his mouth full, Dan can only nod and gesture, meaning he will do one thing at a time. But the artist goes to pick up a piece of jerky, comes back, and thrusts it into Dan's hand.

"You see any changes in them? The colors and the way I handle the brushes?" the old man asks.

Dan nods.

"See that? What a departure from my old works! See there? It starts from a single stringed melody and ends in a storm of music with only rhythm—no melody anymore. Anti-melody. It becomes a motion of colors, churning melody and rhythm all into a rich, pure harmony, almost silent . . ."

He pauses, panting. Dan looks up from the paintings and sees that the old man is pale and frail, staring at his own creation incredulously. It is scary, it really is, Dan thinks.

"They did me a great favor by leaving me alone. Their evil helps me discover the motions of my brush that I have meant to find for so long. They can send me to jail, or plunder my wealth, but I've found what I set out to find. I'll die happy."

"You won't die . . ."

He points to a brownish-red patch of color on one of the paintings and smiles: "Bet you can never guess where that color came from. Never seen a color this rich and with so many depths, have you? I hadn't either until last week. It is the color of fermented red tea. The inspiration struck me like lightning when I accidentally dipped my brush into a teacup that had started reeking."

Dan nods, thinking of the soy sauce company that makes tasty soy sauce with human hair from surgical wards.

"Do you like the jerky? I didn't eat anything but this for days when I worked. Because I hate to see those faces around this house. Faces of conspirators. Do you like the jerky?" he asks again.

Dan says he likes it. He tears at it and chews with relish. He doesn't have the heart to tell Ocean Chen the meat has been kept too long and some pieces already have green shadows of mildew.

"Has Miss Ruby come back?"

"Her mother is very sick," the old man says. Then he smiles. "I know why she doesn't want to come back now."

Dan keeps quiet.

"She wants to wait and see. If I come out of my legal troubles intact, her mother will get well, and she will come back to me. If it goes the other way, she will say, sorry, my mother is too sick and I have to stay by her until she dies or recovers. Or she will say, hey, it is not my fault I left you; I didn't know you had evaded taxes. She doesn't really care if I did anything wrong or not; she only cares if I get caught, and how much it will cost me.

"I enjoy being alone, though," he says, shrugging. He has the smile of a very lonely person.

They begin packing the new paintings after the household staff has gone to bed and turned off the lights. Each time Dan fails to keep the paper from rattling, or bangs on furniture while moving things, or doesn't speak softly enough, Master Chen crosses his lips with his index finger, making a fierce "shhhh!" When Dan gestures to argue that all the people are fast asleep, the old artist squeezes his eyes shut, erecting his two fingers above his ears, meaning they are sleeping with their ears pricked up like antennae. It is two in the morning by the time they finish loading the car. They set out and turn onto an unlit country road, bound for the cottage of Ocean Chen's old friend.

The dawn is looming as they enter a hilly resort area. It takes them almost another hour to find the cottage among a scattering of country houses. By the time they arrive at the cottage and Dan unloads the car, the roosters in the villages are crowing. In a much improved mood, the master goes into the cottage's kitchen looking for something to eat. He comes out covered with dust, holding a dusty shape in his hand.

"There's a smoked duck in the kitchen!" he exclaims, happy as a child. "I am sure I can find some liquor here somewhere."

"Ruby said you can't drink," Dan says.

"Bullshit. Is it a duck? Looks like it. Wash it, will you? Hope it's not too rancid. It was hung from the ceiling, so the rats couldn't get at it."

Dan sets down the paintings he has been putting away in a closet and goes to clean the creature that looks like a duck. The old man watches him brush off the dust and wash it in the sink. He follows him like a child, asking him if the meat is too dry and how long it would take to cook it. Dan lets most of his questions drop.

At eight o'clock in the morning, the master says he wants to go back to his villa. Light-headed from lack of sleep, Dan drives, with the old man dozing off in the backseat. At the entrance of Ocean Chen's villa, the master's driver glares at Dan as he half-carries the old man out of the car. The secretary comes out to greet them, guessing rapidly where the two of them went during the night.

Ocean Chen goes directly to bed. Dan can't sleep, despite his fatigue. He goes to the kitchen, aching for a nice cup of hot tea. The secretary follows him, as if needing someone for a chat. When Dan asks if there is anything he can help with, the secretary chuckles and says no, he doesn't need Dan's help. Then why is he following him everywhere? Well, he has to. Joking, Dan asks if the secretary thinks he will steal MSG or sausage from the kitchen. Well, it's not just Dan that he follows; he has to watch every visitor the master receives, so please, no hard feelings. Every visitor? Yes; no exceptions. Nothing personal, he is just doing his job. Dan thought his job was answering phones and filing paper. That's right, but he's been assigned another one on the side. By whom? Well . . . Miss Ruby doesn't trust anyone but the people who have worked here for years. Did Miss Ruby tell him that? That's exactly what she said. So here he is, carrying out Miss Ruby's orders. Sorry if Dan feels offended.

Dan stares at the teakettle that has blown its whistle. He lets it blow, thinking Ruby must have gotten both Dan and the household staff to play this spy game against each another. What a tricky woman, with her beautiful skin charted by faint blue veins through which flows such cold blood.

The old man wakes up after lunch and calls Dan to his studio. He locks the door behind them and looks scared. He points at an empty wastebasket he is holding.

"Look, they are all gone. All the sketches."

"I thought they were just blank sheets with some ink strokes and lines."

"My paintings are nothing but lines and strokes."

His fear is increasing. His not-so-clear eyeballs appear totally round, not at all eclipsed by his thick eyelids.

Dan feels sorry for him. The old man is having a severe attack of paranoia.

"That's what happens every day here, in my own house, dealing with thefts and guarding against them. In these silent battles both sides have become sneakier. But they always get sneakier faster than I do."

Helplessly he looks at Dan. He is leaving himself at Dan's mercy.

He waits for Dan to come up with some idea, any idea will do. Dan wants to tell him not to trust anyone like this. It's not right to give his entire trust to anyone, and it is wrong to withdraw his trust altogether. But he figures this concept is too complicated for this sixty-five-year-old child.

"Just imagine, they tiptoe around me every time I sleep," the old man says. "I checked the baskets in the other rooms. All empty. They stole them. They unfold them and patch up the torn parts. They steal my seals and authenticate them. Then they will sell them to the galleries after I die."

Dan says it's possible they just dumped them as trash into the public trash barrels.

"Then go check the big trash barrels on the street," Master Chen says. "The trash gets picked up only twice a week. Go to the street corner, and you will see a pair of big, blue barrels. Go through the trash carefully."

The big trash barrels are all empty. Maybe the trash company came one day early. But the old artist doesn't think so.

"They must have stored them away. They will sell them later. Only by looking at the brushstrokes, people know they are my drawings. They will be willing to pay a high price for them after I die. They are looking forward to my death."

The old man isn't easy to be around. Sometimes he drives the people around him nuts. He makes Dan want to kill him right now, even though he knows that, in Ocean Chen's heart, the old man is a child whom anyone can hurt.

The whole evening Ocean Chen paces the floor of his studio and stops short once in a while, shivering with fear. "You'll see who, after my death, will study my trash and try to decipher my brush movements.

They will try to see how many failed strokes happened before a complete picture emerged. They'll try to discover how my pictures were conceived and miscarried, and how many abortions occurred before the birth of a real work of art. I hate that. I really do. I only want my paintings to be seen in their final form, mature and whole."

It dawns on Dan that it could also be Ruby's trick. She's been playing with the old man's paranoia. She must have conveyed her suspicions about the household staff to the old man, while telling the staff not to trust any visitor, so she got everybody to work for her by watching everybody else, to guarantee that no paintings would go out of this house in her absence. That sweet, dimpled face is a facade hiding a secret police headquarters.

The third day, Dan walks outside and calls Little Plum on his cell phone, telling her he will stay another week with the old artist. She says a beautiful woman came to see him yesterday. Is her name Old Ten? No, her name is Happy. Dan is relieved but amazed. In Little Plum's eyes Happy is beautiful. She appreciates Happy the same way she does all the brutally modern things, from multilevel highway interchanges to vast automobile dealerships, from the immense shopping clubs to McDonald's.

He calls Happy's cell, then hangs it up with a jerk. How did Happy find his residence? He never told her where he lived. He dials her number again, trying to think of ways to beat around the bush and find out how she got his address.

"Hey, don't try to beat around the bush. If you want to know how I got your address, just ask me," Happy says.

". . . How?"

"You thought it was hard to find it while you were trying to hide it from me all this time?" she says. He can see one of her cheeks go

206

up. Her sneer is economical, using only one corner of her mouth that pushes up one cheek.

She tells him it wasn't hard to find out where he lives. The registration number on his ID card indicates the district he resides in. All she needed to do was to locate the registration office in his district and find his address.

If she can do it, then so can the police, Dan thinks.

"You want to ask me how I got hold of your ID card?" Happy says.

"How?" He knows he sounds extremely stupid.

"I just asked one of the receptionists at a banquet," Happy says. "The system is a network nowadays. Every existence is digitized."

Dan feels distressed at getting educated about this network. It must have worked like crazy the night that Little Plum and he were detained at the district police station.

"I don't give a damn where you live," she says. "I looked for you because you will work with me on a new subject."

"I will?"

"You'll like it."

"Okay." Why did the network miss the real information and let them go?

"Aren't you going to ask me what the new project is?"

"What is it?"

Happy turns her voice low and dry. Prostitution in China. It is a taboo topic to the government. Let the two of them blast it open. According to her sources, the owners of some of the most expensive nightclubs are the children of high officials. She has been working on it for some time, visiting hair salons, massage clubs, nightclubs, and hostess bars. But she has the disadvantage of being a woman. That is where Dan, as a handsome man, comes in handy. Does she mean she wants him to pose as one of the clients? Well, for a great piece of writing that has great value to society and humanity, one has to make sacrifices. Besides, it might not be such a sacrifice for a *man*! Happy laughs like a truck driver who whores regularly in tawdry little salons along country highways.

He hears a noise on Happy's end.

"What are you doing?" he asks.

"What do you think I am doing? I rolled over laughing and knocked over a thermos coffee cup," Happy says.

Dan can hear her moving her coffee table and sweeping up the shards of the broken insulated cup. He hopes she isn't in her night-gown and barefoot, or she might get hurt by the tiny glass splinters.

"You really think you can get lucky, don't you?" she says. "We probably only have enough money for little necking and kissing. Or a little fondling."

He hears her sighing. He can see her sinking back down onto the sofa, sprawling her long limbs and skinny body for maximum com-fort.

"Are you in or are you out?" Happy asks.

Is she going to pay him to do this?

"I know you're thinking about money. I will put up some. Sixty percent," she says, waiting. "All right, seventy percent. You pick up the rest." She listens to the silence on Dan's end and says, "If you don't want to do it, I can find another partner."

He needs to think about it. What's to think about? she demands. All he needs to do is get acquainted with the girls. He can do that without even getting sexy about it, if he doesn't want to. He will get the girls to trust him and pour out their hearts, then pay them for their time. If there is no physical contact, their fee is significantly lower. They might even waive their fees altogether, if they fall in love with him like the little fool at the foot massage club. Grip their affection and win their trust, which he is good at, and everything will flow from there.

"You can start with the story of the little foot massager. She told you about her sister, didn't she? We may use the story of her execution as a centerpiece and structure the other girls' stories around it. What do you think?"

"Okay."

"You've been in touch with her since she disappeared, haven't you?"

"Since she *what?!*"

"Come on."

"She disappeared?"

"Into your protection . . ."

"I swear by Chairman Mao, I didn't know . . ."

"I went there yesterday, and they said she had left."

"Did she leave anything . . ."

"Nothing but a jar of pickled cabbage."

Old Ten had told Dan she made the best pickled vegetables. She promised to make him some.

"I thought you must have known where she went," Happy says.

After finishing the phone call, he goes back inside and tells Ocean Chen he has to leave. He has an important interview to complete. The artist is at a loss, like a child abandoned on the street.

At one o'clock in the morning, Dan comes out of a foot massage club, exhausted. He has combed through almost all the massage clubs in Beijing since he left Master Chen's country house. Maybe he shouldn't have stopped visiting Old Ten altogether after their dinner at that Sichuan restaurant, at least not so abruptly. Is she disappointed by Dan's true identity that he volunteered to her? She might have taken Dan's self-revelation as a refusal to help.

Now he is on an elevated crosswalk over a broad avenue, looking at the city relinquished by crowds of respectable professionals to throngs of beggars and drifters. She disappeared with all the debts he owed her. All around him is a galaxy of lights and neon, throbbing and pulsating, swallowing up a girl called Old Ten.

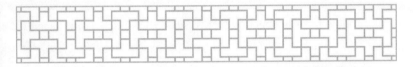

AN ARTICLE APPEARS in *Shopping Guide Weekly,* a popular Beijing magazine with several million subscribers. The current issue features a model home of President Wu's real estate development. With computer magic, it belies the flaws and crudeness of the construction. The headline reads: "The Builder Who Builds for the Working Class."

"Take a look," Happy says, pointing at some sentences she has highlighted. "Do they sound familiar to you? Only now they are even more disgusting."

Dan is shocked. The "author" stole 70 percent of Dan's manuscript and reconstructed it into the publication. Although it wasn't Dan's creation entirely, he spent two nights taking sentences and paragraphs out of hundreds of sales flyers, and another two nights piecing them together.

"Do you still have your original draft?" she asks.

"I think so," Dan says.

"Let's go confront the bastard."

After following her for a little while, he stops. He has never felt so bad. But he is actually more disturbed by the fact that he could have been the swindler writer who helped President Wu trap people into buying the buildings with cracked walls and gaps in the floors, with land-lease deeds attached to a lawsuit. He himself could have been the trap-maker. He could have been the one to put the disguise of a great saint on a criminal who owes his construction workers two years' back wages.

"I don't want to go," he says.

"What about the apartment he promised you? You could use a nice little apartment for a change. You are living in a shithole as far as I can tell. Let's demand that he keep his word."

"I don't want to see him."

"Why not?"

"Don't know."

"Look, Dan. I will do the talking. I will shut him up and make him pay. You just stand aside and enjoy the show." She goes to her car and opens the door for him. "I know what will hurt him most."

First she takes Dan to a department store. She goes to the men's clothing section and picks out a leather jacket and a pair of Esprit blue jeans. Hanging the garments over his shoulders, she pushes him into one of the fitting rooms.

"What are you doing?" Dan tries to fight her.

"Try them on."

"Why?"

"Don't tear off the designer labels on the sleeve, okay? He can read nothing but the famous designer labels on clothes. He goes around doing nothing but impressing others. We will impress him today."

They talk with a door between them. Before he has buckled his belt, she yanks the door open and drags him out. Walking around him, giving a tug here and a pull there, she examines him seriously, her dark red lips pressing tightly together.

"Boy, do you look important," she says.

When they get into the car again, he starts to sweat. She lets him drive while she is busy making phone calls.

"I can't let you buy me things," he says.

"You can buy me something, too, if you want to."

"Can we return them?"

"Oh, shut up and enjoy it."

"But . . ."

"Hello," she says to her cell. "It's me. Do you know the chief editor of *Shopping Guide Weekly*? Good. Give me his number . . . I'm writing it down now. What's his name? . . . Lee? I don't need his first name."

She hangs up and dials the other number. "Chief Editor Lee?" she says in a perky voice. "How have you been since last time I saw you? Remember? In the function held by . . . the textile exporters? . . . Don't you recognize my voice? It's Happy Gao! You asked me to write for your paper at the function and you forgot all about it!" She pouts, giving the receiver a coquettish, naughty smile.

"The thing is, I found out that a major article in your real estate section is a huge lie. You guys have been cheated by the developer, President Wu. He deserves twenty years in jail, and even that would be a very lenient sentence for what he has done. He is a criminal. And you made him a hero overnight. I know someone who has investigated him thoroughly."

"I didn't investigate thoroughly . . . ," Dan says.

She puts her finger across her lips.

"You are? Where are you having lunch then?" she asks. "Oh, okay. I can wait for you in your office. Take your time; I will keep myself entertained." Before she hangs up, she starts yelling at Dan. "Hey, next time I'm intimidating people, don't talk to me, okay?"

"They'll find out it's not true."

"True or not, it makes no difference to the bastards."

They arrive at the formidable building of *Shopping Guide Weekly* at a quarter to one in the afternoon. The receptionist tells them the editor in chief went to a restaurant at President Wu's invitation. Which restaurant? It is called March, April, May, very well known for its high prices. When did the editor in chief leave? About half an hour ago.

Happy's chin gives a little whip, meaning that Dan should follow her. Outside the office, she says she has a brilliant new idea. She will go to the restaurant alone while Dan organizes the construction workers. If he can't gather them all, a few representatives will do. Just tell the workers their boss is hiring new workers and it is their last chance to get their wages. She will pretend to interview President Wu at the lunch table, waiting for Dan to get the workers ready outside the restaurant. It's going to be a fine little demonstration for Chief Editor Lee and President Wu to enjoy after an expensive meal.

Happy waltzes with excitement along the corridor to the elevator.

As soon as Dan gets out of the taxi, he hears music. It comes from a loudspeaker hung on a telephone pole by the construction site. The folk music sounds gay and festive. The elevator is not in operation, so Dan hikes up the twenty-eight floors. Fortunately, every floor is so low that it only requires twelve steps; President Wu designed the ceilings to be lower than the legal height, so the working class will be under low ceilings, feeling like giants shouldering the sky, a metaphor for

213

his own social class that Dan once learned. Following the jovial noises, he finds a group of workers playing a simple gambling game on their bunks. An aroma of stewing lamb wafts out of the doorless kitchen.

"Who are you looking for?" one worker asks.

Dan recognizes him as the leader of the workers. "Hello!" Dan says.

"There you are!" the leader gets up, all smiles. "Mr. Journalist."

"How are you?" Dan asks. The new leather jacket makes him very self-conscious.

"Hanging in there." The leader digs in his pocket for cigarettes.

Dan makes a gesture that he doesn't smoke.

"I see you have nice food now." Dan sniffs, smiling.

"Well, the boss sent a truckload of lamb the day before yesterday and also some money."

"He paid you?"

"Not in full. It is two months' worth of wages. But he will pay the rest as soon as we complete the buildings."

The boss sent his apologies with the lamb and the two months' wages, begging their forgiveness. His failure to pay them on time was caused by his financial misfortune: the bank had canceled his loan. He was heartbroken to know that the workers had no money to send home to their old mothers, wives, and young children. He promised he would work his way out of his financial difficulty if they would pardon him and give him a little more time. Without their pardon, he might have to declare bankruptcy, which would mean he would never be able to pay them. The only salvation for the workers is to finish the projects, so he can pay them with the money he will get from selling the buildings. By evening, there will be a banquet of sweet potato wine and stewed lamb to signify solidarity between employer and employees.

"Do you believe him?" Dan asks.

"We have to," the leader says.

Dan pulls out *Shopping Guide Weekly* from his pocket and hands it to the leader. The leader reads it slowly.

"He sounds like the richest man in the world, doesn't he? He is talking about building ten projects in Beijing for low-income people," Dan says. "He has invited the editor in chief of this newspaper to lunch right now. The lunch alone costs two years' worth of your wages."

The workers playing the gambling game start asking one another what is going on. Dan passes the newspaper to them.

"What do you think we should do then?" the leader asks.

"If you guys want to, I will take you to the restaurant," Dan says. "You can ask him which is true: the newspaper or what he told you."

"You mean all of us go there?" a worker says.

"Sounds like a riot. The police will throw us in jail if we do that."

Some workers from other living quarters have come. They fill up the windows and doors.

"If the demonstrators are fewer than twenty, the police won't care," Dan says. "You can choose twenty representatives to go."

"I don't want to be a representative," a middle-aged worker says, stepping back.

"Who wants to be a representative?" the leader asks them.

No one answers.

"Don't look at me, I am not a representative!" a young worker says.

"If we go there, the boss will get mad and never pay us," an old worker says.

"What if he decides not to pay us because he thinks we are the ones breaching the agreement?"

215

"Hire a lawyer and take him to court," Dan says.

"How much does it take to hire a lawyer?"

"Plenty," one of the workers says. "A relative of mine went broke because of a lawsuit."

"Count me out if you guys go to lawyers. I don't even have money for my children's school fees!"

"Let somebody else take the boss to court. I'll save my money for the train fare home."

"If we don't offend the boss, we have a chance to get our money back, right?" the leader asks Dan.

"I don't think so," Dan says.

"No matter what, we won't get our money back?"

"Not if you don't fight."

"We don't want to fight."

"Why not? It is *your* money you're fighting for, dammit!" Dan says. He doesn't understand why he has become so angry all of a sudden.

"If anything happens, are you going to take responsibility for it?" the leader says.

"What will happen?" Dan glares at him.

"Who knows," the leader says. "Anything can happen. If the boss is pissed off by the demonstration, he'll go ahead and hire new workers. If that happens, are you going to take the responsibility?"

"Why should *I* take responsibility?" Dan asks, pointing at himself. "It's *your* ass I'm trying to save! Why should *I* be responsible?"

"Hey, what do you get out of it if we riot against our boss?" one of the workers demands. Then he yells at his workmates, "Why does this stranger come to help us if he sees no interest in this?"

"See what he's wearing: leather and wool!" A worker makes a point to rub Dan's leather jacket with his callused fingers.

"Hey, take your fucking hand off me!" Dan pulls away, disgusted. "You pathetic things, you're only worth a pot of stewed lamb! You know what? I think you should let him go on, sucking out all your sweat and blood and bone marrow until you're nothing but human husks!"

Someone pushes him. He lurches forward, his hands clawing at the air, tripping over a foot. Laughter ensues.

As Dan sits in the taxi, he tries to recall how he got out of the building that smelled gamy with stewed lamb. He was so angry at the workers that he almost fell and rolled down the rail-less stairs. He remembers the leader calling to him after he reached the yard. The man yelled that he was sorry; he knew that what Dan had done was out of goodwill. His helmeted head leaning out of a window, the leader shouted thanks to Dan's furious back; he said he was grateful that Dan had come here trying to help.

Dan dials Happy's number with a shaking finger. Trying to control his irritated voice, he tells her what happened in a couple of dry sentences.

"So you got thrown out," Happy says in a subdued voice.

"I didn't . . ."

"What's the difference? Haven't I told you that peasants are the very root of corruption in China?"

"Cut it out," Dan says.

"Listen, I can't talk to you now. I ended up interviewing the bastard over lunch. I've got to go back to the private dining room. When you get to the restaurant, come right on in. You might enjoy the last of the main courses."

Then she tells him the name of the private dining room in the restaurant. It's called the "Peony Pavilion."

Ten minutes later at the restaurant, Dan is led to the Peony

Pavilion. President Wu, without breaking his eloquent lecture, looks up and waves at Dan, as a forgiving host would greet a tardy guest. Editor in Chief Lee becomes tense at seeing Dan's darkened face.

"It is my goal to keep housing prices below three thousand yuan per square meter. You are not a real builder if you only build for those who have a monthly salary of ten thousand."

"You've said that already, Mr. President," Happy remarks.

"Have I?"

"You've said it three times, in fact."

President Wu laughs. "Good lines are supposed to be repeated many times, right?"

"What gets repeated most are lies," Happy says, challenging him.

President Wu lets it drop. He turns to Dan, as if just catching his breath to give Dan an official acknowledgment. "Hey, old friend, come and sit by me! Waitress! Where is a mao-tai glass for this gentleman? Bring the menu to me, will you? I'll order some more dishes."

Happy kicks Dan's feet under the table. It is time for Dan to attack. He looks at President Wu, who seems honestly happy to see him, pouring him a glass of mao-tai and loading his plate with a pile of food from every dish.

"You're looking good, old buddy," President Wu says. He lifts his own glass and toasts Dan, downing all the liquor in it in one gulp. He shows the bottom of his glass to Dan, all smiles.

Dan finds himself smiling at President Wu without wanting to. Then he sees the big jade ring. He tries not to stare at it, but he can't help it. He can't help but picture the fleshy finger, bearing a phlegm-colored jade ring, toying with the pink lips of a girl who could have been Old Ten's sister. He fantasizes the image with increasing rage.

"Did Miss Wang show you my present to you?" President Wu asks.

Dan wakes up from his daydream.

"I told her to show you the present I had promised you," he says. A smile of complicity comes to his thick-cheeked, full-jawed face.

Does that mean he is going to give him an apartment after all? Compared with Dan's building-top encampment, an apartment is a palace, in spite of all those cracked walls that need patching. But can he trust President Wu? Of course not. How many times has he made promises to his workers? With that kind of sincerity, he could have promised you a perfect world called communism.

"A present? How nice!" Happy says, glaring at Dan. "Congratulations." So you already received the apartment without telling me? she thinks. No wonder you didn't want to confront him.

He turns his face away, giving her only a third of his profile. She kicks him again under the table. His jaw twitches, so that she sees it really hurts.

"May I know what that present is?" she asks President Wu with a charming but unfriendly smile.

"That's between him and me," President Wu says.

"Dan and I have no secrets between us," Happy says, turning to Dan. "Am I right, Dan?"

Editor Lee is fidgeting visibly. He glances at his watch.

"Sorry." Lee stands up, pushing his chair back. "I have a meeting at three."

"No, you don't!" Happy says, giving him a smile. "I checked your schedule for this afternoon on your receptionist's desk. Are you running away from me?"

As if to rescue the editor, President Wu stands up and stretches out his hand. "Don't let us keep you."

Happy jumps to her feet and drains the remaining liquor in her glass. "Enjoy your secret present, Dan."

As she calls to the waitress for her trench coat, Dan tells her to wait; he is leaving with her.

"Thank you for your present, President Wu, but I can't accept it," he says, blinking his eyes at the plate in front of him, as if anticipating a blow. He loathes himself for this fear. He tries to stand up forcefully but slumps back into the seat, having miscalculated the space between his seat and the table. Awkwardly, he gets up again, his legs squished so far down in the heavy chair that he can't straighten them all the way. "I want nothing from you, absolutely nothing." He tries to say something more impressive, but no words come.

He walks out of the restaurant with Happy. He stops in the doorway, watching Happy say good-bye to Chief Editor Lee, who is getting into his car, a white-gloved chauffeur standing by. The chauffeur puts his hand on the top of the door frame, cushioning it in case the editor's head should bang on it. Happy then turns back to Dan before the car drives away.

"Hey, buddy, I'm proud of you," Happy says.

"Oh, shut up," Dan says.

"I am. You are such an incorruptible person. Not everyone can resist an apartment as a present. That fellow couldn't, even though he has plenty of places to live," she says, thumbing toward the editor in chief's car, now merging into the traffic.

"How do you know?"

"Didn't you see how he looked when you were talking about the present? He looked as if he'd been caught in the act of fucking someone else's wife." She puts her trench coat on his arm and runs to a cigarette stand by the street. "I'm celebrating your virtuous act by breaking my cigarette ban."

When he starts driving, she pushes her seat all the way back and lets it recline. She says she was waiting for Dan to denounce President Wu in front of Chief Editor Lee for defrauding his workers of their wages. That would really have been a spectacle. He was going to. What held him back then? He had structured words and sentences of denunciation before he walked into that private dining room called "Peony Pavilion." But he didn't. He almost did. He almost pointed a finger at the bastard: If you really are so filthy rich, you shouldn't be owing your workers two years' wages. If you have compassion for low-income people who can't afford pricey apartments, then you should first be compassionate toward your workers. Dan doesn't notice he is livid with anger, poking his index finger at the windshield from the steering wheel he is holding. But why did he chicken out in the end? He really was ready to expose him in front of Chief Editor Lee, to show how the bastard kept his workers in misery while posing as a savior of the working class. Dan would have said it, had he not been so disgusted. It's only normal to be disgusted by a bastard like President Wu, isn't it? But he was disgusted at himself as well. Why? she asks. Dan says nothing.

Happy turns on some music and lies down. It is a woman singing a foreign song in a whiny voice.

"Do you like this music?" she asks.

Dan says yes instinctively.

"She is a singer whose talent didn't get discovered until she was thirty. Do you know about her?"

He nods.

"What's her name?" she asks. "Is it Whitney Houston? Oh no,

I think it is . . . it's just on the tip of my tongue. Do you remember her name?"

He thinks for a second and shakes his head.

"Oh, I know. It's Happy Gao!" she laughs, her feet flying up and alighting on the dashboard. "I caught you pretending to understand music!"

"Sounds nice, though," Dan says.

"I could have been a singer. Could have been many things, not that I am good at any of them, but I simply can't keep my focus on anything. I got kicked out of university because I had too many unpopular pastimes: smoking, drinking, dating around, calling professors names, and participating in student demonstrations. They did me a favor throwing me out, though. I was way too far behind in the classes that bored me to tears."

Out the window Dan sees a middle-aged woman handing out a flyer with a picture of a foot printed on it. When did this "foot era" start? He came to realize how much care and fuss and love were lavished on people's feet after he first met Old Ten. Since he stopped seeing her, he's often found himself contemplating signs and flyers with a foot printed on them. He was surprised to notice that just about every other storefront in Beijing is a foot massage parlor.

"Nobody's perfect."

He turns to look at Happy. She points her sharp chin skyward.

"What do I mean? I mean you don't have to be perfect to fight for the truth." Her foot starts kicking at a little glass swan glued on the dashboard. He wishes she wouldn't go into her didactic mode. He wishes she would stop kicking that poor little swan. It makes him nervous. "My dad is the most imperfect person in the world. He's boring, vain, deceptive; a devil in a dysfunctional family. But he is a great man with scholarship, a good fighter when he believes the truth has been distorted."

He really worries that the swan will be smashed at any moment. Why does she buy things in order to destroy them? The first time they met, she destroyed his pack of cigarettes. Lately he has met more and more people who make him nervous. They all have such quirks: Ocean Chen pulls at the bristles of his paintbrushes, President Wu flings matchsticks, Ruby toys with her beaded slipper; they do these unnerving things to calm themselves down. It is hard for him to understand what makes them neurotic, since they have everything: houses to live in, cars to drive, money to spend, people to command, and pigeon tongues and crab claw tips to eat.

Happy sits up and her feet fall from the dashboard. Dan heaves a sigh of relief, knowing that the swan's slaughter has been called off for today. Happy chain-smokes in silence until they arrive at a short pedestrian tunnel under a highway interchange. It is between the Third and the Fourth Ring Roads, and the people on the street are a mixture of farmers and city residents. The scene in the tunnel is vivid and colorful. It is full of stalls with goods for sale: everything from roast chestnuts to barbecued lamb; baked sweet potatoes to socks; dresses, hair decorations, fake Polo perfume, and imitation Louis Vuitton bags.

After they get out of the car, two young women come toward them from deep inside the tunnel. The women walk slowly past the stalls, trying to make eye contact with the men. One of them is wearing a pair of tight blue jeans with golden embroidery on the side. The other has long, straight hair and a round face, looking like a high school student except for her full figure.

"See them?" Happy tugs at Dan. "The lowest type. Foreigners call them streetwalkers. Go strike up a conversation with them."

"You said the story starts with Old Ten's sister," Dan says.

"But you've got to understand all kinds of them. Go buy them stockings and barbecued lamb, and you can own them for the night." She presses some bills into his palm.

"No, I can't do it."

"You don't have to *do it* with them. You just *talk* to them. Ask them where their hometowns are, how many people in their families."

"Let's start tomorrow, okay? I'm just not ready today."

"Just go up and ask them directions to someplace."

"Look, Happy . . ."

"Or ask them what time it is. Tell them you have a plane to catch. They love traveling salesmen. You have a nice country bumpkin accent to make them believe you're from some godforsaken province," Happy says, giving him a push on the back.

He enters the tunnel and moves toward them. They walk in identical fashion, shifting their weight from one leg to the other, so when their hips go left, their waists go right. Now he is about five paces away from the two streetwalkers headed toward him. He turns to look at the fruit stall, to delay the encounter. As a tidal wave of traffic rushes past the opening of the tunnel, the space shakes and the dust wafts in, fogging the scene under the highway bridge. He will buy them dust-spiced lamb. He will pick up a few pairs of dust-sprinkled stockings for them. Then he will strike up a dusty conversation with them about their miserable lives. Another two paces and he will say, "Hi!" He sees how their warped high heels tremble under their weight and how their fingernail polish is chipped. Misery doesn't have to look hunch-backed, cripple-legged, or famished-faced. It can be a perfect female figure trying too hard to look sexy. Once again, he blames all these miserable creatures for his mood that has suddenly turned dark. He is better off not knowing them. All of a sudden, he finds himself missing his simple life with the deafening roar of the canning machines. He used to be so happy and content to work shifts in the factory, where no one made him scavenge through people's misery.

The two girls become aware of his attention. The one in embroidered jeans takes a few steps forward, shifting her weight from side to side, and makes it look as if she is about to brush shoulders with him. He will have to say something when they pass each other. What shall he say? The way she walks is so miserably ugly.

"Fifteen."

Only after he passes her does he ask himself: Did I hear what I thought I heard? Fifteen? Her price? Or her age? She is definitely over thirty. So it must be her price. She is straightforward and honest about the relationship they are going to establish; any face-saving rigmarole is superfluous. Fifteen yuan. Not much more than a few skewers of barbecued lamb.

Next thing he knows, he is walking back toward the opening of the tunnel, where traffic moves through the pale afternoon in roaring streaks. He will punch Happy out if she dares to stop him. There is nothing more miserable than this naked number "fifteen," a naked need to sell oneself for a price just enough for barbecued lamb.

Giggling like mad, Happy follows him as he walks away from the tunnel.

"That's why I like you, Dan. You can't do it unless you fall in love with them."

He keeps looking at the traffic.

"I'll let you take your time and find someone you can fall for," she says.

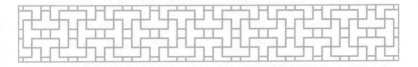

ON SUNDAY MORNING Dan sees it on TV. The talk show host is interviewing the owner of the nudity banquet restaurant, which opens to the public a week from now. The owner is a woman about forty, very poised and elegant. She talks about the sensuality of nudity and food, which was greatly appreciated in ancient China. She will invite a number of artists, including painters and photographers, to the grand opening night. Of course, journalists are on her invitation list as well. She welcomes controversy, which always gives rise to opportunities for inspiring, intelligent discussions.

The food? It is going to be the best collection of seafood. The freshest and the rarest, shipped over by airplane the same afternoon, directly from the fishing boats along the shores of Beidaihe. The girls? Well, they have to be college students who have never had any diseases other than colds and flus. Their ages? From eighteen to twenty-two, all virgins of course, selected from among thousands of candidates. They come from all over China, with records of their school grades and behavior scores. They had to pass a gynecological exam and have their figures measured to make sure their breasts, waists, and hips meet the standards. No one wants to pick up food off bodies that are all skin and bones. Their skin color matters a lot, too. It has to look white and tender, smooth as tofu, half-translucent like fugu, the rare Japanese blowfish delicacy. They will look better than any food displayed upon them, so you'll realize that the best food is not for your mouth; it is for your eyes and all your senses. And rest assured, they will be paid so well that they need not worry about their college tuition for next semester. So you won't say the banquet is too pricey when you know the girls' wages. And hygiene? Well, they must be waxed first. Then they get bathed twelve times over the course of the day in water perfumed with twelve flowers. They must stop eating and drinking for eight hours before they are carried to the chill boxes. Then they must take a sedative and lie atop ice and flowers for one hour as the food is placed on their bodies. You won't see their complete nudity until the food is gone. Then they will wake up from the sedative and participate in the last part of the banquet. The artists invited are those well-known ones. The journalists? They will have to have their journalists' union or company's introduction letter to prove they are not banquet bugs.

Dan steps into his shoes.

"Where are you going?" Little Plum asks.

He ignores her and continues tying his shoes.

She has been repairing the book-shaped souvenir, which has fallen apart once again. The black marble that the fake gold trademark is set on became detached from its wooden mounting. This is how they found out that the marble is also imitation. It is just a square piece of metal coated by a wood-mounted plastic shell with marble patterns glued on it. At the very least the great publisher shouldn't have used such cheap glue.

"Don't bother with that piece of shit," he says.

"Got to have *something* to hang on the wall," she says.

As he makes it to the door, she watches him.

"It's Sunday," she says.

"So?" he says, smiling.

Stopping at the door, he vaguely knows his motive for going out. He might go to the guy who forges documents. He might be able to get the letter of introduction made before the grand opening of the nudity banquet. Happy says he carves all kinds of chops and seals. He can instantly carve them out of anything, even a daikon radish or a bar of soap.

"I'm going to the clinic for my stomachache," he says.

She smiles, as if to say "The hell you are." He smiles, too, knowing she sees through his lies.

"Made four hundred fifty-six yuan on those wigs last month," she says. He reads her as saying, "Quit being a banquet bug. Until you find another job, I'll make as many wigs as I can."

"But be careful; you're a little cross-eyed now," he says, crossing his eyes so hard he feels they might trade places behind his nose ridge. She hurls one of her slippers at him, and it lands on his shoulder. He laughs and waves good-bye.

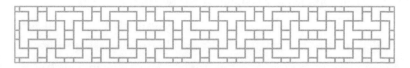

DAN MEETS THE document forger in a teahouse. Over a cup of tea, they conclude the negotiation, and Dan follows the forgery artist to an attic room atop the teahouse. On the way up the termite-hollowed ancient stairway, Dan asks the forger his name. Happy, he replies—he is working through Happy's introduction, so he might as well be remembered as Happy. He is a quirky little character with a big beard and a tiny pair of tinted glasses.

It is quite spacious for an attic room. A slanting skylight on the roof is covered with dust, and overlooking Beijing's alley life there is a little balcony that could take you back to 1920. An enormous hardwood opium bed, engraved with intricate carvings and under a majestic canopy, occupies the major part of the room, like a lion crouching in a dog's cage. Sitting on the floor and flipping up the bedspread, the forger stretches his legs into the dark space under the bed. When he withdraws his legs, Dan sees a wooden box coated with hairy dust that the man carries between his feet.

Inside the box is a huge variety of seals and chops.

"What do you want? Ministry of Culture or Film Bureau?" he asks.

Dan looks at him.

"You're a nice-looking fellow. You look like someone from the Film Bureau," he says.

"Can you make it for a media company?"

"Anything you want. You need a fake identity to get your girlfriend an abortion?" he asks. "You don't have to tell me. I can give you a stamped blank sheet, with letterhead. But I'll charge five hundred more."

"Why?"

"Because you might use it to enter Zhongnanhai to assassinate a Party leader. Or go to the Great Hall of the People to shoot a People's Representative. I don't mean to protect them; I only want to stay in business and steer clear of politics." He picks up a round chop.

"Make it for a newspaper," Dan suggests.

"Will the *People's Daily* do?"

"Do you have anything less well known?"

"Beijing Daily?"

"Well . . ."

"Here we go: *Chinese Railroad Daily.*"

"Fine."

"Do you want it blank?"

"No."

"Yeah. I wouldn't want to pay five hundred extra myself."

While the forger sets up the computer and the printer, Dan asks him if he is the owner of the teahouse. Yes, he replies. He needs a place to conduct his dark, lucrative business. He asks Dan what name he wants on the recommendation letter. Dan Dong, Dan replies. He tells Dan that if he needs an ID card to match this fake name on the letter, he can arrange it in two days. It doesn't actually take him that long; it's just that he is too busy making marriage certificates right now. Why is it that the guys always get the girls pregnant in this season? Guess it has to do with summer vacation. They were in heat all summer, he figures, like hens and roosters. Dan finds him rather garrulous. After he prints the letter out, he presses the round chop into red, oily ink and presses it hard on the paper. His expression is far more serious than those who have the power to press real seals.

The recommendation letter reads, "Dan Dong is a reporter of *Chinese Railroad Daily,* specializing in food and leisure. Your assistance to his work is greatly appreciated. Salutations, *Chinese Railroad Daily.*"

After Dan pays the fee, the guy takes off his glasses and tells Dan not to move. He cups Dan's skull with his long, cold hand and turns it slowly.

"You have a good head. Like a beautifully carved piece."

It feels creepy. Dan thanks him and takes his leave. As he's on his way down the dark stairway, the forger stops him. Dan has forgotten his wallet. A faint light goes on in the stairway.

"Your bone structure looks even better in this dim light. Look this way. Good. Such good contours."

He throws the wallet to Dan. It drops on a stair. As Dan straightens up from picking up the wallet, he finds the man still gazing at him.

"That's why I said you look like someone from the Film Bureau. You might consider show business. You could be a very good extra, and if they give you a line or two, you can be promoted to playing a supporting role. Why not give it a try? It's all faking, and it's much easier than faking a reporter. Besides, they pay well. An extra gets fifty yuan a day, plus three square meals. Once you get promoted to playing supporting roles, you can make tens of thousands."

Dan asks him how he knows about it. He has done it. He did it for a while after getting out of prison. He had gotten caught forging documents? No, he got caught playing politics.

"If you don't have anything better to do, go there. You will see a lot of pretty men and women in front of Beijing Film Studios who dream of being movie stars. They recruit extras there every day."

Dan is elated when he walks out of the teahouse. The gray morning feels sunny, and the doves' cooing sounds romantic. The quirky guy turned out to be an angel. Dan won't be bossed around by Happy and have to nose into people's misery if he can make money as an extra. He will no longer need the "money for your troubles" at the risk of imprisonment. He won't have to understand Ocean Chen's profoundly confusing paintings, or his infinitely intriguing circle of people. He won't need to smile and drink banquet liquor with people like President Wu. He won't even have to feel guilty and full of heartache for people like Old Ten and her sister. Extra; that's what they call it. He loves the name of his new profession.

Over an hour later, Dan is among the future extras. The recruiting office, made out of a converted mail room, is just outside the walls of the film studio compound. The door opens only to let someone out or call someone in. Five girls in colorful nylon down-filled jackets are sitting on the folding stools they have brought with them, drinking water out of plastic bottles. Expensive cars come in and go out through the studio gate, their blinds drawn. The girls guess which male star is sitting behind the closed curtains. They laugh at their own silly whispers.

Dan finds a place under a pine tree to take shelter from the wind. He is not prepared to wait out in the open during this season. A young man says he hopes they will recruit him soon, so he can be on board by the time they serve lunch. The girls laugh. Dan laughs involuntarily with them. It is a happy place that makes you feel young and healthy, away from reality.

The door opens. A middle-aged man wearing a canvas vest with multiple pockets leans out, yelling, "You girls! Did you prepare the lines I gave you?"

"Yeah," one of the girls says.

They all stand up, suddenly shy and timid.

"We need two prostitutes. All of you are welcome to try out. But if you don't want to take off your clothes, don't bother to come in," the man says.

In a nervous clatter, the girls fold up their stools and rush inside the office.

"Don't forget your letters of recommendation," the man says.

The men outside shout to the girls, "Hey, *your* lunch is taken care of. Save some pork bones for the rest of us!"

The girls are too nervous to tease them back.

"You guys, drop your cigarettes! And don't take off your shoes when you wait in front of this film studio, okay? Have some respect," he says. "We need ten bandits. Do any of you want to try?"

The male extras cheer, swarming over to the office. Dan stands up, following them.

"Listen: the bandits on this show are supposed to be skinheads. Those who don't want their heads shaved should stay outside."

Some of the men hesitate and walk back to where they were sitting. Dan looks at both groups and decides to stay outside. He doesn't want to scare Little Plum with a bald head.

When the door opens again after two sleepy hours, an old man comes out. He has bloody makeup on his face.

"What did they have you try out for, Grandpa Bai?" someone asks. "A corpse again?"

"Not as good as a corpse. A corpse just lies there and rests. I like that. They had me try out for a beggar, getting punched out the whole time."

The old man's voice and accent are familiar to Dan. He follows him with his eyes as he walks closer. He wants to run when he recognizes him as one of the old peasants.

"Is that you, Reporter Dan Dong?" the old man calls out to him. He has excellent eyesight and memory for a man of his age.

"And you are . . . ?" Dan says, standing up. He knows he does not pretend well.

The old man stops and stares at him. The bloody makeup makes him look grotesque.

"We waited a whole week and you didn't show up. We were penniless when we left that rathole they call a hotel."

"If I'm not mistaken, you are Uncle Bai, right?" Dan says, feeling truly stupid.

During the formalities, Uncle Bai keeps looking at him accusingly. The painted knife wound crossing his face makes Dan nau-

233

seous. Behind this perfect cosmetic job, Uncle Bai stares at Dan, even though he says he understands if Dan failed to write the article. It might cost him his job once the article is published.

"But Uncle Bai, the article *is* going to be published, by *China Farmers' Monthly*. It is coming out this week."

The old man looks surprised. "You did keep your promise after all?"

"Well . . ." It is mainly Happy's writing.

Uncle Bai comes up and grabs his hands. His wrinkled lips move a few times before he curses: "Damn!" He wishes the article had come out earlier. It would have made a difference of life and death. He has a long story to tell Dan. He suggests that they go to the little restaurant by the recruiting office, where they can have some liquor and a simple lunch. What about his masked face? The restaurant was established for these extras, and the waiters and waitresses are extras themselves. Sometimes they serve you with spooky masks on.

They sit at one of the four tables and drink white sorghum liquor. Steel Bai, Uncle Bai, and Uncle Liu went back to their village after they had spent all their funds. The village heads came to them the night they arrived home. Steel Bai was detained immediately. The Party secretary said that according to Chinese law, they had committed crimes: slandering Party leaders; living in vagrancy that affected city security; evading taxes; and attempting to riot against the Party's leadership. They must either pay a fine of forty thousand yuan or else go to jail. In view of their status as respected village elders, the Party secretary gave them two days to raise the money for the fine. Uncle Bai wanted Uncle Liu to flee with him at night, but Liu said no, he wasn't afraid. Why should he be? He was innocent, and his conscience was as clear as the well water of the village.

"So I ran away alone. I hid at my in-laws' house in a neighboring village for a couple of days, and then the news came to me. They went for Uncle Liu two days after my departure. Uncle Liu didn't let them take him easily. You should have seen how stubborn he used to be. An old bull, that's what he was. He would gore you with his old horns if you made him mad. They started to tie him up but he struggled loose. He charged forward all of a sudden, holding a kitchen knife he had tucked under his quilt. Next thing he knew, he was riddled with bullet wounds and thrown onto the police jeep. He didn't make it to the hospital. He bled to death on the way."

The story makes Dan's teeth chatter. He has to keep drinking the spicy liquor to stay warm.

"Oh, how I wish he'd lived to read your article," Uncle Bai says after a long silence. "I hope your article will get Steel Bai out of detention."

"Did you come to Beijing to hide?" Dan asks. He feels tipsy enough for more tragedy.

"No. I am waiting."

"Waiting for what?" Dan asks. He knows he sounds peevish, but he can't help it. Is there anything more hopeless and miserable than this old face covered with such a horrifying mask?

"There's got to be someone with power who will listen to me, or read your article," he says. "I am waiting for him to save us."

"Yeah, right, he will save you," Dan says. He is pouring another glass of liquor and watching it spill over. With his neck going forward and his lips reaching out, he sucks the liquor off the table loudly.

"He will."

"Who is he?"

"He is sitting right before me," the old man says. The solemnity the bloody makeup gives him is more than his facial expression could ever achieve.

Dan blinks his eyes at him for a while, then lets out a bitter chuckle, the liquor streaming down his chin. Peasants. Just like his own parents, Uncle Bai takes anyone to be his savior. No, actually, it is as if he believes anyone *could* be his savior if Uncle Bai wills him to be. Buddha, Jesus, Chairman Mao, Chairman Deng, Chairman Jiang. Now it is he, Dan Dong the banquet bug, who is filling the savior's role for the old peasant.

"Your article is going to save us. It's going to make the powerful men see what happened in our village. That's where revenge for Uncle Liu begins."

Dan eats and drinks in silence, and the old man's face has become nothing more than a red blur in his quivering view. Dan feels better now. Alcohol works wonders. Especially when you face misery.

"Do you get to play the damned corpse all the time?" Dan asks.

He is so loud that all the customers are turning to gawk at him.

"No. You don't get to play anything for days until they have something for you. Sometimes they don't want you after you try out. Only when they want someone ugly or sorry-looking, they come to me. Only good-looking guys or butt-ugly guys stand a chance. I wish I were uglier, so I could get more roles."

"You get fifty yuan a day though," Dan literally yells.

Uncle Bai hushes him, glancing apologetically at the irritated customers. "Depends. If they just have you lie or sit there, you only get twenty to thirty. And you have to pay fifteen percent to the go-betweens they call agents. If they have you beaten up, not really beaten up, but occasionally get in one or two blows, you get fifty. It all depends. If I don't get a job for days, I feed myself on my own blood."

"What?" Dan shouts.

People shudder at his loudness and groan.

"I go sell my blood. The film people feed you good meals when you work for them, and you fatten yourself up as much as you can so you will have blood to sell. Good deal, isn't it? You grow your own blood and milk it."

Dan can't help thinking how much cholesterol the old peasant's blood contains. The hot dumpling soup has started melting the bloody color on Uncle Bai's face. It really looks nightmarish.

"How often do you come here?"

"Every day, if I have no place to go. Normally I have no place to go."

"Where do you live?"

"Usually at the bus station." He sees Dan's hand shaking hard. "You all right? Looks like you're drunk . . ."

Dan wants to assure him that he is okay. He gives him a stupid smile, as all drunks do when they want to prove they are sober.

"You are drunk. We should get drunk," the old peasant says. "I've been waiting for this day. What those bastards are getting, they're getting thrown out of the Party and into prison. That's what they're going to get. All my waiting is worth it, right? The Party leaders will look into the matter after reading your article and say, how dare these beasts who feed on peasants' blood call themselves Party cadres? Handcuff them all! . . ." The old man slurs more and more, until his words are replaced entirely by a snore.

Dan carries Uncle Bai to the place under the pine tree. When the middle-aged agent calls him to work, Uncle Bai roars at him that the Party is going to expel all those ancestor-fuckers who call themselves Party cadres. The agent ends up dragging an old man from a nearby farmer's market to substitute for Uncle Bai, begrudging that the whole morning's makeup job on Uncle Bai has gone to waste.

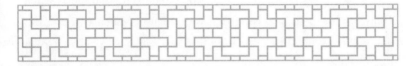

THE GALLEY PROOF of Ocean Chen's profile has come out. It is going to be the lead story in *Reader's Weekly*, a publication with twenty million subscribers. Happy treats Dan to a South Pacific restaurant called Pink Chamber on "Bar Street." It is a Sunday night, and bars on Bar Street are packed with expatriates from all over the world. Although the wind turns hard and occasionally churns up fine yellow sand, a sign that Beijing is well into autumn, chairs and tables, with umbrellas flapping in their centers, are still outside on the sidewalk. In a blast of music, strings of lights tied between trees on both banks of the street wink and blink at the crowds with dizziness in their eyes. Under the neon ads for Budweiser, Heineken, and Johnnie Walker, bar owners are trying to convince passers-by that their bar serves better cocktails, or has better bands, or shows something with "color." They give special emphasis when uttering the word "color," so one understands that "color" is the color of flesh. From windows, one can glimpse one or two female singers with intoxicated facial expressions and agonized body movements. Dazed, Dan doesn't know where to direct his eyesight. "Hello, big brother and big sister!" Two black boys, both eighteen or so, come to Happy and Dan, whispering in perfect Mandarin, asking whether they want marijuana or other drugs. There are pimplike Chinese men standing almost in the middle of the street, acting as touts for various bars, soliciting the men and women passing by.

Pink Chamber is a three-story building painted pink and with pink window shades and pink lanterns. Dan looks at it before going in with Happy. What pleases him is that, unlike the restaurant he went to with President Wu, there are no "human statues" by the door. Nor are there any golden lions or palm trees with cloth trunks and plastic leaves. As Dan catches up with Happy on the stairs to the second floor, he finds that the building is actually like the factory building that he and Little Plum inhabit. It is a crude concrete structure decorated with the most feminine materials and colors: soft satin cushions in hot pink for the chairs, gauze draperies in peachy pink on the windows, and silk lanterns that let out a pink glow, making pink shadows of men and women wearing pink smiles. And the floor is made of a kind of foggy glass. Easing himself down on a chair, Dan is oddly touched by the atmosphere. He can't say if it is pretty or not. He has never seen such a combination of roughness and fragility.

"You can read it when you get home," Happy says.

"Huh?" Now he knows why this place looks so charming. Sexy, that's what it is.

"The galley proof," she says, handing him a few printed pages. "I don't like my stuff read over the dinner table. It has to be read seriously and with respect."

After the dishes are ordered, Happy cranes her neck and looks around. Their table is on the second floor by the balcony, overlooking a fountain in the middle of a fish pond on the ground floor. Some fat, reddish fish swim in the turbid water. Overhead is a glass ceiling, which is also the floor of the third level. If the glass floor were sheer enough, Happy says, they could tell the colors of the girls' underwear under their miniskirts.

"They probably wouldn't mind. Their miniskirts are their ads," Happy say. "Those hairy foreigners are used to whores in miniskirts."

The soup comes. The flavor is almost unbearably pungent at first, then it loses its sharpness gradually after you overcome the initial discomfort. The penetrating sourness and spiciness, as well as the exotic fragrance, become mild as your senses sharpen. Dan has never known such exciting, rich pungency until now. It is a flavor, or combination of flavors, that you have to suffer to enjoy.

"Look, there comes a miniskirt. So young," Happy hisses, leaning forward to Dan. He smells rather than hears her words carried on her smoky breath.

He turns around to look and sees a slim-legged girl holding a foreigner's arm, stepping up the stairs.

"These are higher-class whores. They can speak some English. You should hear their English, so thick with their country accents. And they tell you they are college students."

She can be very caustic. She forgets Dan is one of the country bumpkins who have drifted to Beijing. The second dish doesn't have much character, and he is looking forward to the next one. His cell phone buzzes. Someone has sent him a text message. "Want to have a romantic adventure with a girl? I think I'm the right choice for you."

"What's that?" Happy asks.

"Don't know. Wrong number, I guess."

Happy takes the cell phone from him across the table and reads it. She smiles mysteriously while keying in a reply.

"Hey, what are you doing?" he asks.

Ignoring him, she sends the message out.

The answer comes back in several seconds: "I'm one meter sixty-seven tall and weigh forty-nine kilograms. I'm nineteen years old, a freshman at the Central Drama Institute."

"Let's proceed," Happy says. "Where do you want to meet this girl?"

"What's her name?" Dan says.

"Never mind her name. They all have a thousand names. By the way, you are not Dan Dong the freelance reporter either. You are a businessman and have a big company."

"What does the company make?"

"Buildings. You own a lot of buildings like that son of a bitch President Wu. These girls think they are hot."

"Okay."

She starts to key in an answer for him and, as her finger moves, she reads the words out loud: "Sounds like you are a very pretty girl. I can't wait to see you." She goes on with the message, giggling. "First, I would like to invite you to a romantic dinner at Pink Chamber. Come right away. Don't worry about the taxi fare. I will take care of it. If you need to know the exact address of the restaurant, let me know."

The answer says she knows Pink Chamber well. In fact, her place isn't far from it. She will be there in about fifteen minutes.

"You know what? I think she is one of the girls sitting right in front of those bars out there. All she needs to do is to walk across the street and up the stairs. But she will pick up a taxi receipt, twenty or thirty yuan, from the sidewalk and have you reimburse her."

"Are you going to be here when she comes?" Dan is already nervous.

"Of course not," she says.

She goes to the window facing the street and looks out.

Dan feels a knot in his stomach. He is losing his appetite at the prospect of such a meeting. He can't think of a thing to talk about with this girl. Should they talk about her drama classes? Or about recent soap operas? How much nonsense and how many lies does he have to prepare to fill these minutes?

"I think she is coming," Happy says, turning from the window. She hurries back to the table, tidies up the food on the plates, and replaces the used chopsticks with fresh ones. "There is plenty of food. If you like her, you can order a dish or two for her. Let her order drinks if she wants. Alcohol sometimes makes people tell fewer lies."

Dan grabs her arm. "What do I do for living?"

"You build a lot of buildings and sell them."

"That's right."

"The profession is called real estate developer."

"Real estate developer."

No sooner has Happy retreated to a table by the window than a woman in her late twenties shows up at the entrance. She looks around, trying to engage the eyes of all the men, either sitting alone or with other men. Then she walks toward Dan tentatively while working her fingers on her cell phone pad. Dan's cell buzzes. The message reads: "Lift up your head and here I am."

Dan lifts his head and there she is, smiling a twisted smile at him. Dan is the kind of man who feels preyed upon by a woman with that sort of smile. He stands up and gestures for her to sit across from him, on Happy's ex-seat. When the girl crosses her legs, her bell-bottomed jeans draw up a bit, and he catches a glimpse of the two little pillars of her high heels. How can she walk on them without breaking her ankles? Dan pours some tea for her, and she chirps her thanks. You can't tell if she is pretty or not; she has a suspiciously straight and Western-looking nose.

"How are you?" she says in English.

If Dan had a shred of fantasy about her, it is gone at hearing this. He just smiles and nods.

"Glad to meet you." She persists on in English.

Are all the whores on Bar Street so phony? He nods at her again without smiling. She is disappointed; from his lack of English, it's obvious he is not an executive of any of those foreign joint-venture companies who keep their wives abroad.

"Eat, please. The food is getting cold," Dan says.

She thanks him and picks up the chopsticks. She has very good table manners, her lips pressed painfully tight when she chews. He sneaks a glance at Happy, who gives him a hard look. When the girl holds up her bowl, a string of big, amber beads around her left wrist emerges.

"Those glass beads are pretty," Dan says. He doesn't have any knowledge of gemstones.

"They are amber," she says, stretching her arm across the table for him to examine. "My mom gave this to me. She is a Buddhist."

"Are you a Buddhist?" He doesn't know if he should hold her wrist or not.

She giggles, withdrawing her arm. "If I say I am, I cannot order drinks tonight. Do you know Lao She's philosophy? It says: 'Be a Muslim when pork is too expensive; be a Buddhist when lamb is too expensive; and be a Catholic when tea is too expensive."

She loses Dan for a while as he digests the remark. Then he laughs. She isn't nineteen, and she's too old to be a drama student, but she is witty and smart. Dan finds himself beginning to enjoy her.

"What's your name?" Dan asks.

"Summer Dream." She looks at him. "Of course I wouldn't tell you my real name. We are not here to fall in love or anything, are we?" she challenges him.

Dan laughs. He wouldn't have imagined laughing like this with a woman in her line of work.

"I wouldn't fall in love with any man," she says. "Not now. Not in the foreseeable future."

"Why is that?"

"Because I enjoy what I am doing. I pity those wives whose husbands come to me for what they miss out on at home. I don't want to be one of those wives. You really get to know women through men, and you know how not to be them. A fleeting passion is much better than no passion. I try to be an interesting companion for decent men who suffer something I call sexual aesthetic fatigue with their wives."

Dan suspects she is well educated.

"Maybe I am not a decent guy," Dan says. "How do you know?"

"I have very good information sources. The men introduced to me are not garbage. And I have keen intuition."

Dan wants to order some new dishes for her, but he doesn't know the menu well. He excuses himself and gets up. He eyes Happy to follow him as he passes her table. He picks up a menu from the serving cabinet, watching Summer Dream's back, and pulls Happy behind the silk curtain.

"Tell me what to order."

"That means you like her," Happy says, studying the menu. "That's dangerous. You can't like every whore you interview. You'll end up with a minced heart."

"Okay, then, *you* go ahead and interview her," he says.

Happy laughs. Dan watches the girl's back through the curtain. A foreign woman is asking her something.

The foreign woman is still talking with Summer Dream when Dan returns to the table. Summer Dream's English is fluent as far as he can tell. Not only does she talk; she also makes foreign gestures, shrugging her shoulders and rolling her eyeballs. Dan watches her. So it takes all this to make a whore for the rich.

The two dishes turn out to be too spicy for Summer Dream's taste. She orders a simple pad thai for herself. She never drinks or smokes. She doesn't do self-indulgent things to ruin her looks and well-being. If you treat your job seriously and your clients responsibly, she says, you should lead a sensible life.

"What do you do?" Summer Dream asks him.

"Hum? Oh, I do . . . I build apartment and office buildings and sell them."

"Really?" She stares at him.

"Why?"

"How do you make those cement blocks that you use to build walls and floors?" She puts down her chopsticks and rests her chin on the back of her hands, her elbows on the table.

"You mix the cement powder and pour the mixture into molding frames. Then you lift the frames off and let them dry. And there you have cement blocks."

"Sounds like a peasant making dirt bricks."

"Same technique."

She smiles.

"Seriously—what *do* you do?"

"I told you."

"You don't even know how those cement blocks are made."

Dan smiles, but she no longer does.

"Then *you* tell me how they are made." Dan's smile feels heavy now; it is the thick-skinned smile of President Wu.

A tension has built up.

"Where are you from?" he asks.

"What do you mean?" she says, smiling again.

"For instance, I'm from Gansu Province. Just about everyone in Beijing is from somewhere else."

"I'll tell you when I get back from the ladies' room. Be good now. Don't charm any other women while I'm gone." She tilts her face to one side and touches his hand across the table. Then she stands up, smooths her long, bell-bottomed jeans, and leaves. A few paces away, she stops and turns back, giving him a very sexy look.

Twenty minutes have passed and she has not returned. Happy goes to the ladies' room and a cleaning lady tells her that no one has come in for the last thirty minutes. Summer Dream must have figured out that Dan is a journalist, if not a police detective.

As Dan repeats their conversation and Happy makes notes, he sees a pair of mini-pillars moving across the foggy glass ceiling. A pair of huge shoes are following. He thinks he sees the bell-bottomed jeans' legs, too, but he is not sure. Summer Dream has found another decent man and is ready to become an interesting companion for him. He watches the pillarlike heels moving to the far corner. He is jealous. He likes her, even though she is a bit phony.

"Not bad, the interview," Happy says, closing her notebook. She sees a teary-eyed Dan mechanically stuffing his mouth with the spicy food, and pulls a tissue from her bag.

"Are you lovesick or something?" she says, handing the tissue to him.

"It is just too damned spicy." He points at the dishes that Summer Dream didn't touch, sniffing and rubbing his eyes with the tissue.

"I hope the next girl will be as well-spoken as she is," Happy says.

"*What* next girl?"

"Buddy, your luck in romance has barely begun!"

She has given Dan's cell number to an underground service that collects wealthy men's numbers and resells them to prostitutes. From now on, Dan's cell phone will be flooded with text messages from women in the sex industry. That's what they call it: the sex industry.

On the way home, Dan's cell phone buzzes again.

"How are you?" the text says.

Dan replies that he is fine.

"No, you're not fine. You're lonely."

There is no point in arguing. Ahead of him is a subway station under some kind of reconstruction. Beijing is forever an uncompleted city, with a thousand architectural ideas going against one another. Some ditches filled by one company today are only for another company to dig open tomorrow.

"I know many fun places in Beijing. Do you want me to take you to them?" the message says.

The steep subway stairs are desolate. He descends while answering that it is too late to go anyplace.

"It's not ten o'clock yet. Fun places are no fun before ten."

This one is more aggressive. He asks if they can meet tomorrow, at two in the afternoon.

"You are so cruel, wanting me to wake up so early."

Dan is amused. He asks when she normally wakes up. Six o'clock, just in time to watch the first evening news show on CCTV.

The messaging is cut off as he reaches the bottom of a flight of stairs in the subway station. There are only five people going in the direction he goes. All of a sudden, Old Ten is on his mind. He finds that she has been on his mind all the time, like background scenery revolving unnoticed until it is illuminated by solitude. Then the longing overwhelms him. Is she somewhere sending men text messages? How will he know if it is Old Ten hiding behind these messages, even if she sends him messages from the vast anonymity? Is she going to know that Dan is the man receiving her seductive words? If Happy's project does help give voice to silenced victims like Old Ten's sister then Dan will meet these girls and interview them. With his affair with Old Ten over, he won't be disgusted with himself if he helps her. To him, conscience is something that makes you disgusted with yourself when doing certain things in a certain fashion. He doesn't recognize his conscience; he only recognizes that distinctive disgust. He has to admit Happy's idea isn't bad, centering the story around the execution of Old Ten's sister. He will help Happy to write it. He will interview as many prostitutes as she needs. When the article comes out, will he know Old Ten's response toward it?

Preoccupied, he follows a pigeon that somehow has entered the subway, trying to find her way out. She shoots into the tunnel and disappears into the dark uncertainty for a while, then shoots out of the tunnel across the platform, darkened by dust, more desperate and frightened, with less balance and accuracy, her wings' neurotic clapping echoing loudly. Dan looks, feeling for the bird. It is a most frightening nightmare for a pigeon, repeating her route as if under some unbreakable spell, circling in a mysterious, dark orbit. The more she tries to break free, the more deeply she is trapped. There she goes once more, dashing into the tunnel, her body askew. She will fly until her energy is exhausted and she drops dead.

To distract himself, he gets out the galley proof of Ocean Chen's profile. He slips down to the granite floor and sits against a column to read it. His train arrives, and he boards it and continues reading. Old Ten is forced into the background again. He finds Happy's writing very good indeed, so insightful and witty, presenting a great artist with lovable defects and eccentric merits. As the train approaches Dan's destination, he shudders at the last paragraph.

It says Ocean Chen has many young friends with powerful fathers who will help him out of his current legal dilemma. Since tax law is still something new to Chinese citizens, it could be argued that the artist's predicament stems from mistakes rather than felonies. With his powerful friends' help, reclassifying his legal position is as easy as the turn of a hand. In China, everything depends on how to interpret things, and who interprets them.

When Dan arrives at his station, he starts dialing his cell phone while climbing up the mountain trail of subway stairs. He is totally out of breath when Happy picks up the phone.

"What's up?" she says lazily. The background noise is very loud.

He gasps more and swallows hard. "You . . . you can't *do* this!"

"Can't do what?"

"Can't betray him!"

"Pardon me?"

"You *must* take out the last paragraph off that damned article."

"Says who?"

"You used me. I told you Ocean Chen was getting a call from the son of so and so, and they were talking about his tax scandals. I was happy that someone could help the old man out . . ."

"I'm happy, too."

"I guessed that he would just pay a big fine and walk out of the legal mess with the help of that son of a chairman."

"That's not hard to guess."

"You can't use something I overheard."

"Anything you didn't want me to say, you should have told me before I started writing."

"You make me feel like the kind of person I always want to kill!"

"Did Ocean Chen try to avoid you when they talked on the phone?"

"No! He trusts me . . ."

"So it's not something you learned by eavesdropping."

"But you must take it out," says Dan. He is so angry that he feels beads of sweat seeping out beneath his thick hair.

"Too late. It is going to print tomorrow." She sounds like a witch declaring victory over someone she has tricked.

"You must pull the article back."

"Must I?" she says, a menacing tone rippling in her voice.

"Yes."

"Tell me what will happen if I don't." She is nasty.

"I don't normally beat a woman. But that's *normally*," he says. He is pleased with himself, showing a little bit of the hoodlum nature that he has suppressed for so long.

"While we're at it, let me tell you something. Your article 'A Normal Day in Bai Village' has been pulled from the next issue of *China Farmers' Monthly*. In other words, it has been banned before its publication. I didn't have the heart to tell you. I thought I'd tell you after I found another publisher for you. That is, if you're nice to me."

He stands in the windy night, staring at the shadowy buildings of the Beijing suburb. He has told Uncle Bai that the article is coming out next week. He closes his eyes, seeing the old face distorted by the bloody makeup, smiling with so much gratitude and worship.

"I will get it published. I can go to those provincial publications. Sometimes those publishers have the guts to expose stuff like this. In the past, some of the most controversial stuff first appeared in those publications. They sometimes got shut down by the government for a while, but when they reopened, they would be the most popular publication in the country."

He says nothing. Uncle Bai has been selling his blood. He has been waiting for someone to give voice to the silenced villagers. He has been playing a corpse, lying in the autumn dampness for hours or letting people punch him out, in order to see this article appear as the first blow of revenge for Uncle Liu.

"If you want my help, you have to help me," Happy says. She has been talking all this time, while he has had Uncle Bai on his mind. "How are people going to know it's you who fed me the information? They won't know it. Ocean Chen isn't going to suspect you. He has so many people around him, it could have been any of them who overheard him."

"I hate it. You know? I really do."

"I understand. But let us make a contribution to human civilization with just a little tarnish on our professional ethics."

It is as if a big piece of spoiled food has been forced down his throat. He says, "Okay," and rings off.

DAN GETS UP before daybreak. He rushes downstairs after washing. The morning traffic has not started yet, and the air is still clear. It is a chilly morning, and the vegetable farms are gray with frost. He walks a mile to the subway station, noticing that his mood has improved.

He arrives at Ocean Chen's house and sees cars on the front lawn. The artist has some guests staying over, and none of them went to bed before four o'clock. Dan decides to take a walk to an open farmer's market, where he can have some stinky-soybean soup and deep-fried dough sticks. He has not eaten breakfast in a farmer's market for so long, and its smell permeates the air for miles, making his mouth water.

After he finishes the food, he asks for one more order to take away. He can reheat it for his own lunch if Ocean Chen doesn't care for it. But the old artist is overjoyed at smelling the stench.

"What smells so good?" he yells from his bed. "It woke me up!"

With a quick shuffling sound, he appears at the doorway. He says he has been deprived of this kind of food for so long by all his wives that he has almost forgotten that such a delicacy exists. Nobody knows him but Dan. And nobody cares what he likes but Dan.

Dan sits down on the sofa, leaning forward, his elbows on his knees. He says to himself, let the old man enjoy his breakfast. He doesn't want to spoil Ocean Chen's appetite with what he will say. He knows his chance of being forgiven is slim after he says it. He has betrayed the old artist's trust, using the information he gained improperly. He is well prepared to be thrown out after he tells the truth. Then he feels his courage to bring up the subject subsiding. Ocean Chen starts asking him what he has been doing. He answers with what has happened to the article "A Normal Day in Bai Village," knowing the old man isn't listening. To his surprise, the artist responds appropriately this time.

"What? The old peasant got shot to death? What is this society coming to?" He puts down the plastic container. "What are we Chinese coming to? Good for you to expose it! When is the article coming out?"

"They banned it."

"Those corrupt sons of bitches! They call themselves the *China Farmers' Monthly* and they don't have guts to speak up for farmers?!"

"No publisher in Beijing wants the trouble," Dan says.

Ocean Chen loses himself in his thoughts for a while, then says: "Well, then, we can do the back-door stuff, too, can't we?" He stands up, his mouth smeared with the gray viscosity of the stinky soybean soup. "Our back door is nice and big, wide open to all the secret shortcuts that lead to miracles."

Ocean Chen hurries down the corridor, yelling to the bedrooms at the other end, "Hey, time to get up! Somebody got killed and you still sleep like pigs!"

A door opens, and a woman in a white lounging gown comes out, rubbing her hair and complaining; she has a severe headache from overdrinking and lack of sleep. It is Ruby. She came back when the crisis died down, just as Ocean Chen had predicted. She gives Dan a vague acknowledgment with her chin and goes to sit on the sofa opposite the TV. Dan knows that, in her mind, she has written him off because he has not been a good informer. From another bedroom come the noises of a television and music being turned on. The young man Dan met at Capital Hospital pulls the door open, and his bare torso leans out as he calls, "Coffee!"

A maid pops up out of nowhere, a tray in one hand and a cof-feepot in the other, and hurries to the young man.

"Don't come in. I have no clothes on," the young man says.

As the tray and the coffeepot exchange hands awkwardly through the half-open door, the young man asks Ocean Chen who got killed.

"An old man like me!" the master says.

"But not you, though."

Ruby laughs, switching on the TV in the living room.

The young man disappears behind his bedroom door for a minute or two, then reappears, yelling: "Juice!"

The maid makes another magic appearance out of the blue, with a pitcher of orange juice and a glass. The young man finally comes out into the living room, claiming he now can be considered sober and awake. He picks up the TV remote control and asks who the old victim is. Anyone he knows? Ocean Chen tells him a syn-opsized version of the story. The young man flips through the channels, saying the story is outrageous indeed. Why didn't the relatives of the old man go to the local law enforcement? It was a police officer who shot him. Then they should go to the provincial law enforcement. But the provincial law enforcement upheld the local law enforcement's decision to arrest Steel Bai and Uncle Liu in the first place. The young man stands there, trying to find a channel while expressing his rage, saying how shocked he is by such a tragedy.

"Dan wrote an article about the event, but it was banned," Ocean Chen says.

"Who is Dan?" the young man asks, his eyes still on the TV screen.

"He is a reporter. You met him."

"Did I?"

"Anyway, his article was banned a couple of days before its publication."

"Hey," Ruby whines to the young man. "Would you please let me watch TV?"

"How many kinds of shampoo do you ladies need, anyway?" the young man asks. "Every channel sells shampoo." He keeps surfing the channels as he tells Dan: "Go to another magazine or newspaper. There are thousands of them out there."

"Nobody dares publish it," Dan says. "It's a touchy topic."

"Why is it touchy?"

"It is about village party leaders abusing farmers . . ."

"Oh, farmers. They are still in the dark ages."

"Don't you talk about farmers like that," the artist says. "Your father used to be one."

"That's why I can't find anything in common with him."

"Would you help him get it published?" the artist asks, pretending not to see the looks Ruby gives him.

"Name a newspaper or magazine," the young man tells Dan.

"Any one will do," Dan replies.

"Okay. Give me your phone number, and I'll have them call you."

"How do I send the article to you?" Dan asks him.

"Why do you have to send it to me?" The young man is getting impatient.

"I thought . . . you'd want to read it first."

"I don't want to read it."

Dan looks at him.

"Call me tomorrow so I don't forget." He gives Dan a card. It bears only his name and phone number embossed in tiny gold print on an otherwise blank background.

DAN TOUCHES the recommendation letter inside his pocket. It bears the round, red seal of *China Railroad Daily*. He lingers outside the restaurant and observes the registration area right by the door. The bejeweled female owner is greeting the guests like a queen, standing under a huge chrysanthemum arrangement in the shape of a throne. From inside the glass door and outside along the front steps is a flood of all kinds of chrysanthemums, gushing down to the sidewalk. They are congratulatory gifts from the dignitaries of the city. At the foot of the stairs, Dan sees an enormous flower basket of multicolored chrysanthemums. It stands out from the rest with its size and bright colors. It is from President Wu. There goes another two years of a worker's wages.

What if the police set traps in this nudity banquet? They probably know some banquet bugs would take a chance and come here. Dan counts the reporters who have registered, his hand grown damp holding the false recommendation letter in his pocket. He sees the little man hurrying up the steps, the photographer by his side. Is he as apprehensive as Dan? A woman reporter passes Dan, cheerily telling him how good he looks. He is wearing his black leather jacket atop wool trousers, an outfit of Happy's design, with a deep red tie he has bought especially for this occasion. He has changed his eyeglasses to a pair with thin silver frames that give him almost a businessman's elegance. He has learned so much, eating banquets for a year and a half.

A long limo pulls up. Dan sees that the person of such importance is none other than President Wu. He is wearing a white suit that makes him look gigantic, accessorized with a black bow tie and a pair of leather shoes that squeak with each step he takes. He offers noisy greetings to his acquaintances and non-acquaintances, flirting with the owner and the registration girl.

"You are late, President Wu!" the owner says.

"I know!"

"You knew we wouldn't start without you."

"That's right."

"The penalty for your late arrival is three cups of sake!"

"Make it ten!"

They laugh.

"Ladies and gentlemen, let's start right now," the owner announces. For a split second her image is bleached and frozen in hundreds of flashbulbs.

Dan passes through registration smoothly. The girl is too excited to check his documents thoroughly. When he signs his name, he spots a business card of his fake former company. The little man is still using it. As he reaches the reception area, he hears haunting music. The lights are dimmed and replaced by candles. Waiters in snow white silk push six carts covered with snow white silk sheets. A chilly breeze runs through the crowd. The atmosphere and the music make it seem as if under the white silk lie bodies just out of a morgue.

Then the waiters begin unveiling the carts. Pinching the corners of the silk sheets, their thumbs and index fingers are effeminately deft, leaving the rest of their fingers to flex open like orchid petals. As the silk sheets rise, the flowers and food begin coming into view. Then the faces of the maidens, which will stay under sheer veils until the last moment. The naked maidens are buried under abalones, scallops, prawns, and an array of various kinds of seafood sashimi. The owner explains that their beauty will be gradually appreciated as the food is taken off their bodies.

The guests begin circling the maidens whose skin and flesh are bearers of the most expensive seafood, as if making a farewell viewing of the deceased in a funeral parlor. They don't speak; they just breathe words into one another's ears. Nobody makes eye contact, and if someone is caught resting his eyes on any of the maidens, his eyes shift immediately to the floor. Even the slow, haunting music, which is supposed to create an unreal and ethereal reality, makes the crowd anxious and restless.

The owner notices the tension hanging heavily over the banquet hall. In a cheery voice she says that all the girls are university students with the highest grades who might someday become employees or secretaries of the CEOs and board chairmen here at the banquet tonight.

The guests laugh nervously.

As the food is taken piece by piece, the maidens' nakedness begins to surface.

If you look at Dan now, you will find him standing weak-kneed, holding a translucent plate with a variety of food on it. You've never seen him so unenthusiastic at a banquet of such rarity. He takes slow steps around one cart, his face pale and his eyes dull, his mouth moving as if chewing on a piece of wax. His instinct recognized the maiden's body earlier than his eyes, despite her veiled face.

The owner lectures the guests on erotic art in Chinese history and Western civilization. The crowd becomes more restless when the food is almost gone, except for the small parts remaining on the female private parts. President Wu steps forward and jokingly lifts up a big piece of lobster meat, then steps aside to reveal a gentle slope underneath. People gasp. The rouged nipple rises before their eyes.

President Wu makes a suggestive gesture, holding the white lobster meat in front of his mouth and touching it with his lips.

"Um, delicious," he says in a perishing voice.

Some people start to lighten up. They push one another, teasing and laughing, and swarm over the maidens. The music becomes gay and naughty while some of the candles are put out. Hiding behind jokes and playfulness, the guests' chopsticks reach out for the biggest abalones and lobster meat to uncover the maidens' essential secrets.

Her body is now entirely exposed. It doesn't look as fresh as Dan remembers it. It might have been chilled too long. But he thinks it is the most beautiful nudity among the six maidens. Dan steps up and whispers, "Old Ten."

Nobody hears him but Old Ten. He whispers to her again. Her body shivers subtly. Dan stands transfixed, gazing at her body, which all of a sudden becomes abashed. A naked body that expresses shyness so well.

He knows he shouldn't stand gazing at her like this. Motionless as it is, he can see, under her silky skin, her struggle to escape his gaze. It blushes in frustration that his gaze nails it right where it is. He sees her legs pressing tightly against each other, her arms stiffening with a fierce intention to cover her breasts.

He walks away.

The owner's wife announces the sleeping beauties are ready to turn back into normal college girls. Dan goes to a corner shaded by a treelike chrysanthemum flower arrangement. Following hand-clapping and cheers, the girls rise from their coffinlike carts dripping with shreds of fish, oyster juice, and chrysanthemum petals. They step forward and curtsy gracefully.

The waiters come out with gauze capes and wrap them around the girls' shoulders. Then the girls move in tiny dancers' tiptoe steps toward every guest and curtsy like princesses. Old Ten is obviously distracted, her eyes searching in every direction for Dan. He retreats a little further into the shadows. She seems relieved, as she believes Dan is gone.

President Wu makes some joke, and Old Ten laughs with the crowd. So Old Ten doesn't know President Wu. He approaches Old Ten and shakes hands with her. She turns her smiling face up toward him, her body bathing in the warm rays of his laughing eyes. He wasn't the one who caused her sister's misfortune. It was another hand wearing a big, fat jade ring that trashed Little Plum. There are plenty of presidents and chairmen and CEOs. Old Ten will let one of them pick her, then trash her.

Dan walks toward the door without looking back.

Two men come toward him. Then he hears the swift footsteps of two more behind him as well, coming from inside the restaurant. The men don't look severe or ferocious; they even smile a bit. Maybe they don't want to make a scene and spoil everyone's good time.

"Would you please come with us?" one of them says.

As if he had a choice. Dan nods and walks out with them, one on either side and two behind him. He is considerate enough to make it easy for them and for everybody in there. Old Ten is having dessert with her audience by now. Perhaps President Wu is asking her which university she studies at. The relationship will begin with nothing true except her naked beauty.

As Dan sees the police jeep ease out of the parking lot and drive toward them, he hears the clinking of handcuffs at the ready. Without warning he is seized by a violent sickness. He roars, doubling up, and begins throwing up. There seems to be a powerful pump down at the bottom of his stomach, and solid and liquid substances spew forth out of his mouth, hitting the ground with terrific impact. For a moment he considers where these resounding roars must come from, so mighty in their reverberations. They sound as if they come from a deep, huge maelstrom of stormy water threatening to flood. Tonight he had very little to eat, only a few pieces of seafood here and there, before he saw Old Ten. His stomach should have emptied out by now. But he keeps on vomiting, squatting low, his legs parted wide. He feels the exquisite banquet food he has been eating for a year-and-a-half going out of him. Gradually his mouth is full of sour flavor. It is the flavor of the spoiled cabbage buns he had in the army. While the cooking squad was discussing whether to feed the buns to the hogs, he stole them and shared them among the soldiers from poor farmers' families such as his. He has to move often so his feet won't be submerged in his own vomit. His heaving roars subside, yet he is still not through puking. The juice from his stomach is no longer sour; it is bitter. It must have gotten down to his childhood now. The bitterness is that of tree bark with which his mother made gruel. The ferocity of vomiting turns his stomach inside out, not missing a single furrow or fold, the way Little Plum turns chicken gizzards inside out to clean them before stewing. A sharp pain has started, and it gives him a terrible pull each time he lets out a mouthful, followed by a sweet and fishy taste of blood, as though what comes out of him is a small part of his very being. His organs keep turning and churning, and he feels he is throwing up the whole dietary history of his thirty-four years of life.

The policemen stand as far away from him as their duty permits. They are so disgusted that their Adam's apples jump and quiver. Dan's roars are replaced by moans, and he balances himself by leaning part of his weight on his arms, propping himself on the ground, almost like a beast squatting on its four limbs. The policemen see him give the ground a push to stand up. He lurches as he straightens his body. He looks hollowed and spent, smaller than their first impression, like a big pile of loosely bundled rags that stands up and moves.

"I need to say something to my girlfriend." In an acid-etched voice, he pleads to the plainclothes police officer on his right. "I don't want her to worry about me."

"We thought you had a wife. What's her name? Little Plum or something?"

"Please don't say her name here. She's too good a woman for you to mention her name in this filthy place," Dan says.

"We don't want you to make a scene."

"I won't. Or you can give me a more severe sentence. You can even shoot me right on the spot. I am a dead fish caught in your net."

The four officers look at each other, and the one on Dan's right moves his chin to signal his consent.

Dan approaches President Wu in an easy manner, smiling casually. President Wu is delighted to see Dan's willingness to reconcile. Dan takes his watch off his left wrist and puts it around the knuckles of his right hand. President Wu says something, but Dan misses it. He is too preoccupied by what he is going to do. You wouldn't believe how wonderfully quick and forceful Dan's attack is, unless you knew his history as a semi-gangster in the factory, and that he had gotten in wonderful shape after his army training. He used to worship righteous men with gangster qualities. So when people hear the thud, President Wu is on the floor, his face entirely flat on the marble floor, soaking in blood.

It is too late for the police to stop Dan. When their reactions catch up, Dan's feet have kicked the president's head several times, like a soccer player kicking a punctured ball that won't bounce.

Old Ten doesn't shriek like the other women. She stares at Dan as he is pulled away by the police officers. Dan feels her eyes following him when they handcuff him beside a collapsed chrysanthemum arrangement by the door. In a shower of yellow and white falling petals, flashbulbs flash at him, a few belonging to cameras as filmless as his own. He feels oddly good to be on the other side of the cameras, real or fake. He wants to repeat Ocean Chen's drunken lines: "You man-eaters! You shit-eaters!" But his voice is ripped by his roars and corroded by the sourness and bitterness of his vomit.

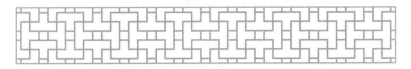

"MY PATIENCE IS running out, okay?" says Officer Lu to Dan.

"Okay." How can that be? You have plenty of patience. You lay in wait for me, pursuing me better than my own shadow. You had the patience to let me out of that detention room so that I might lead you to a banquet bug colony.

"Do you understand what that means?"

"Sure." Who doesn't?

"What?"

"It means you're going to beat the shit out of me." There isn't much to beat out of me, though, since I tossed up all my food two days ago.

"Confess, and you can spare yourself some unpleasantness."

"What time is it?"

"Why?"

"Nothing." It is about the time Little Plum is supposed to go to the hospital for a test. Yesterday she came to give Dan clothes and some pork buns that she had made, and she told him, in a blushing whisper, that she was going to have a pregnancy test today. She must have sat on the bench outside the lab and kept her crochet needle poking and pulling, working on a wig, believing she would make all the money she and her family will need with the hooked tip of that needle. Officer Lu, you should have seen how fast her hands are, they work themselves into a blur! Once I asked her, what if the demand for wigs drops? She said it won't. She'd been watching soap operas; eight out of ten of them are costume dramas set in ancient China, because ancient dramas are safe from government censorship. I asked what that had to do with wigs. She said it meant the shows won't get canceled by the censors, and all the characters, male and female alike, have to wear wigs. "It's just that I broke my watch punching the president out."

"You actually used your watch as a weapon?"

"I should have taken it off. It was a good watch. Heavy-duty and all. I spent most of my army discharge bonus on it. It's the only thing I own that's worth something." But I'm glad it served a good purpose. And it did prove to be heavy-duty.

"So why did you break it?"

"I wasn't careful, I guess." To make sure the blow was hard enough. And leave something on the president's face for him to look at every day when he shaves. "What time is it, please?"

"You want to turn back the clock, don't you?" Officer Lu smiles, getting a little philosophical. "You want to go back to the day before you took your wife to that shark fin banquet. You parasite! Is this what you're wishing for right now? To rewind all the way to the beginning, when you were first mistaken for a journalist? Do you wish you had corrected their mistake?"

"You are right, Officer." If I could retrieve all the steps I've taken, going all the way back to the beginning, I would keep a much lower profile, eating more quietly, not participating in any bull sessions, not showing off my knowledge of corruption in rural areas, not pretending to be a smart-ass and attracting attention from Happy and others, so I could be left alone to eat more and to eat in peace. "Would you please tell me what time it is, Officer?"

"Ten-twenty in the morning. You'll soon realize your time is worth nothing."

"I'm sure I will." My Little Plum must have gotten the lab results by now. I am a father to a tiny creature in her womb, and that's all that matters to me.

"And you'll pay for it if you waste *my* time."

"Sure." I know you are angry at my conceited smile. But I bet you felt the same way when your woman told you that you were going to be a father. You felt that nothing else mattered anymore.

"Let's try to make some progress here so we won't have to beat the shit out of you."

"I've told you everything, Officer."

"What are you waiting for? Waiting for that old painter to come and get you out? Dream on! You think with a piece of writing about him you can get out of here and become a newsman?"

Dan sits silently, his hands on his lap. Why would I want to become a newsman? Finding pathetic characters and unearthing their misery: that's what a newsman does. No one can get girls like Old Ten out of misery, just as no one can keep those beautiful moths from throwing themselves into the flame. They can't help it: it's their nature. Any attempt to help only puts me in a bad mood.

"You think with a little writing here and there you could call yourself a reporter and continue dining your way through life? Dream on!"

Dan looks at him. I am through dreaming to be a reporter. Why would I want to go to Ocean Chen and coax him for help so the reportage on Bai Village could be published? And Ocean Chen himself had to go for help to the young man with a big daddy. Lately I am easily disgusted. I was disgusted to see the young man's sleepy willingness to help. I was disgusted with myself when I tried hard to be one of these people who so thoroughly baffled me. I've never known for what obscure reason I am liked or disliked. I am through pretending to understand them.

"Who are your accomplices?"

"Huh?"

"Don't play dumb!" the officer shouts, throwing his pen at Dan, who doesn't duck, so it makes a tiny dot on the front of the shirt he wore to the nudity banquet.

Dan studies the tiny dot on his shirtfront for a moment, then bends and stretches his long arm to retrieve the pen.

"Leave it there!"

He does. He withdraws his arm, sits back, and faces forward. His movements are accurate and obedient, like a good soldier's or a good dog's. Good dog.

"You will tell us who the other banquet bugs are, and you will testify against them in court," Officer Lu says. "I know you bums cover for each other and do good teamwork. Let's make a deal: expose two of your teammates, and we'll take one year off your sentence."

Dan feels his eyes brightening for a second. The police officer, who is a semi-psychologist to the people sitting across from him at the interrogation table, notices the fleeting brilliance in his eyes. He knows Dan is tempted. He waits for his proposal to be fully analyzed and calculated. He plucks another pen out of his uniform pocket.

"I'm ready whenever you are," Officer Lu says.

Dan looks at him. He is tempted. If he cooperates, he could be free before his child learns to ask its mommy, "Who is my daddy? Where is he?" Once he is free, he would find a humble job to help out Little Plum before she becomes cross-eyed from crocheting wigs. Officer Lu has been talking about taking him back to the banquets and having him point out the other freeloaders. He believes delinquents of the same kind can easily identify one another through their survival instinct. If Dan identifies more of them, he will be rewarded with two years off his sentence. That's very kind of him. Well, after all, they are the People's Police and sympathize with ordinary people who have made mistakes.

Silence falls. Both of them can almost hear the noisy discussions in their heads.

"You should know better than to pass up this offer," Officer Lu says. "Do you trust me?"

"Yes." As far as I know, Dan thinks, you cops are famous for never keeping your promises. "I trust you," Dan says, raising his golden retriever face.

Dan listens to Officer Lu elaborating on their leniency policy and thinks of the little man and his phony photographer. Even if this cop did keep his word, Dan still wouldn't want to betray the other bugs. Somebody's got to do it; eat all that superfluous food. Or it will just fill the waste buckets, or make hogs' feed—not good feed, though, compared to the popular feed that makes hogs reach their full size in just a few months. Dan would be happier knowing that the good food had gone to people who appreciate it. Besides, it would be too much work for Dan if they demanded that he testify. And he takes pride, as a good gangster, in never betraying anyone.

"Sorry, Officer," Dan says. "I wish I could help."

"What?"

"I would have helped," Dan says, "if I hadn't enjoyed eating so much that I paid no attention to anything or anybody else. Officer Lu, you should have seen what I ate in my childhood. Ever tried boiled peachtree worms? They don't taste too bad compared with tree bark. And the flowers of the scholar tree are tasty. You boil and soak them well, then dip them in chili paste. The children in my village used to say it tasted just like chicken—as if they had any idea what chicken tastes like. But what tastes best are acacia flowers. Pick them before they are fully open and knead them with flour, if you have any, and make little pies and steam them. The trick is to pour hot water, instead of cold water, into the flour, so the dough swells up like a pregnant woman's belly. That way you end up making more dough with the same amount of flour, and it tastes better—sweeter and puffier. It was a regular food festival for the children to have acacia flower pies in my village, where all the trees are skinned and shaved—"

"Oh, shut up!" Officer Lu says.

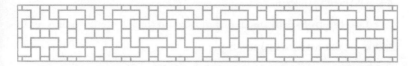

THE TALK SHOW HOST looks up and sees Dan Dong walk across the prison's visitation area toward him. Dan doesn't seem to recognize him as everyone else here does, policeman and visitor alike. The TV host has spent twenty minutes signing autographs on the paper they handed to him—sheets from writing pads, pages of notebooks, shopping receipts, traffic tickets, napkins, and facial tissues—when Dan comes in with the host's assistant. Long-limbed and wide-shouldered, Dan Dong strikes the host as a typical Northwest man who impresses you with a certain *gravitas,* a man who would never be frivolous.

"Glad to meet you, Mr. Dong."

Dan smiles, not comfortable with the way the talk show host addresses him. Dan is still in his own clothing, a camel-colored sweater over khaki pants. The talk show host knows that Dan won't have to wear a prison uniform until he is sentenced. Dan's eyes are deep and frank, set not for a crowded city but for gazing over great distances. He has a way of transmitting his *gravitas* through his handshake.

"I hope you don't mind my having chosen you as a major character in my TV documentary dealing with the banquet bug phenomenon, which reflects the corruption and decadence in society," the talk show host says.

Dan Dong smiles, saying he doesn't mind. The smile is languorous. He asks if he may know the reason the talk show host picked him. Of course he may. It is because Dan is a "reserve worker," an unsolved problem for the government and a phenomenon that constitutes a negative, dangerous force in society. And yet those workers used to be told that they were Atlas carrying the weight of the country, that they were the vanguard class of socialism. Ironic, isn't it? Is that the reason he qualifies for the leading role among the banquet bugs? That's right. Thanks.

As they are about to launch into the interview, two policewomen come to ask for the talk show host's autograph.

"My wife is a fan of yours, too," Dan Dong says after the policewomen leave. "I probably would have been as well if I hadn't been so busy eating banquets. But I loved the food. You can't say you've come into this world for nothing if you've eaten food like that."

There Dan goes with that quiet humor of an old farmer, which makes you think you might have missed something he slipped in under his frankness. Something funny or caustic. So Dan did recognize him after all, the talk show host thinks, but he did so without making a fuss. The host sees an unusual disposition in this banquet bug that sets him apart from the other bugs. That is how he has fooled quite a few people, including Ocean Chen. The old artist told the talk show host that he doesn't believe Dan Dong is a banquet bug, and the police must have made a mistake, as they often do. But his fiancée said there are so many strange people buzzing around the master every day that she has no recollection of this particular bug, Dan Dong.

The talk show host tells Dan that he himself has been to some of the banquets in various disguises, wearing wigs and beards and different eyeglasses and cosmetic masks. He was a banquet bug, too, in a way. Dan smiles, asking what dishes impressed him most. The talk show host says he is an anti-banquet person, and he never pays too much attention to what he is eating. Why does Dan smile? Oh, nothing. Please—this is an interview: he has to answer questions. Okay, Dan replies. A person who can afford to eat all he wants, and to eat whenever he feels like it, tends to be anti-banqueting. He thinks so? Yeah.

The assistant asks Dan to repeat that sentence. The little light on the recorder wasn't blinking, so he has to check whether it missed it. The talk show host tells the assistant, well then, use the writing pad and your ears and memory instead. He hates for anyone to break the mood and flow of a conversation. He turns back to Dan Dong. Now the other visitors are leaving, and the talk show host makes no response to their waves and adoring smiles.

"The police knew I was gathering material on banquet bugs, so they gave me your file three months ago. That was after you took your wife to the shark fin banquet."

"Yeah, I reckon so."

"Whatever possessed you to bring her to that banquet?"

". . . don't know," Dan says, staring at his long, big-jointed hands lying on the tabletop. His lips open, stop, and close up. One minute later he says, "I was stupid. I really was."

The talk show host believes he was going to say something else but changed his mind.

"Is it because you love her very much?"

"I like her all right."

"Does she love you very much?"

"You see, we don't say it that way. We are country folks. Words like 'love' and 'passion' are words in those songs. The songs you hear everywhere. They make you think of a guy moaning without pain. They embarrass me. We say everything to each other except those words. Somehow, I feel cheap if I say it to her."

"Very interesting. Then what would you name the feeling you have for her?"

"Don't know. I just feel for her. I feel with her . . ." His finger moves slowly on the table, drawing melancholy circles. "Just imagine a person going through her life without knowing what shark fin is. To her these things don't exist: sea snails, pigeon breast snowballs, Black Forest cake . . . Isn't it terrible? It's terribly unfair."

"So that's why you risked it. Do you think it was worth the risk?"

"I could have prepared her better. I was stupid. I wanted her to taste those wonderful dishes before I quit."

"Quit freeloading?"

"Yes."

"Why quit?"

"Got tired of it. It's a real pain when people start to bother you. They just can't leave you alone to enjoy good food."

"But you had started writing. And writing pretty well, as a matter of fact."

Dan says nothing, just smiles. Dan lets the host understand he doesn't want to argue.

"You'd actually begun to understand what journalism is all about, and the responsibility it brings."

"Had I?"

"It's a pretty good piece, your article about the peacock banquet. Your descriptions are vivid and unique; the way you write about the smells and textures of the food. And especially those lines describing Ocean Chen's gestures and speeches. You could make a good reporter with that kind of writing. A good food critic, perhaps. Too bad there isn't a profession like this in China. It has something to do with the hypocrisy of our society—there are certain things you just do but don't talk about. Have you written anything else other than this piece?"

"No."

"What about the reportage about the village party leaders' corruption?" The talk show host interviewed Happy Gao two days ago, and she told him about the impending publication of the article, with cuts and changes.

"But it became somebody else's writing in the end."

"Could you explain that?"

"Happy Gao said I couldn't get beyond my peasant limitations when I touched on this topic. I was corny and all. So she almost rewrote it. It's her work."

The talk show host smiles. Dan Dong: the honest banquet bug.

"I know you also wanted to write something for that girl whose sister was sentenced and executed. Are you lovers?"

"No."

The talk show host smiles again. The bug isn't so honest after all.

"But I know for a fact that you are." He interviewed Old Ten, and she claimed she had never known anyone named Dan Dong. But he finally got her to admit to her relationship with Dan.

Dan says: "She was the lover of Dan Dong the journalist, not of Dan Dong the banquet bug."

The talk show host likes his explanation.

"Did you write anything for her?" he asks.

"I told her I couldn't write for shit."

"That's not true."

"But I felt I could after I broke up with her."

"Why is that?"

"Don't know."

"Well, you did lay the groundwork for Happy Gao to write the reportage about the peasants. You should give yourself credit for that."

Dan Dong nods. The talk show host sees another effort Dan makes to suppress something he wanted to say. Happy Gao said the reportage had been banned several times until a very important person came to her and Dan's rescue. She didn't want to give this person away, but the talk show host figured he must be one of Master Chen's connections.

"You might stand a chance on appeal. With these publications, no matter how obscure the magazines, you can argue that you are a freelance reporter. Are you going to hire a lawyer?"

"You think I can afford one?"

"Find someone who's not too expensive. Happy Gao told me she has a lawyer friend who offered to work on contingency. Maybe you can become a real reporter when you get out of here."

Dan smiles again. The talk show host is now familiar with Dan's smile of disagreement, and he is a little tired of it. It's hard to open Dan up and get the truth out of him.

"You never wanted to become a reporter?"

"In the beginning, yes. In the end, no."

"Why?"

"It's too much work."

"Do you mean that it's too much work to promote fake products? Or that to publish certain articles, you have to ask for help from powerful people?"

"Not ask. Beg."

Happy told the talk show host that Dan Dong was depressed that the powerful person didn't even read the reportage before he lent his help. He didn't need to read it. He didn't care. He just reached out his indifferent hand and pressed it on a newspaper, and it was done, although some important phrases were missing from the final version. "So in the beginning you didn't realize how difficult it would be to get out a piece of truth in this country?"

"No. And I thought, if you have nothing to believe in, believe the newspapers. They always tell the truth."

The talk show host sees the bug sneaking in a yawn as he answers. He must have been deprived of sleep last night. It must have been tough for the bug, going through an all-night interrogation.

"I thought those newsmen were lucky sons of bitches who get to eat like kings every day. The first time I went to a banquet, I couldn't stop eating, even to catch my breath! So I thought to myself, I would do anything to eat like that. I don't mind playing a newsman. I could have played a dog! Those dishes—they are *incredible!*"

The talk show host sees Dan Dong's head lift slightly, his gaze fixed on a spot beyond him, on a wall bearing a slogan written in red: "Leniency for those who confess; severity for those who resist!" Dan's eyes are the eyes of a youth giving in to his own vision of romance or adventure. Dan is a passionate banquet bug. It makes the talk show host ill that someone could love food to this extent.

"But it's a parasite's life."

"Yes."

"Should anyone lead the life of a parasite?"

"No."

"Do you want to correct it?"

"Yes."

"You can if you try. You correct it by becoming a real journalist. Study in prison and get some kind of degree."

He sees Dan's vision dim. Dan shakes his head and smiles. He keeps shaking his head and smiling. The talk show host guesses what the bug doesn't want to say is "That's too high a price to pay to eat." He is an arrogant parasite for sure.

"How did your wife react to your arrest?"

"She's all right. She's always all right. The time I first brought her to Beijing, she found out I was not a well-to-do man as I had told her. When she was washing my clothes, she saw a slip of paper in my pants pocket that was a receipt for a monthly deduction from my salary issued by the factory accounting office. I had owed the office money for a salary advance for some years. She was all right; didn't make a scene or anything."

"Does your wife regret that you were caught only because you brought her to the shark fin banquet?"

"She regrets that she can't see me every day."

"Is she going to wait for you for seven years?"

"Sure."

"You are so sure."

Dan nods and smiles. It is a different smile.

"She is still very young, isn't she?"

"Twenty-four."

"You are ten years older than she is?"

"Yes. But she is like a little mama, managing everything just fine. Nothing is a big deal to her, not even my being in jail. You know how mamas treat their children. Mamas are a little crazy. They believe their children do bad things for good reasons. Their children are their lives, so you can't tell them their lives are totally rotten. They wouldn't believe you, anyway. That's how my wife seems to me: a little mama. She would treat me the same if I were the president of the country, or a prisoner."

The talk show host looks at him, not totally certain whether he has understood him completely.

"Is she happy that your writing got published?"

"She is. But nothing is big deal to her."

"Do you mind if I interview her?"

"You'll have to ask her if *she* minds."

"Okay . . . Would you do me a favor?"

"Sure."

"While you're on camera, don't say anything about the powerful person who helped you publish your reportage."

"I'll say whatever you *want* me to say."

"Good."

225 ff
269 ff